DEBRIEFING DARLY

Also by Amy Virginia Evans

Fantastically Fabulous February
Solstice Celebrations
Resin
I Love You, Eugene

DEBRIEFING DARLY

Amy Virginia Evans

DEBRIEFING DARLY

Copyright © Amy Virginia Evans 2024

Printed in the United States of America

ISBN 978-1724939005

For Ali and Zoe
   —finding their way with integrity and grace

"Changing society takes time. Feminism ebbs and flows. What saddens me is that young women have to re-invent the wheel again and again. Mary Wollstonecraft said it. Susan B. Anthony said it. Simone deBeauvoir said it. Germaine Greer said it. Gloria Steinem said it. I said it. But nobody believes it until they live it! We could learn from our foremothers but since we have repudiated their wisdom, we must keep beginning over. The real answer is to trust older women. They know. The generations must nurture and support each other. That's the only answer."

Erica Jong

"I feel proud, and I feel mad as hell. We are still dealing with the same issues."

Gloria Steinem New York Times 2022

"My feelings are of frustration and rage and deep disappointment when I look at how far we've slid back on two things: reproductive rights and nonsexist child rearing and education."

Letty Cottin Pogrebin (Co-Founder Ms. Magazine), New York Times 2022

ABSTRACT

Darly could do nothing but wait as her interim advisor read her study proposal. Much was riding on his approval and support, and she was anxious to confirm he was on board. She had considered every question he could ask, every roadblock he could erect, and every attempt he would make to dissuade her. What she had not considered was that Dr. Ian Brown would be so attractive.

She had ample time to observe his unstudied appearance—the haphazard beard stubble, a muscular calf beneath a rolled up pant leg, the way he twirled a pencil in his elegant long fingers. She guessed he was around thirty years old.

Meanwhile, the steady tick tock of the vintage school house clock seemed to grow louder. For fifteen minutes, the only other sound in the small office had been the occasional creak of wood as Ian adjusted his lanky frame in the office chair.

Just breathe, she told herself. This unexpected attraction to the man in the room was a complicating distraction.

When she saw that he had reached the last page in the black binder, she lowered her eyes to her lap, as if that had been her focus all along.

"I'm impressed, Darly." Ian's smile was engaging. "You're getting a head start on your bonus study before summer term begins. Interesting abstract, too: assessing the long term impact the Women's Liberation Movement had on that era's generation. How many responded to your questionnaire?"

"Two-hundred-fifty."

"Clearly, you've struck a nerve. The second phase will include only five of the women?"

"Yes. I have to decide which ones."

"Keep in mind the department's standards. Not to mention the formidable editors at The American Sociological Review. I assume you plan to submit?" Ian raised his eyebrows.

"Perhaps."

Although Darly seemed confident, the prospect of her research being judged by experts was daunting. Publishing the manuscript was a lofty goal she preferred to keep to herself, for now. *If you share your power, you can lose it.*

She glanced at the clock, noting her allotted thirty minutes had passed. As a show of respect for her advisor's time, she reached for her bag, acknowledging the end of the meeting.

Ian responded to the prompt. "All right, Darly. We'll see you next time."

Darly's hand was already on the door.

"Have a great weekend," he added.

"You, too."

She hurried down the hall. She must stay focused. *Discipline is essential for success.* Her future was limitless, now that she had completed the first year of Boston University's doctoral Sociology program. Despite being one of the youngest in the program, twenty-four year old Darly Lane had been granted a temporary office and a small stipend during the quiet summer session. This season was the perfect opportunity to further distinguish herself from her peers. She wasn't going to squander it.

That night, Darly met with the SocioLites, a group of female PhD candidates who gathered monthly for drinks. They were celebrating semester's end. Darly had planned to ask the group for advice about her permanent advisor, the arrogant Dr. Simon Grady. He had the power to endorse or derail her candidacy. After a glass of wine, it slipped her mind. Fortunately, Grady was on sabbatical until fall. There was an entire summer until then. In the meantime, there was Dr. Ian Brown.

Early the next morning, she spread two-hundred-fifty completed questionnaires over the sun-dappled wood of her apartment's living room floor. Random selection, she reminded herself. She called in her roommate Gracie to reach in five different directions until she held five questionnaire sheets in her hands. These participants would become the heart of her research. Darly turned over the papers and read the names out loud:

Heidi Belanger, Sherall Savard, Pamela Cardin, Dolores Quimby, Kimberly Dolan.

PARTICIPANTS

#1. HEIDI BELANGER
   (Name) Heidi P. Belanger
   (Age) 58
   (Marital Status) Married
   (Children) 2
   (Occupation) Volunteer
   (Address) 20 Auburn Street, Charlestown, MA

The two-page questionnaire appeared on Heidi's computer screen.

Dear Respondent:

As a Sociology PhD student/researcher, my primary focus is to understand how people react to one another and how individuals react to society. A specific area of interest to me is how the Women's Liberation Movement of the 1960s and 1970s influenced the development of women of that same era. Five respondents will be randomly selected to participate in a series of in-depth interviews. Please indicate if this is of interest to you. All information will remain confidential.

Please return the completed form to me via email or mail to: Women's Study, P.O. Box 412, Boston MA 02215.

Thank you.

Darlene Lane

Doctoral Student

Department of Sociology, Boston University Graduate School of Arts and Sciences

Heidi clicked the response link and filled in the data. She scrolled to the first question.

Q: *Do you think the Women's Liberation Movement helped or hindered your development?*

A: *Yes, the Women's Liberation Movement helped me and many women in every way. I may have been too old to benefit from the part I needed most (girls' sports equality), but I am glad there are girls who are luckier today.*

She rested her hands on the keyboard. A wound reopened as she recalled her childhood years playing baseball. Under bulky protective equipment, she had honed her catcher skills alongside her brothers and their friends, but her participation abruptly ended at age thirteen when she could no longer disguise her transformed body. She had considered these boys her friends, but the dynamic had changed. She now braced herself against humiliating comments from both bench and sideline, and eventually found herself banned from the sport she loved.

During the following years, Heidi watched bitterly as her brothers continued to participate on their school teams and receive accolades in the media. Although she complained vehemently about the unfairness of her exclusion, she eventually surrendered her anger and accepted her lot. When her parents encouraged her to try cheerleading instead, she dutifully embraced this socially appropriate place on the sidelines—cheering on boys' teams.

Heidi read the next question.

Q: *Is marriage a good option for a woman?*

She considered her answer, wary of the direction this questionnaire was leading.

A: *Yes, I feel that marriage presents a good option for most women because it provides a secure place for her in the family and community.*

Heidi answered the other questions with positive responses. PMA. Positive Mental Attitude. Her cheerleading coach had drilled that into her. Anyway, what was the use of dwelling on things she could not change?

In the space for comments, she typed a few affirming lines. She gave her consent to participate further as well as her interest in meeting other respondents if she was selected for the final study.

Throughout the day, her responses haunted her. Why such reluctance to answer honestly? Heidi had spent most of her life pleasing others. It was something she genuinely wanted to do. But she was beginning to realize that she had suppressed her own ambition to support goals that were not her own. Now it was all catching up.

PMA? Rage, rage, go away. Come again another day.

#2. SHERALL SAVARD
(Name) Sherall Savard
(Age) 59
(Marital Satus) married
(Children) 2
(Occupation) Sales
(Address) 91 Mt. Vernon Street, Boston, MA

Sherall popped a fresh piece of NicAway gum into her mouth. She savored the satisfying rush as she scrolled through messages. When she arrived at the updated status of her best client, she grinned. Thanks to her influence, he had increased his order thirty percent from last year. She would top the sales group for a fourth consecutive quarter.

Sherall had a never-fail work philosophy: "Find it. Get it." It was unfortunate that it also caused some collateral social damage. She had a way with clients, but coworkers gave her a wide berth. Stepping on toes was the price others had to pay for doing business in her proximity. Sherall wasn't trying to be popular.

Scrolling through more messages, she arrived at a link to a Women's Liberation Movement survey a colleague forwarded. After a cursory view, she committed to the concept, flying through the questions and narrative response:

She added a comment at the end:

The things you ask are usually overrated by everyone. Do you want honesty? I'm a seize-the-day kind of person. Probably not the type you were expecting. I think it would be a kick to meet the other women in this study.

She tapped send, then tossed her phone into her purse.

Sherall headed to a new sales call down the street from her office. She didn't need more clients, but she liked to feel life spinning. One adrenaline rush after another.

#3. PAMELA CARDIN
(Name) Pamela Cardin
(Age) 58
(Marital Status) Married
(Children) 0
(Occupation) Homemaker
(Address) 115 Chestnut Street, Weston, MA

Sitting at the desk in her spotless kitchen, Pamela perused her email, including a daily check on spam. Sometimes there was something interesting there. Today it was a B.U. survey about women. She would complete it before her husband returned. Bruce wanted to know everything she did, including who she told what. It wasn't always a rule she followed, but she tried not to push it.

Q: Were you personally involved in a consciousness raising group?

A: No. I heard about them when I was in college but I did not attend. I think that kind of group would still be relevant today, though.

After Pamela completed the questionnaire, she turned to her journal. It didn't take long to compose a new poem, which she then read out loud in her smooth voice.

Cashmere is soft when dry.
Its fiber can break when wet.
A heart beats for blood—
And for love.

Closing the cover, she fastened red ribbon around embossed leather and returned it to where it was always stored, in the guest bedroom cedar chest. Many journals were there under neatly folded wool sweaters.

Pamela's life goal was singular: security. Early years in an orphanage fueled her search for emotional stability and a sense of belonging. When charismatic Bruce Cardin arrived, she clung to him, desperately seeking the affection she needed. Romancing her sweetly, she responded with gratitude, oblivious to his selfish intentions. He eventually insisted she narrow her world to focus solely on him and his goals. She diligently maintained their home and her elegant appearance to entertain business clients. She had an enchanting manner that countered her husband's aggression. Pamela was initially eager to partner with Bruce to build their team together. She had imagined someday passing the company onto their children.

It was always a team of one, though. To Bruce, Pamela was merely a beautiful line on the curriculum vitae he presented to associates. Although their relationship was never healthy, it had recently taken a dark turn.

She yearned for freedom but had lost her way. With some control over her life, she hoped to feel part of a kinder world.

It helped to leave the house. With only a few items on today's list, her time elsewhere would be brief. First, she would wait for the pool crew to arrive and ensure that the work complied with Bruce's stipulations. She would next drive to their tiny town center to drop off and pick up her husband's suits and shirts at the dry cleaner. She would stop at the butcher to purchase his favorite choice cuts of meat that had been reserved in his name. They considered him a connoisseur. Lastly, she would swing by the accountant's office to sign tax documents. Bruce always filed late.

#4. DOLORES QUIMBY
(Name) Dolores "DoDo" Quimby
(Age) 57
(Marital Status) Divorced
(Children) 1
(Occupation) Photographer
(Address) 123 South Street, Boston, MA

In the bright studio window facing South Street, DoDo quickly checked her email, noting the star next to a Boston University survey a friend had forwarded. She liked to help other women whenever possible, so she set about completing the questionnaire before the morning's photo shoot:

Q: Did you experience any hostility at your early career workplace?

A: It depends what you mean about workplace. I worked as an apprentice in my early years. I had to rely on the goodwill of experts who were willing to teach a woman. Not all were receptive.

DoDo loved being a professional photographer, both living and working in an old Boston Leather District building. Although the marred wood floors were creaky and the windows drafty, the convenient consolidation of life and career in one place more than compensated for its shortcomings. The furnishings were sparse. One wrinkled black leather couch was pushed up against a side wall. Two mismatched and dented metal stools stood alongside the kitchen counter. The entire living room wall was covered with shelves full of photography paraphernalia.

The bedroom at the end of a narrow hallway was bleak and uninviting. Even in this most personal area, the trappings of comfort were minimal. DoDo told herself she liked everything that way. She was all about the essence of things.

At the jarring sound of a buzzer, she walked to the wall and pressed a button to release the lock at street level. When the sound of light footsteps on the stairs ended, a willowy young woman opened the battered wood door.

"Is Dodo Quimby here?"

"I'm Dodo, Jessica. The agency sent me your portfolio. Let's get started."

The morning shoot was underway.

#5. KIMBERLY DOLAN
(Name) Kimberly Dolan
(Age) 59
(Marital Status) Married
(Children) 5
(Occupation) Administrative Assistant
(Address) 28 Withrow Street, Newton, MA

Kimberly stood at the window, watching her youngest daughter climb into a classmate's car bound for Newton South High School. Eighteen year old Meghan was unable to drive herself for a second day because her candy-red Audi was getting a repair for negligent damage. As always, she took her frustration out on her mother, and although Kimberly was accustomed to the treatment, it was never easy to bear misplaced wrath. Meghan's four older siblings behaved similarly, despite reaching adulthood. Kimberly wondered when she could expect them to mature and treat her with deference. Her husband Gary was another story. She doubted he would ever respect her.

On her computer that morning, Kimberly completed the Boston University questionnaire, then saved it to proof and return later.

Q: Did you choose a career or family, or both?

A: I did not actually choose either but I tried to do both to the degree I was able.

Kimberly almost deleted the entire survey because the prompts to rate her life had disturbed her precarious equilibrium. Adding to that was guilt about being less than forthcoming with her ratings. She lied in the categories of "Marriage" and "Family Dynamic," hesitant to paint a negative picture of her children or husband. How could she forgive herself if they discovered she had been disloyal in her memories? She hoped other respondents would be more forthcoming. Although she did not want the PhD student to lack important information, she was not yet ready to tell her true story.

But, she was getting closer.

Kimberly tied her sneakers and set out on her usual ten mile morning run.

Later that day, she returned to her computer, rolling a frozen water bottle under her foot to soothe an evolving injury. Kimberly located the questionnaire and made her final edits.

Impulsively, she printed a new version, daring herself to answer the questions truthfully.

Halfway through, she fed it through the shredder. Too raw. The original version would have to do. She sent it to Darlene Lane, then leaned back and buried her face in her hands.

••••

Outside her apartment on the outskirts of Boston, Darly waited for the MBTA bus. Living in the heart of the city was beyond her budget, so she often took an earlier bus to enjoy the vibrant atmosphere prior to heading into her office for the day.

At the Boston Common, she walked through the gates and wove her way into throngs of people moving in every direction. The grass was green, daffodils and tulips were heavy with blossoms, and promising shoots speared through the dirt. The colorful advent of early summer heralded an explosion of activity. People who had walked these paths for months dressed in sensible rugged boots and puffy down parkas, shoulders bowed to the wind, now lifted their heads and smiled at one another. Coats came off, Red Sox hats were donned, and the aura transformed from somber stoicism to maniacal glee.

Darly made her way over winding paths and under budding weeping willows, looking edgy with her spiky brown hair and mirrored aviator sunglasses. On her petite frame, she wore a navy jacket, pale yellow tee shirt, and tight jeans. A faded canvas messenger bag straddled her chest.

Near the entrance to the Swan Boats, Darly settled herself onto an empty bench to observe the public—a sociologist's favorite laboratory. A few yards away, a wizened official held a small group back until the next boat safely positioned itself dockside. Under his direction, impatient children eagerly pulled parents' arms to claim coveted seats on the fanciful boat. Senior citizens dressed in pastel colors heaved collective sighs of relief once firmly settled onto their benches. Darly watched the boat glide away from the shore and begin its figure-eight circuit around the pond.

She walked up to the park building to buy a ticket. She was the only one in line. The old man working there was chatty.

"Did you come here when you were little?" he asked.

"No. I grew up in Michigan. But, I love Boston."

"I'm glad you decided to take a ride. It'll only cost you $4.50."

Darly nodded politely, handing him her money, and turned to gaze at the pond.

"Do you know the history?" he persisted, gesturing toward the boats.

"No, I don't. It seems like they've been here forever."

"Over one-hundred-twenty years. The man who started it died after only one year and then his wife took over. Her name was Julia. She had four kids to support. Every year, she had to get local businessmen to agree she was fit to run this place."

"Because she was a woman?" Darly asked.

"Guess so."

He pulled a ticket from a big roll.

"Her husband got the swan idea from a German opera. It's about a knight who defended an innocent princess with the help of a swan."

Darly rolled her eyes. "Fairy tales."

"You're not old enough to feel that way. Young ladies should have dreams." He handed her the ticket.

She walked to the edge of the pond where another swan boat glided by. Darly took in the tranquil atmosphere of the still water.

A line on the dock finally formed, so she joined the queue until it was her chance to step onto the boat's stern and sit on a freshly varnished bench.

One of three senior women seated in front of her turned and smiled.

"Are you a student?" she asked.

"Yes. I'm working toward a PhD."

The friends swiveled to look at her.

"Good for you," said the woman.

"What are you working on?" asked another.

"How the Women's Liberation Movement changed the lives of those who lived through it."

The three friends looked skeptical.

"Nobody wants to talk to us. It's like people think we go from young women with babies to old women in wheelchairs, and there's nothing in between."

"You got that right," one said.

Darly continued. "These days, many older women are rejecting rules. They don't seem to want to do what society expects."

"I suppose it seems that way," the woman in the middle said, glancing back at her friends.

Darly asked, "What do you mean?"

"Sometimes, I think *we* are the ones who expect so much."

"From a career, for example?" asked Darly.

"Career, mothering, being a wife. The whole thing."

"Was that true for any of you?" Darly asked.

"Expectations?" the woman on the left asked. "I guess so. Maybe we would do what we really wanted if we thought we could get away with it."

"Not have people criticize you?" Darly asked.

"Yeah," the first woman said. She pulled her sunglasses down her nose to look at Darly. "Not have people make us feel guilty just because we want to do something for ourselves."

"Do you feel like that?" Darly asked.

"I don't know," she answered. "Honestly, it doesn't do any good to think about it." She pushed her sunglasses up and turned away.

Back at her desk, Darly typed an email to the five study participants her roommate had helped select from the hundreds spread on their apartment floor.

I'd like to thank each of you for agreeing to elaborate further on your thoughts and experiences relative to the 1960s/1970s era second wave Women's Liberation Movement. All of you expressed an interest in meeting other research participants. With that in mind, I have reserved the Sociology Department conference room from 12-2 on May 14th. The conference room is located on the 2nd floor at 96 Cummington Street. (Behind Warren Towers - BU East T stop) A light lunch will be provided. I hope you can make it. Please email me at this address to confirm.

Thank you.

Darlene Lane

Darly had read a few of the seminal feminist books, but she intended to get also get through those that were piled on her bedside table. Friedan, de Beauvoir, Woolf, Millett, Greer. They had belonged to her late mother and would serve now as her guides while she explored the five study participants and their mindsets. She hoped that these women's stories would move her research from abstract to concrete, would bring color to the broader themes, and help her more fully comprehend what women felt during the years of the women's movement. Could they see what change was to come? Was it exciting? Did they embrace it, or were they ambivalent?

Her private hope was that these women might help her understand her own mother and who she might have become. Darly was only six when she died. Her father had told her many stories about how she organized others, marched in protests, and participated in consciousness raising groups. As much as she loved her father, she doubted he could empathize with a woman's journey. He did his best to fill the void, but Darly's wound grew deeper as she waded through womanhood. As she approached the age her mother was when she died, the sorrow and anxiety had become acute. What would happen when she finally reached that age? Her talisman would be gone. Would there be nothing more to learn about her mother because her mother's life had ended there? She would have to face the future without that guiding ghost, because the ghost would be younger than her. Darly would become the mother.

The May 14th meeting date arrived. Darly propped the conference room door open with her foot as she balanced a pyramid of halved sandwiches, six-pack of seltzer water, and her heavy messenger bag. Once she reached the large table and carefully rested everything on top, she collapsed onto the nearest chair and wiped sweat from her brow.

Darly was grateful for good weather. She wanted nothing to deter the five women from attending this meeting. Her research suggested that some post-menopausal women avoid challenge, struggle with lethargy, face issues of regret, and occasionally self-medicate with alcohol. Darly also anticipated a possibility of bitterness directed at her youth and a perception that she lacked understanding or maturity. She forecasted potential envy for her appearance, for her impressive achievements, and for her freedom from personal attachments. Hopefully, she and Ian had covered every other possible scenario that might occur. She planned to stay one step ahead of the participants by understanding and respecting their unique perspectives and using well established motivational techniques to counter apathy. Ian had approved her inquiry strategy, factoring in the possibility that the session would fall flat if the women chafed against revealing personal information to a group of strangers.

As a final review, Darly mouthed the participants' names as she counted them on her fingers: Heidi, Sherall, Dolores, Pamela, Kimberly. She peeled plastic wrap off sandwich trays, lined up seltzer cans, and fanned napkins into an artful display. She booted her laptop and pulled the completed questionnaires out of her messenger bag. She tested her university issued recorder and set it on pause.

A tip-tap of unmistakably fine leather soles grew louder in the hallway until a striking brunette woman arrived at the conference room door. Her light brown skin had a hint of honey and olive. Expertly arched dark eyebrows framed enormous green eyes. She wore a deep rose-colored leather jacket over an ivory silk blouse, slim fitting straight black pants, and flats with silver buckles. The woman moved gracefully forward to introduce herself.

"Hello. I'm Pamela Cardin. Are you Darlene?"

Darly shook the manicured hand, noting the soft skin and fine bones. Before her was the most stunning woman she had ever seen. "Yes," she finally answered, recovering her composure.

Pamela, long accustomed to the reaction, offered a gentle smile. "I hope I'm not too early. It looks like I'm the first to arrive."

"No, you're right on time. Come in."

Pamela surveyed the room, then walked over to the window to peer down at the busy highway spectacle. From the outside, her life probably looked perfect, just like the occupants in the vehicles below her now. No one knew what she endured. And, what did she know of the struggles of others?

"I wonder where all of those people are heading," she murmured.

"Me, too. I don't even own a car. It's so hard to park in the city," Darly replied.

Pamela nodded. "Yes, it is. Fortunately I found a spot right near the entrance on Cummington." She pulled sunglasses from atop her head and stowed them in her designer purse.

At the sound of more footsteps echoing in the hallway, they both turned toward the door where two smiling women appeared. The first was a short, muscular strawberry-blonde with an open and friendly face.

"Hi, I'm Heidi!" she announced.

Behind her was a willowy woman with wavy chestnut-colored hair who wore a scarf twisted artfully around her neck.

This is—" Heidi blushed, having already forgotten her new companion's name. She felt out of her social league. Why had she worn sneakers?

"Kimberly Dolan," the taller woman obliged.

Darly introduced herself and Pamela, gesturing toward the window where the beautiful woman stood.

Heidi said, "I have a horrible memory."

"I think everyone over fifty has that problem!" Kimberly laughed. She had enjoyed walking down the hall with Heidi who seemed to automatically accept her even though she knew nothing about her. She was grateful to enter the room accompanied by someone so nice, even if she forgot her name.

"I'm glad you could come. Please help yourself to a drink." Darly pointed to the table. "I'm still expecting two more. They should be here any minute."

At 12:05, a gangly woman walked through the door. Dressed in faded canvas pants, a camera slung over her shoulder, her otherwise drab appearance was hijacked by exceptionally bright blue eyes. A loose braid of grey hair dangled halfway down her back. She looked around at the others, smiled broadly and said, "This must be the old lady meeting! I'm Dodo. Dolores Quimby. At your service." She spread her arms wide and bowed to the others. It was her favorite introduction and it always elicited a good reaction.

Darly stepped forward. "Great to meet you, Dodo. I'm Darlene. This is Pamela, Kimberly, and that's Heidi."

The women nodded and smiled. Name tags were filled and affixed. Audio recording consent forms were signed.

"We're still waiting for one more, but I think we can get started on lunch. I'll give you a little background while we're eating."

The five women settled around the table and helped themselves to sandwiches.

Darly turned to her laptop and opened the file marked US 50+ Women's Study. She cleared her throat and began.

"The first thing I'd like to do is welcome you and thank you for agreeing to meet today to help with my research. You probably want to know a little about my background. As you know, I'm a Boston University doctoral student working on a PhD in Sociology. I'm pursuing a career in academia and research. I got my undergraduate and graduate degrees at the University of Michigan in Ann Arbor. That's where I'm from."

She surveyed the faces of the women sitting around the table politely munching on sandwiches.

"So," Darly continued, "I've always been interested in women's issues, but I want to better understand how American women benefited from the Women's Liberation Movement. I want to learn how they took advantage of those opportunities. That is my primary research focus. This will be somewhat of an informal study though. I'm following regular research modalities, but my outcome criteria will be more anecdotal than analytical. We all have our theories, but everything must be documented. The study will be monitored by an adviser who..."

A glaze settled over the women's eyes.

Fortunately, the sound of footsteps running down the hallway broke the spell, and in another moment, one last participant burst through the door, almost a half hour late.

"Oh god, I hate Comm. Ave.!" she laughed. The tall woman shook off her blazer, revealing a sleeveless blouse unbuttoned just far enough to display an ample, exceptionally firm bosom. A red leather pencil skirt stretched around slim hips and slender legs. The look ended with alligator embossed pumps. She sat in the nearest chair, plopped her Chanel bag onto the table, and leaned over to grab a sandwich. All eyes were on her and she knew it.

"You must be Sherall," began Darly.

"Yep, Sherall Savard, Esquire. Except I got tired of practicing law. I'm in sales now, but I'm still licensed. Gotta keep my options open." She made a quick assessment. It didn't look like she would get any new clients from this group. Of course, that wasn't why she came to this meeting. It was just a habit of hers to assess new acquaintances in those terms.

Kimberly slowly pushed a marker and name tag across the table toward the other woman.

Sherall chuckled. "I don't need one of those. You guys will remember *me*, right? It's Sherall. S-H-E-R-A-L-L." With each letter spoken, she looked around at an individual face. "Unusual name spelling aids recollection. Just remember, SHE and ALL. That's what I'm about. So, what did I miss?"

Ruddy skinned Heidi glanced at elegant and exotic Pamela, who escaped the scene by looking down at her sandwich. Cooperative and well-dressed Kimberly's eyes focused on leader Darly. Daring but dowdy Dodo rested her chin on her hand, and shook her head, smiling at Sherall.

Darly's heart rate soared with the appearance of this new participant. She had anticipated an interesting character but not someone quite so *rude*. Straightening herself in her chair, she continued.

"Well, I was telling the other women about my background and filling them in on the study."

"Okay, great. Keep going. I'm starved." Sherall helped herself to another half sandwich. She could feel her hangry mode threatening.

Darly took a deep breath and cleared her throat. "So, what I'd like from all of you is a broad sense of how the women's movement affected your lives." She looked around the table with her most professional affect. "Does anyone want to begin?"

The women stared at her, then looked down at their plates, then at each other, then back at Darly. Finally, Sherall and Dodo burst into laughter.

Dodo asked, "Darlene, how old are you?"

"I'm twenty-four." She had not planned to reveal her age to the group. Why was it relevant? "And please, call me Darly."

"Since you're only twenty-four," Dodo continued, "you probably can't imagine how different things were for us than they've been for you."

"In what way?" she responded.

Kimberly offered, "Well, for one thing, I remember having to wear a dress to school every day, even when it was freezing cold."

"I thought only us kids in Catholic school had to do that. When did you get to wear pants?" Heidi looked over at Kimberly.

"Probably sometime around eighth grade. We had a student council fundraiser where the girls could pay to wear pants in seventh. I remember it was ten cents."

"That is *so* pathetic. What a bunch of wimps we were," Sherall commented.

Kimberly winced at the visceral reaction to her recollection.

"It wasn't like we even knew it was an option, though," Heidi said.

The others nodded.

"So, how did you feel about that restriction?" Darly asked.

Dodo looked incredulous. "Feel? We never went there. Can you imagine if we actually felt something about how we had to act? We'd go crazy."

Sherall shot Dodo an admiring glance, then said, "Everybody eventually did, didn't they?"

"Went crazy? You got that right," Dodo responded. She reached around and twirled her grey braid like a lasso for comic emphasis.

"Pamela, we haven't heard from you, yet. What was your experience?" asked Darly.

Those who looked toward Pamela registered the massive yellow diamond sparkling on her left hand.

"I guess I didn't mind having to wear a dress. I always kind of liked to feel fancy when I was younger. It became less fun as a teenager, though."

"That's because you're already gorgeous," Sherall joked. "The rest of us had to work to get noticed, right ladies?"

Pamela cringed. This pattern was typical. In a mixed group, males would talk to her and females would talk about her. She still hoped to be accepted by these women.

Petite Heidi spoke next. "It took a long time for everything else to change, didn't it?" Her feet barely reached the floor beneath her chair.

"Such as?" Darly encouraged.

"Well, like sports, for example," she responded. Was it appropriate to bring up her baseball experience? It seemed childish to whine about it now.

"I played basketball in high school," offered Dodo.

"That's really great to hear. I agree that there were some sports for girls, but they seemed to be sort of for a *particular* kind of girl."

Realizing the inference of her statement, she quickly continued. "What I meant was that my friends made fun of me when I said I was going to try out for the softball team," Heidi clarified. "I really wanted to continue playing baseball like my brothers."

"What did you end up doing?" asked Kimberly.

"Cheerleading."

"Ha! I *thought* you were a cheerleader," commented Sherall.

Heidi shrugged. It wasn't the first time she had received that reaction. At least cheerleading had given her a template to keep her body fit.

Kimberly quickly offered, "Somebody has to support the teams. And cheerleading is physically challenging. It's even considered a sport today, you know." Her oldest daughter had been a cheerleader. She loved watching her cheer at the games they attended.

"That's true. Okay, so anything else?" asked Darly.

"Does everybody remember not wearing a bra?" Sherall looked around the room, laughing raucously.

"And, those pucker shirts with the little bubbles that were skin tight?" added Dodo.

"I'd love to have *my* old figure again," said Heidi.

Smiles and wistful glances passed between the women.

"There is something I really do miss about our younger era," Pamela began. "It seemed like we were more honest about our bodies. We didn't use so many tricks to fool men."

"I say, thank goddess for those tricks today, though!" Sherall laughed, pointing one manicured nail toward her ample cleavage.

"Well, I guess some of those things do help us as we age. But, can you imagine caring about tiny details when we were young?" Pamela continued, shaking her head.

Heidi leaned into the group. "On my way here today, I saw an entire salon dedicated to eyebrow threading."

"And, what about waxing?" Sherall asked. "Those salons are full of women *and* men. I used to get a Brazilian wax, but—Ow! That had to stop. They're sadists at those places."

"How about work and your jobs?" Darly attempted to steer the conversation.

"How much time do you have?" Dodo cracked.

"What kind of work do you do?" Sherall asked Dodo, popping a piece of NicAway gum into her mouth.

"I'm a photographer."

"Have you done that for long?" Sherall chewed vigorously. It was a little rush she savored.

"Since I was eighteen. I didn't start making any money until I was in my late thirties."

"What do you photograph?" Kimberly asked.

"I started out with street scenes, then I broke into portraits and fashion. Back then, girls weren't interested in women photographing them. They wanted men. The younger ones usually still do."

"How did you get around that?" Kimberly asked. She worried about being too forward, but easygoing Dodo seemed happy to reveal additional details.

"I just kept at it until I was taken seriously. It wasn't always easy."

"I hear a lot of women did that," Heidi said. She wished she had a similar story to tell. She wanted to be admired and to have earned more money. It was probably too late, though.

"Hey! Remember those stupid ties we wore with our suits?" Sherall asked.

The women groaned at the recollection.

Dodo said, "We all should have stayed true to our nine-year old selves. *That* is the age when you're most authentic. Before society tries to break you."

Darly noted the time. It was almost 2:00 and the room had been promised to another group. Outside the door, Professor Alan Berrios paced, his glasses perched low on his nose. He caught Darly's eye through the window and dramatically pointed to his watch.

She was disappointed that she had to end the discussion. She had not gathered the information she needed.

She broke into the lively conversation. "Unfortunately, our time in this room is up. There are specific topics I need to cover. Would you like to meet again as a group, or would you prefer individually?"

The five women looked at her, eyebrows raised expectantly, lips turned up into smiles.

"Does that mean stay as a group?" Darly asked.

Heads nodded.

Heidi had an inspiration. "My cousin owns a little restaurant on Boylston Street that has a private room. We could meet there. The room would be free and I know he'd give us a good deal on food. We could all pitch in."

This was unexpected but Darly was pleasantly surprised. "Wow. That's a great offer. I thought we'd have to meet here again. Is the restaurant something you all want to do?"

"It'd be marvelous to be able to order a drink." Sherall said.

A cluster of professors had now gathered outside the door. Darly needed to wrap up.

"Heidi, when you talk to your cousin, would you please send me the info so I can contact everyone to set a firm date? I'm happy that you all want to meet again as a group. I'm looking forward to hearing more of your thoughts." She turned to the short stack of paper next to her. "These are some questions to help you prepare for the topic of our next discussion topic: Ambition. It would be helpful if you could consider them beforehand." Darly distributed the sheets. "There is also a voucher for a BU theater discount as a token of my appreciation. I wish I could offer you more, but my budget is pretty tight. There will be a similar B.U. venue voucher for each session. I'll be in touch soon regarding our next meeting. Until then, have a great week, everyone!" She stopped the audio recorder, closed her laptop, and slid everything into her bag.

The participants left the room, chatting and laughing as they made their way down the hall.

Darly heaved a sigh of relief. Except for not covering all of her material, the meeting far exceeded her expectation. The women seemed genuinely interested in her research. She had imagined that they would be older. Less flexible. More reserved. Their animated chatter surprised her. None of them had met before, but they acted as if they had. They still felt like strangers to her, though.

• • •

"So, what are they like?" Ian asked Darly at his office the next day.

"Not what I expected."

"In what way?"

"Well, for one thing, they're all completely different."

"People can be."

"Yeah, but they seem to celebrate their differences."

"That's a good thing, isn't it? You must know women like that. Maybe your mother or some of her friends?"

Darly looked down at the questionnaires resting on her

lap. She wondered what her mother would think of her study participants. As always, she wished she could ask.

"My mother would have been fifty-seven today."

Ian looked stricken. "I'm so sorry, Darly. I didn't know."

"It's okay."

He reached over and touched her hand, then removed it just as quickly.

Darly composed herself. "Anyway, they're a pretty likable bunch."

"Go on."

"Well, there's Heidi Belanger. She's short and athletic looking. Maybe a little sad about her past, and sort of hesitant with the other women. I think she feels a bit inferior. She's from Charlestown. A high school cheerleader. I don't think she went to college."

"Let's call her Tired Cheerleader."

Darly reacted. "How did you do that?"

"What?"

"Just categorize her like that? You were spot on."

"It's a knack I have. Nicknames make things easier."

"Okay. Are you ready for the next one?" she asked.

"Shoot."

"Pamela Cardin. When I first saw her, I couldn't even talk for a minute. She is the most gorgeous woman I've ever met. She has dark hair and a beautiful face. Very exotic looking. You can't take your eyes off her. She hardly ever smiles, though. I get the feeling she has a ton of secrets."

"Sad Beauty."

"Hmm. Sad Beauty." Darly made a note of the

nickname on Pamela's questionnaire, then took up the next form.

"All right. Here's Dolores Quimby," Darly said, holding up the questionnaire. "She's really a kick. Very friendly and down to earth. She's a photographer, doesn't wear makeup, and pretty much dresses like a man. She'd be completely drab if it weren't for the bluest eyes. They just pop out of her face."

"She's your Aging Free Bird."

"Right on, again," Darly responded.

"Next?" Ian leaned back in his chair and linked his fingers behind his head.

"Don't get cocky," she teased.

He smirked.

She was beginning to really like this guy. Was she being too chummy, though? At the end of the day, he was her interim advisor. What if he liked her, too? The thought made her dizzy. She forced herself to focus.

"This next one is hard. Kimberly Dolan. She hasn't revealed much about herself. Mostly, she's extremely nice. It seems like she always wants to be helpful and rescue everyone."

"What does she look like?" he asked.

"Pretty average looking, but fit. Extremely. Very neat."

"I'm going with Guilty Perfectionist."

"Seems presumptuous."

"You'll let me know as the study progresses."

"I will."

Sparring overshadowed their work but Darly enjoyed it. Maybe she could let down her guard just a bit. Ian was only her temporary advisor, after all. Dr. Grady was the one who held the real power.

"Okay, you'll love this last one," she continued. "Sherall Savard. That's S-H-E-R-A-L-L. She went to law school but now she's in sales. She looks like a bona fide cougar but I think she's married." Darly reviewed Sherall's questionnaire for confirmation. "Yes, she is."

"I'm going to go with Attention Addict."

"Attention Addict! Love that."

"That's five, right?" he asked.

Darly nodded.

"What about Darly Lane?" Ian asked.

"My nickname?"

"Yes. That will be a real challenge. I'm on it!" Ian shut his laptop. "I'm also starved. Let's go to Noodle House. My treat. We can talk about the rest of this next time."

"I— Uh— Okay. Sounds good." Darly gathered her belongings, then waited in the hallway while Ian locked the door to office 126.

METHOD

TOPIC: AMBITION
Why did you choose your career path?
Who influenced you?
Have you realized your potential?
What obstacles did you overcome?
When will you retire?

Darly's ambition was clear. She was on the fast track to earning her PhD to teach at a major university, and eventually do research at some renowned think tank.

She had always been an excellent student. Her father, Aaron Lane, a professor himself, was supportive of her academic and career goals, but had reservations about why she was so intent on her own PhD trajectory. Was it the goal she should pursue? He diplomatically voiced his concern only once, and Darly heard her father loud and clear. His unease stemmed from the fact that her mother had been scheduled to defend her doctoral dissertation just before she was killed by a distracted driver while out walking. Because Nora Brumm-Lane was well liked and respected socially and professionally, the university discussed the possibility of conferring her degree posthumously. But, time passed, faculty became distracted by other issues, and the idea lost traction. Everyone told Darly that her mother had been robbed of her dream. As Darly grew older, she started to make it her dream as well. It felt important and right to fight to the end of the process for her mother, and for herself—of course. As a bonus, it was another way she could hold her mother close, at least in spirit.

Nora Brumm-Lane's scholarly research was packed in notebooks and journals in Darly's father's basement. He had recently allowed her to see it. She pored over the papers with studious attention. She was aware that Nora's research and proposed thesis had since been validated by other academics. Darly considered it brilliant material.

Darly wondered if her father realized that a few of Nora's personal journals were packed in the boxes with other papers. Although she felt guilty reading accounts of her mother's and father's relationship on those pages, she was eager to learn all she could. She could not resist exploring their contents. During her last visit home, she slipped three of the journals into her suitcase so she could keep them close and read them at her leisure.

One day, she stumbled on an exciting entry. Her mother expressed a desire to leap to the future to examine the outcome of the women's movement. She was curious about the fruits of her own labors. Because Nora Brumm-Lane was passionately involved in the movement herself, she was convinced that all who were touched by it would have spectacular lives full of amazing careers and relationships. As an assistant professor, she made it her mission to convey her enthusiasm about the vast possibilities for women's futures in her students. She used phrases like "women should," and "a woman is responsible for," and "opportunity is everywhere and should not be squandered." Mostly, there was the theme that a woman should do as much as possible to be successful and to pave the way for other women to follow. Tragically, Nora was unable to witness the impact of her words, but Darly felt like *she* was one of the women for whom her mother had blazed a trail. She took Nora Brumm-Lane's vision to heart.

There were a handful of less positive journal musings as well. Comments in Nora's distinctive handwriting hinted that raising a young child while on an academic fast track was more complicated than she had expected. She would occasionally express frustration that her husband Aaron did not understand all that was required of her. One hastily scribbled post described how upset she was about having to beg a female colleague to teach her class because she did not have the heart to leave Darly with a babysitter when the child was sick. In Darly's reading, comments of this nature registered as minor footnotes. Her own inexperience made her less sensitive or able to comprehend the nuance in her mother's lamentations.

Darly believed that massive progress had been made for all women since Nora Brumm-Lane's entries. She was supremely confident that women in contemporary society could be counted on to manage all facets of life.

The journals inspired Darly to further explore the themes so important to her mother. That was why she decided to use this summer to complete the mini study. She would return to her primary PhD research in the fall. Like Nora Brumm-Lane, she firmly believed that the past struggles of women would have been well worked out by the future. And, the future had arrived. She would do the work her mother could not.

••••

Darly wondered how her study participants would respond to the topic of Ambition.

Although she didn't know the participants well, she couldn't resist speculating. She was surprised that several of them were low achievers. If doors were opening for them as young women, why didn't they walk through them? The cost of education was more affordable when they were in their twenties than current tuition prices. Were they distracted, or lazy, or just lacked direction? Maybe they didn't plan when to birth children for optimal career progression. Or, maybe they married too young. At the end of the day, they were just excuses, and she was prepared to hear them all.

Darly composed the follow-up email she had promised to send.

Hello Heidi, Sherall, Pamela, Dodo, and Kimberly.

Thank you for taking the time to meet last week. The information you shared was helpful and I hope our gathering was enjoyable for you. Heidi has secured a special room for us at her cousin's restaurant, Vivere, at 132 Boylston Street, Boston. Please let me know as soon as possible whether Tuesday or Wednesday would be best, and whether you would prefer a lunch or dinner meeting.

Also, please take a moment to review and complete the sheet I distributed last week so I can collect them and you can give some advance thought to the topic we will discuss.

I look forward to hearing back and seeing you at our next meeting.

Darlene Lane
Doctoral Student
Department of Sociology
Boston University Graduate School of Arts and Sciences

PAMELA CARDIN

"Bitch."

"I didn't think it would bother you, Bruce. I'm sorry. Please forgive me." Pamela pleaded.

"You know how much I hate Glenn. That asshole is trying to steal my clients. Now, he thinks he can steal my wife."

"But Bruce, I didn't plan to sit next to him. The seats were prearranged," she added, following him from their garage into the mudroom.

"You didn't have to suck up to him like that. You could have talked to Dan on your other side."

"I'm really sorry." Pamela walked faster to keep up with him as he made his way down the hallway to their kitchen. "If I had known about Glenn, I never would have been nice to him."

Bruce turned, and faced her. "What could he see in you, anyway? That dress looks like shit."

Pamela looked down at her gown. The clerk had assured her that teal was a good color this season and even her seamstress had said the gown fit so well that it only had to be slightly altered.

"I'm going to bed." Bruce turned and left.

As soon as he was gone, Pamela clutched the counter. The vicious tone tonight was new; more often his comments were merely callous.

She tried her best to please him. Pamela took care of herself by visiting the dermatologist every quarter, the esthetician twice per month, and recently consulted a plastic surgeon about a mini-face lift. Bruce had instructed his personal trainer to design a workout for her and she faithfully executed the routine in their home gym three times per week. Personal shoppers at both Neiman Marcus and Nordstrom were on retainer to regularly update her wardrobe. Housekeepers cleaned every other day. Dust settled nowhere. The lawn service she scheduled also managed end-of-season clean-up, snow removal, and exterior holiday decorating. The butcher alerted her when Bruce's favorite meats arrived. The wine shop put aside specific wines that Bruce demanded for their frequent guests so she could pick them up whenever needed. All of this required effort from Pamela. She would gladly do more.

Where would Bruce be without her by his side?

She had boosted the success of his public relations firm. Her elegant charm wowed new customers and helped retain the company's happy stable of long-term clients, but she was qualified to do much more.

After graduating from Smith College with a degree in Communication, she immediately accepted a secretarial position at Rhinegold Public Relations, hoping to rise through the ranks. With her strong work ethic and professional demeanor, Pamela was quickly promoted to administrative assistant to the executive director. It was primarily clerical work but she was able to sit in on conceptual meetings and occasionally offer ideas to the group. She noticed that although others admired her intelligent input, her boss would not share her or nurture her career progression. She was too valuable to him right by his side.

A few years later Bruce joined Rhinegold. Social and digital media did not yet exist. Nurturing a personal connection was the only way to grow a client's business. This was Pamela's strength, albeit in a supportive role only, and Bruce noted how much of an asset Pamela was to the agency. He decided that he had to have her on his future team when he opened his own public relations company.

Because of this goal, his wooing of her was pragmatic. His comments and attention made Pamela feel valued and heard. He convinced her that she was underappreciated at work. After they married, he persuaded her that she would contribute to Rhinegold more effectively by supporting him at their home, versus in the office. When Bruce opened Cardin Consultants, his wife was conveniently trained to do exactly what he needed. Now she was merely an uncompensated helper. She paid a steep price for trusting others whose only interest was their own.

Pamela took a sheet of paper and pen from her desk at the kitchen and moved to the dining room where the mahogany table gleamed in shadowy light. She pulled one of the upholstered chairs away from it and sat down. Gathering inspiration, she put pen to paper.

Ten empty chairs
Waiting for life to appear.

The table without a mark
Knows not the warmth of true conversation.
The grain of the wood is authentic but
The air is more surreal than real.
The woman in the chair
Is similarly covered with varnish,
A poison.
Only she can rearrange the seats.

Q: What obstacles did you overcome?

Pamela reflected on the myth of Sisyphus who perpetually rolled a boulder up a hill, only to have it roll down again. For him, it was a punishment from a god. For her, it felt like everyday life.

DODO QUIMBY

Dodo climbed the creaky stairs to her flat, unlocked the battered wood door, then tossed her keys and gym bag onto the metal kitchen counter. Saturdays were her favorite. All play. She made a point to schedule no Saturday shoots, at least never locally. If she had to work, it was always out of town; preferably, out of the country. At this stage of her career, she was in demand and had a great deal of control over her schedule. It hadn't always been that way.

Around the corner, on a bedside crate, was a tiny photo of a little girl. The round face was framed by auburn braids trimmed with yellow-polka dot ribbons. Freckles spread across her nose. Twinkling bright blue eyes promised a future as a dazzling woman. Dodo picked up the picture and brought the photograph of her daughter into focus. How old was Georgie then? Four? Five? Dodo couldn't remember.

It had been three years since she had last seen her. That part she remembered. Teenaged Georgie refused to communicate with her mother, a consequence of Dodo's sporadic participation in her early life. Her ex-husband Rolf, his mother Ada, and a nanny had raised Georgie. At the time, Dodo's lifestyle choices had not seemed egregious to her, but her heart ached now at the thought of what she had neglected.

When Georgie was small, Dodo had been busy. The success she had worked hard to achieve had finally arrived, and her business was growing exponentially. Raising a child along with demands of long hours, traveling, and networking to build her reputation, proved incompatible. There was no disputing that Georgie's father had been in a much better position to work near home and pick the baby up from day-care and preschool. Rolf and the nanny he hired accomplished this feat flawlessly. Dodo's frequent absences created an air of unease between husband and wife. When they found time together, awkward formality replaced intimacy. They had become strangers. Dodo wondered if Rolf was seeing someone else during her time away. Her ambivalence about this possibility added to their troubles. Over time, Rolf grew bitter. His wife had left him with the bulk of parental responsibility and she didn't seem to care. There was eventually little in their marriage to hold them together except Georgie, until even that bond disintegrated. Dodo knew that the burden of fault was hers—having chosen a brilliant career over being a good wife and mother.

She set the photo down.

There had been several casual romances since her divorce. Flings, really. She was not an attractive figure that men gravitated toward. When she looked in the mirror, she saw only the plane of her forehead, the angle of her cheekbones, and the bridge of her nose. Her world was one of light and lines, with artifice and clutter filtered out. As her artistry evolved, she discarded the quest for beauty in her own appearance, preferring to focus intently on capturing the elegance of form in others. In the fashion world where she worked, beauty was abundant. It was her gift to showcase it.

Dodo was a quick learner. She began as a photographer's assistant. Her mentor gave her increasing latitude, admiring her raw talent and determination to master advanced techniques. With sharp skills and growing confidence, she ultimately broke those ties and went solo, living frugally and using her earnings to upgrade and maintain her equipment. Within a year, she was solidly booked with domestic shoots, and soon after that, felt the satisfaction of turning those opportunities down in favor of international assignments. This broad network of associates and clients kept her fiscally solvent, and constant creativity fueled her soul.

She was busy and fulfilled in many aspects. Dodo was independent, financially successful, adventurous, and strong, but estrangement from her child made victory feel hollow.

Q: Have you realized your potential?
Career, yes. Life, no.

HEIDI BELANGER

"Three aces!" Heidi's husband, Jim, spread his cards on the table top.

"Are you kidding?" his brother threw his cards down.

"Jim always wins at Jim's house, right Heidi?" another brother called over to her in the kitchen.

"You guys would know better than me," Heidi answered loudly so they could hear. "Next Friday, it'll be your turn to win at your house, Sean." Heidi rolled her eyes toward her five sisters-in-law gathered around the kitchen island.

"Hon', bring me another beer, would you please?" Jim called to her. "I'm celebrating."

She opened the refrigerator door and pulled out several bottles of beer.

Nan, the oldest sister-in-law, refilled the basket of pretzels and handed them to her. "These guys are bottomless pits."

Heidi carried everything into the family room. Her brother-in-law Jack was wearing one of the tee shirts she had designed and printed for their most recent family reunion picnic. He cycled through those shirts whenever he played poker with his brothers.

"Nice shirt," she said to him.

He winked back.

As she handed Jim a beer, she said, "Don't forget about your game tomorrow. At nine."

"What would I do without you?" Jim grabbed Heidi by the waist and pulled her toward him.

"Be late for your games?" she asked, eyebrows raised.

The others laughed, helping themselves to the newly supplied refreshment, then returned their attention to their cards.

Heidi plucked empty bottles from the table and picked up dirty napkins and plates from around the room. Friday night poker parties rotated between all of their houses, so she was only required to host every sixth week. The sisters-in-law always helped with cleaning. An added bonus was catching up on the latest activities of numerous nieces and nephews.

But lately, something felt different. Heidi had struggled for months against a nagging malaise she did not understand. She hid her melancholy. It was an intimate matter she felt she could not discuss with her husband, sisters-in-law, or even her own four sisters. She knew she would find no sympathy for her complaint.

Her life appeared idyllic. Every detail had progressed just the way it should. Even Justin and Jordan, her two grown sons, had managed their transition to independence, living away from home, unless a job collapsed or they broke up with a girlfriend. The Charlestown house mortgage was fully paid and they had the rustic cottage at New Hampshire's Island Pond, too. Jim had every toy imaginable to keep him happy. For almost twenty-five years, he had been employed by Harvard University's facilities maintenance department. Soon, he would be eligible for a healthy retirement, thanks to the union.

She was only twenty-two when she and Jim married. They were in love. A wedding seemed the logical next step. Her mother had also married young, going on to raise four daughters and two sons. Heidi's mother was deliberate in her strategy. She knew it was the best way for a woman to build a successful life in her era. Heidi and her sisters had been imprinted with a clear understanding that they should also make themselves indispensable to their own men. They became convinced that traditional roles were the best form of security. If one kept secret the mysteries of laundry, cooking, shopping, and general plate-spinning, men were presumably helpless without wives. The more the wives supported them, the more they would support their wives. Symbiotic synergy.

Now that her boys were grown, Heidi's life revolved mostly around Jim's big personality. Baseball in the spring led to summer activities at their cottage. Jim wielded his jet ski on the water in the warm months. In the winter, he switched to snowmobile riding and ice-fishing with his brothers and brothers-in-law. Or, the men organized a pickup truck convoy and drove to Ragged Mountain in New Hampshire to use their season ski passes. If the weather was bad, they would default to the couch to watch football on an enormous television at someone's home. The wives were the support team for this lifestyle.

Heidi enjoyed the lively mixture of congeniality and competition, enthusiastically supporting all the men in her life. She nurtured a convivial atmosphere and they loved her for it.

These sidelines were starting to feel unsatisfying. She couldn't quite put her finger on it. She was only certain about one thing—Heidi wanted to play her own game.

Q: Who influenced you?

For Heidi, there was a more relevant question. Who dissuaded you?

KIMBERLY DOLAN

Kimberly startled awake. Her reading glasses, wedged beneath her shoulder, had fallen to the floor. It was her pattern to rest on the couch waiting for Meghan to come home from a party. It was 1:15 am. Her daughter had violated her curfew, maintaining her own pattern to disobey her mother.

Husband Gary was long asleep. Kimberly knew how much he needed his rest because he frequently reminded her. She had always been the one to wait on the couch for all five of their kids who usually tried to sneak in without waking her. Of course, she heard them, but she let them tiptoe by. Her sole concern was that they made it home safely, not what shape they were in or what they did while they were away. Meghan was now the only child who lived in their house full time, and she would go away to college in the fall. It was important to Kimberly that she continue to be a conscientious mother for the sake of her youngest.

She had done the best she could by attending her children's games and events, even during tax season. She helped Gary with his accounting firm in the early years, before the business blossomed. There were times when she was up all night preparing government forms, but still made her family a hot breakfast and sent them off to work and school with nutritious lunches. It was easier now in many ways. But, she was older now.

Long ago, she had enjoyed all things domestic. An excellent cook and seamstress, she had a flair for creating a perfect ambiance in any room. It was a transferable skill. When parents of her children's friends saw how clever she was at designing holiday crafts, they encouraged her to sell some. She found great success at a few school fairs, but it was difficult to complete projects on deadline while constantly tending to her large family's needs. Eventually overwhelmed, she boxed up the collection of tools and materials and stowed them in the attic.

One routine Kimberly did not neglect was fitness. Initially, her commitment to a strict diet and exercise regime was connected to her desire to be a good role model to her children, but as her amount of free time expanded, so did the intensity of her exercise. Kimberly had long ago lost motivation to pursue any other personal goals and plans. She was exhausted, and despite consistent over-training, she knew her fatigue was as much emotional as physical. Nevertheless, the start of a new month also meant the challenge to break a new personal best on some physical level.

She had plenty of free time. This was because Gary had recently informed her she could no longer work at his office. He said his assistants considered her a liability. In their assessment, she had not kept abreast of new technology and was slowing things down. She was completely blindsided by this comment. She loved days in the office spending time with the staff.

One senior accountant seemed to be particularly fond of her. She couldn't imagine he would have said anything negative about her. She had even dared to imagine his appearance at a charity race she ran in was no coincidence. He knew she had been training for it. After she crossed the finish line, they walked a few blocks together. She had begun to look forward to seeing him on the days that she went to the office.

Q: When will you retire?

What was retirement if no one had acknowledged the unpaid work she had done for the last thirty years?

SHERALL SAVARD

The graph on the monitor illustrated Sherall's dramatic sales story. A line from left to right went straight up. Never down. Never across. She was unstoppable, and the start-up company owners loved her for it. It really didn't matter to Sherall what product she was selling. She would study and master it, then convince clients that they desperately needed whatever she offered. She had conquered the techniques of selling so completely that others asked to shadow and learn from her.

Sherral had always been driven to excellence. Her parents never once had to remind her to do homework. Difficult concepts that challenged most students were easily understood by her. Later, as a young woman, she was frequently labeled abrasive and bossy. She refused to modify her demeanor. Their problems were not hers.

Suffolk Law School offered a new channel for her energy. She devoured the contents of the heavy books. Torts, Contracts, Mislaid Property, Bonafide Purchases—all of it equally fascinating. She understood the big picture immediately; instinctively sorting details critical to the mastery of law, storing them in a mind well equipped to access minutiae on demand. Sherall consistently challenged ambiguities until even her professors grew to admire her legal reasoning. She tried briefing case studies in a group, but when she found other students insufferably slow to comprehend, she forged ahead alone.

For a change of atmosphere, Sherall often left Suffolk to study a few blocks away in Bates Hall, the great reading room of the Boston Public Library. This was where she met her future husband, Dr. Scott Green, who she frequently observed sleeping in his wrinkled scrubs at one of the massive oak tables.

He had agreed to pay reduced rent to allow his roommate to entertain his girlfriend in their apartment on Tuesday and Thursday afternoons. One rainy afternoon, he woke from his Bates Hall slumber and propped himself up on the wooden table. Next to him, Sherall flipped through tissue-thin pages of her law books. They struck up a whispered conversation. He found her sharp personality attractive. He could easily relate to another high achiever. Their relationship began in the library, but soon moved down to The Bulkie, a basement-level deli, where they could afford to eat and speak freely.

Scott labored through his medical rotations while Sherall finished law school. She easily passed the Massachusetts Bar Exam. Although they only saw each other once or twice a week, the infrequent schedule suited them. The couple typically had dinner, then sex, then slept a few hours until returning to their individual lives—which they generally found more interesting than each other. A City Hall wedding delivered what they needed to feel they were making progress on life's personal level.

Sherall's courtroom presence as a Boston lawyer was now legendary. She had built her reputation case by case and maintained meticulous records of her strategies. She had found it amusing when junior clerks were sent scurrying for more material as soon as the senior attorneys learned Sherall Savard would be representing the opposition.

Q: Why did you choose your career?
In a courtroom, one wins or loses a case. In sales, one wins or loses a deal. In life? Sherall was stumped.

THE FIRST DINNER
Outside Vivere restaurant, Heidi introduced Darly to her cousin Reggie, the restaurant owner. After he left, the women waited for the others to arrive.

"What a generous man. I'm so glad this worked out for everyone," Darly said.

Heidi nodded. "He said we can meet here as long as we like. The room is only used for family gatherings when business is slow or when they're closed."

The new arrangement took considerable pressure off Darly. With the availability of Vivere, she could meet with the women's group for six additional sessions.

Heidi had taken it upon herself to reach out to each participant via email. The women soon switched to a lively group text. All five agreed to contribute twenty dollars per session for food and drinks. Heidi did not want to bother Darly, so she was not included on the threads.

After all participants were gathered on the sidewalk, Heidi led them through the crowded restaurant and up the creaky back stairs to their special room. She opened the door and let them in.

Dark wood panels covered two of the walls. A fading mural of a family picnic at the bank of the Charles River was on another. Three massive old windows on the fourth wall were propped open with dowels. A gentle breeze tinkled the antique chandelier crystals.

"This is gorgeous!" Kimberly gushed as she entered the room.

The women seated themselves at a large round table covered with a crisp white tablecloth. Red napkins accented each place and a series of candles encased in glass holders circled a low centerpiece of yellow roses. Muffled sounds of pedestrian conversation and traffic drifted up from Boylston Street and the Boston Common.

Seated next to Darly, Heidi whispered, "Don't worry. It just looks expensive. I promise it's still only twenty dollars per person."

A waiter appeared carrying decanters of red and white wine. He set them on the sideboard. Then came a woman with an apron tied across her ample midsection. She set a glass platter of cheese and crackers next to the wine. "This is on the house, ladies," she said.

Heidi rose to kiss the woman on her cheek. "This is my cousin's wife Angela. She's a fan of our project."

Darly said, "Thank you so much for the hors d'oeuvres and for allowing us to meet here."

"I think what you're doing is wonderful. Nobody ever cares about women our age!" Angela beamed, looking around the table as the waiter filled their glasses. "Marco will be back in about twenty minutes with your meal." She and the waiter left the room and closed the door behind them.

Heidi said, "They're going to serve family style so we'll get the best deal. I hope that's okay with everyone."

Darly's smile showed how pleased she was about the way things were unfolding.

Dodo raised her glass toward the others to a propose toast. "Here's to new friendships!"

Glasses clinked and conversation flowed. As promised, waiter Marco reappeared, his arm muscles flexing under the weight of a large tray that he set on the sideboard. The aroma of Tuscany filled the room. A salad of baby greens dressed in honey chardonnay vinaigrette burst over the rim of a Dolfi ceramic bowl. Next to it was pasta stuffed with Ricotta, Burrata, Fontina, and Parmigiano cheeses, topped with shaved black truffles. A platter of herb-marinated chicken, surrounded by roasted potatoes and carrots was positioned beside a large platter of red snapper and colorful early summer vegetables. Warm slipper-shaped Ciabatta rolls nestled in a basket.

"Buon Appetito," Marco said with a bow before leaving them.

"Wow." Even unflappable Sherall was impressed with the offering. "This is truly first rate."

"They've made us an extra special meal," Heidi said. "I've got a buzzer under the table in case anyone needs something."

"Heavenly," Pamela said. "This is such a treat."

"You are fortunate to be a part of this family, Heidi," said Kimberly.

Heidi looked a bit sheepish. "Technically, Angela's husband Reggie is the cousin of my sister-in-law. It took me a long time to get everyone straight, and that's just on my husband's side of the family. My own family is really big, too. Large families are so complicated!"

"Lucky you," murmured Pamela. Her greatest wish was to move beyond her childhood pain as an orphan. She had yet to discover how.

Darly cleared her throat. "I guess this would be a good time to begin our discussion, so we don't end up staying too late. First, just a reminder that you all signed a consent form which allows me to record our meetings. It will help me keep things straight as I collect information. Thanks for agreeing to it."

Darly started the clunky recorder that her department required, then opened her laptop for additional note taking.

She began, "You've all completed the questionnaire about tonight's topic—Ambition. I hope you have some additional comments to share with the group."

"Great topic," Dodo said.

"I need a twelve-step program for mine!" laughed Sherall.

"Do you feel like you *suffer* from it? I wish I had that kind of problem," Heidi said.

"Some people think it's contagious." Dodo looked around the table for consensus.

"I'm probably immune," Kimberly said. "I think I actually avoid the topic. Maybe this meeting will help me catch it." She looked shyly at the others.

Darly gave her a reassuring smile, then glanced at the bullet points on her screen. "Since Dodo brought up the topic last time, let's start with how you all felt when you were pre-adolescent. Does anyone remember being nine years old?"

"Loved it!" laughed Sherall.

Dodo nodded. "Everything seemed so clear then, didn't it?"

"Before the hormones set in?" Darly asked.

"Before we realized we were females and life would always be different," said Heidi. "It suddenly hit me like a brick that my brothers could do whatever they wanted, but I could not."

"Why did you feel that way?" asked Darly.

"I don't know if I understood why, but I felt like people started expecting certain things of me. I knew I wasn't supposed to complain about it. I should want to make life easier for my brothers and father." That same upbringing caused Heidi to feel guilty that she even had this reaction. She had recently allowed herself to consider how unfair that treatment had been to the females in her family. They had never discussed it with each other. They knew implicitly that it was more important to get along, than to make waves and potentially upset the family dynamic.

"I know what you mean," Kimberly said. "I always had to be quiet the minute my dad got home from work. He was king."

"Didn't you want to push back?" asked Darly.

"Not at my house. I somehow knew I'd never be as important as him," Kimberly added. Just like my husband, she reminded herself.

"It was a little different in my family," said DoDo. "My brother was two years older than me. He was the one who was supposed to do great things. I never questioned that."

"And, did he?" asked Darly.

"Do great things? Not exactly. I was the ambitious one. Somehow, I knew I needed to stay a few steps behind him to keep the peace, though."

"Yikes, that must have been tough," commented Heidi. After observing Dodo, Heidi couldn't imagine parents who could ignore her talent and forceful character.

Dodo recalled how deftly she hid her struggle to go against the grain in her profession and her appearance. She was never drawn to personal artifice, but her mother had been, especially on her behalf. Dodo remembered her mother's frequent sighs of displeasure and looks of disapproval about her appearance and actions. Dodo was naturally amiable and pleasing, but chronically falling short of her parents' expectations marred her childhood.

Sherall spoke up. "Personally, I never had a problem with getting what I wanted. It's just the kind of the person I am. I will say that I've pissed off a lot of people along the way, though!" she laughed.

Darly steered the conversation back to her original inquiry. "So when you were girls, how did you see yourselves in terms of a career?"

"You've got to be kidding, Darly," Sherall responded. "There was no real thought of a career when we were that age."

"We were encouraged to be teachers or nurses," added Heidi. "Not that those are bad choices—"

"I remember my mother telling me," Kimberly said, "that being a teacher was the best job for a woman because you could work the same hours that your kids were in school. And summer was off. "

"Well, she was probably right about that," Pamela commented.

"Yes. I suppose she was." Kimberly's voice grew soft. Memories of being mothered and mothering always ambushed her equilibrium.

"Nursing was the other thing." Dodo rolled her eyes. "Do you remember how popular Florence Nightingale was? We were all supposed to want to take care of everyone. It was such a turnoff for me. And, how about the way Florence was portrayed. She seemed so insipid. She was actually the ultimate trailblazer. I wish I knew that at the time. Why didn't they tell us?"

Kimberly sighed and shook her head. "So many women were presented that way in our history books. There's no way we could have known what they were really like. It's a shame. They could have been great role models. We could have aspired to be like their authentic selves."

Pamela added, "The women I remember learning about in school were Florence Nightingale, Clara Barton, Eleanor Roosevelt, and Helen Keller." As a girl, she had devoured every biography about these women. She wanted to understand how they dealt with hardships in life and to learn how to be strong.

"Yeah, but Helen Keller was fascinating because she was a freak," DoDo said. "We pretty much knew we could never be as good as her. And Eleanor Roosevelt was supposed to be great just because she was ugly *and* exceptionally generous. Remember that spin?"

This was Sherall's pet peeve. "If you were docile, doors opened for you. If you had an edge, people freaked out."

"Did that happen to you?" Darly asked.

"Why? Do you think *I* have an edge?" Sherall feigned offense. "People always gang up on me!"

Everyone laughed, but Sherall laughed loudest of all. It wasn't easy, but she tried to assume people liked her, even when she worried they did not.

"Seriously," Darly redirected, "when was the first time any of you contemplated having a career or had an ambition to do something outside of the norm?"

"I don't know if I exactly contemplated a career, but I did dream about seeing the world," Kimberly began.

"Did you?" Darly asked.

"See the world? Just a taste. I went on a school-sponsored summer exchange to France when I was in high school. It was a wonderful experience." Kimberly floated momentarily in memory. She had once believed she would take increasingly long foreign trips until she ultimately become an ex-pat. She would learn other languages, cook exotic foods, and marry someone unusual. She made the mistake of sharing her vision with her mother. She saw pain in her eyes that she did not understand. Kimberly imagined it was the thought of her daughter being so far away. She did not want to risk hurting her mother. She would have to find another dream.

"That must have been fun." Dodo called Kimberly back to the present. "I started what became my career taking pictures when I was about ten. My dad helped me set up a darkroom in our basement. I didn't know how I'd fit into the world of photography, but I just couldn't stop myself. I guess I was compelled to make my own way."

"That was good. And, you're still doing it," Sherall commended her. "The only reason I thought of the idea of law school was because some guy I went out with got so mad about me arguing with him that he said I should be a lawyer, not a *girl*. He said he reminded me of his lawyer father. Damn, he was a good kisser! The kid, not the father. The father couldn't get it up but he did help me get into law school."

The other women stared.

"What?" Sherall stared back, shrugging her shoulders.

Refocusing the group yet again, Darly asked, "Does anyone feel they didn't fulfill their ambition?"

"Darly," Sherall jumped in again, leaning forward this time, "let me tell you. It was like a tsunami when it finally happened to our age group. At first, you weren't supposed to want or try to do *anything* out of the norm. Then, around the early seventies, you were supposed to want to do *everything,* and if you didn't you were a total loser and a traitor to your gender."

Dodo glanced at her with admiration. "God, you nailed it, Sherall."

Heidi said, "I was always kind of embarrassed that I didn't have a big plan. My father made so much fun of 'women's libbers' that my sisters and I didn't dare try to stand out."

"There was a lot of tension at the time, wasn't there?" Pamela asked. "I remember the mailman always dropping my neighbor's copy of Ms. Magazine in the dirt next to her mailbox because he hated it so much."

Heidi nodded. "I believe it. When we started to figure things out, like how women were paid way less than men, we got pretty angry. When my aunt became a single parent after my uncle died, she had to earn serious money. She found out that a guy doing the same job as her got paid much more. There she was, trying to raise her family all by herself! Her boss said she could have a raise if she slept with him. There was nothing she could do about it. She quit and found another job. It wasn't easy. I think she was pretty bitter."

Darly spoke. "That sounds hard. Let's revisit what Sherall said about the tsunami. Was it overwhelming or was it exciting when it all started to happen?"

"Both," answered Dodo. "I mean, we knew something big was happening but we really didn't know how to change things or what to do. The ones who walked point were definitely ridiculed."

Sherall said ruefully. "I can't tell you how often I was hassled just for saying I wanted to be a lawyer."

"But, you stuck with it," Kimberly said. "You should be proud of yourself."

"Thanks. It seems so long ago. Sometimes I forget how hard it was and how much things have changed." Sherall felt almost wistful, remembering those heady days. She always had a constant thirst for challenge—something to keep the adrenaline pumping. Only recently did she tire of the intense pace. This development was surprising and unsettling. Was she losing her edge?

Street sounds below the window had diminished. The mood in the room shifted as everyone took a breath from the conversation.

Darly checked the clock on her laptop. It was time to wrap things up. "I guess we'll have to end it at that. Thanks so much for everything you've offered tonight. If you have any more thoughts on this topic, feel free to email me."

"Darly?" Kimberly asked.

"Yes?"

"Could we get a copy of your report when you're finished?"

"Absolutely."

She stood to distribute the paper announcing the next session's topic: Family.

TOPIC: FAMILY

Why did you choose to have/not have children?
Was your family supportive?
Are you happy about your decision to have/not have children?
How did the decision about family affect your goals?

DARLY

The morning sun was bright, and the air fragrant. Darly boarded the bus she always took from affordable Allston to her tiny BU office in the city. She felt exhilarated about the outcome of last night's dinner with the study participants. Everything seemed *fluid*. She had not expected the women to be so forthcoming. Was it her method, the wine, or just the randomness of strangers who hit it off?

When she arrived home last night, her roommate Gracie was still awake and chatty. They discussed the study over a few glasses of wine. Out of respect for the participants' anonymity, Darly used the nicknames Ian had created.

Gracie said she felt sorry for the women. "Some of them sound lost. Why did they let the massive opportunity of that era pass them by?"

Darly responded, "Not all of them did."

Gracie offered, "It does seem like Sad Beauty and Guilty Perfectionist did. You describe them as pretty competent. Tired Cheerleader is the only one who seems content where she is."

"Maybe there is more to their stories. I know Guilty Perfectionist has five kids. That probably made things harder."

Gracie rolled her eyes. "Oh, come on. She could have used birth control or found a nanny. Where does she live?"

"Newton."

"Then they're rich. No excuse. She chose her husband and kids over herself."

Darly nodded. "You might be right. But, why?"

"Maybe she was lazy or maybe she was scared."

Gracie had something to say about them all. She thought three of them were one-man-away-from-welfare. She said Attention Addict's marriage was probably on the rocks from her outrageous personality. Aging Free Bird was just weird.

Gracie concluded, "They're all old. If they haven't done anything yet, it's too late for them now."

Before Darly met the participants, she assumed they would present as tired old women. That preconception was quickly shattered. Her assessment of them was already evolving. She was eager to learn more about their lives, not just for the study, but because she was personally curious. She wished Gracie could meet them. She was sure her opinion would change if she did.

KIMBERLY DOLAN

Standing in the middle of the kitchen, Kimberly surveyed the spotless room. She had washed the floor, cleaned counter tops, emptied the dishwasher, and folded laundry. The Dutch oven was full and set to simmer; a faint smell of pork, onion, and apple wafted through the room. She turned and walked down the hall.

In the study, she sat at the massive walnut burl desk, nudging the leather triangle corners of the green blotter to center it on the surface. She pulled open the bottom drawer. Toward the back was a box of vellum stationary, and next to it was a similarly sequestered fountain pen. Both had been purchased for a specific purpose. She removed a watermarked sheet of paper, placed it on the blotter, then pulled off the fountain pen cap.

Dear Bruce and Children, she wrote.

Kimberly stared at the blue ink on the page, then put the pen down.

The kids would hate to be called children. She ran the sheet through the shredder.

Dear Bruce, Matt, Kurt, Brittney, Connor, and Meghan,

I know I have not been the kind of mother and wife you wanted me to be and I am sorry for that.

Kimberly tapped the end of the pen against her bottom lip. Bruce would dislike being grouped together with the kids. She fed that sheet into the shredder. She would compose the kids' letter first, then move onto her husband's.

Dear Matt, Kurt, Brittney, Connor, and Meghan,

I know I have not been the kind of mother you would like to have had. I am sorry for all of the things I was unable to do for you and the things I did that you did not like. I love every one of you and always tried to do my best.

None of you ever had the chance to meet my mother but I think you would have liked her. She was almost perfect in so many ways. She woke me up every morning by softly singing, "Oh, What a Beautiful Morning." After that, she would pull back the curtains in my room and tell me I could sleep for fifteen more minutes. She always came back as promised to wake me up again. Every day after breakfast, I'd grab my paper lunch bag off the counter just before the school bus arrived. She always printed my name on the bag in fancy letters using different colored markers to draw cute little figures that showed the things I was going to do at school that day. My friends teased me about those bags, but I felt lucky to have a mother who cared so much about me.

I tried to let you know I cared about you. I went to all of your practices, games, and recitals. I know none of you particularly liked my cooking, but I tried to give you healthy foods and make nice snacks for you and your friends when they visited. I enjoyed decorating the dining room for your birthday dinners, too.

Kimberly stopped writing, capped the fountain pen, and put it back into its case. Blowing across the letter to dry the ink, she carried it over to the bookshelf. The giant dictionary that no one consulted anymore automatically fell open to page 1249. The text on the top left was *subtrahend—sulforaphane. Suicide*, located about one third down the page, was highlighted. Also on that page were eighteen similarly written letters. Someday, she would compose the perfect message, and then—when the time was right—she would end her life, just as her own mother had.

She considered this her destiny. Like her mother, she had given everything to her children. She had loved them so thoroughly, so overwhelmingly, so comprehensively, that they had no need to love her back. There was nothing she could do to change that now.

The problem was that she could never bear to have them unhappy with her or see them unhappy with themselves. As a result, she had a family of self-centered individuals who knew they could rely on Kimberly for anything, even tasks that should no longer be her responsibility. This kept each of them in her life, but not in a healthy reciprocal way. Little love was returned to her as they grew and matured. Now she felt empty and used. Each family member focused on his or her own small world. No one thought to share joys with her.

Others suggested she was experiencing an empty nest syndrome, clucking that she would soon bounce back and adjust to her shrinking household. Her children would become responsible adults at last, they promised. The transition did not materialize as they forecast. Kimberly saw ahead only more sacrifice and constant giving to a preoccupied and self-absorbed husband, thoughtless children, and eventually, a brood of equally demanding grandchildren.

Not a promising future.

Q: Are you happy about your decision to have/not have children?

Kimberly would like to ask her children if they were happy that they had her.

SHERALL SAVARD

Sherall wasn't close to Scott, her maniacally busy physician husband. She wasn't close to her daughter, Lina, in California, or her son, Luke, in New York. She wasn't close to Joyce, her eighty-three year old mother, who had a lively social circle at her retirement home. She wasn't close to her older brother Derrick who had married an Asian woman and lived in Beijing. All five appeared content with their arrangements without her. She wondered if it was too late to change that. If she reached out to any of them now, would it seem odd and self-serving? She should have shown interest years ago.

She could start by visiting her mother where she lived at Hilton Head. It was a short flight, easily managed over a weekend. Her mother would act like no time at all had lapsed between their visits. She was more like Sherall than Sherall cared to admit. Joyce had been physically present when Sherall was a girl, but had also been emotionally absent. Regardless of their past relationship, the idea that her mother would not live forever was nagging at her conscience. Sherall yearned to make peace with conflicting emotions, if only for her own sake.

Next, she considered the difficult challenge in Lina. Her daughter had grown into a stunning young woman whose battles with anorexia were finally conquered. She wondered if she had a steady boyfriend to share her confidences. If Sherall ever met the young man, she assumed he would have a poor opinion of his girlfriend's absentee mother. She would have to bear it. It was well deserved.

Luke was already a man. She knew her husband Scott had been in touch with him. How unfair that a father who neglected his son for a decade could move back into his life without recrimination. She had seen this same scenario frequently with divorced parents. A mother spilled blood rearing her children for years, then suddenly their father reappeared, and everyone treated him like a returning king. No questions asked.

Her marriage was equally problematic. At first, she and Scott considered each other a perfect match. They fed off each other's ambition and energy. Those who knew them marveled at the couple's ability to maintain their breakneck speed in tandem with a marital relationship. Because they spent so little time together, it seemed a miracle when two babies were successively conceived and birthed. Unfortunately, the bond between parents and babies was tenuous. They were never a real family. Nannies raised the children, and thank goodness, *they* were loving people. The first nanny, Mrs. Velasquez, was with them until Lina turned eight and Luke turned six. After that, Carole Mitchell stepped in, shepherding them through boarding school at Choate Rosemary Hall in Connecticut. She returned to stay with them during the kids' breaks. She said she was happy to do it. The money was incentive enough, Sherall thought, but it seemed Carole truly loved the children.

There was a heavy price to pay for emotional negligence, and Sherall considered it her due punishment. Last summer, Luke spent thirty days in drug rehabilitation at McLean Hospital, and there was also Lina's anorexia. Years prior, when Choate Rosemary Hall contacted Sherall about their concern for her daughter, she was befuddled about what action to take. When she told Scott, he sent her names of three colleagues she should refer Lina to, as if a fifteen year old could manage her own health issue. Sherall forwarded the information to Carole Mitchell. She knew she'd take care of it better than either of them.

Q: Why did you choose to have/not have children?
It was the only decision for which Sherall had no answer. She hated herself for it.

DODO QUIMBY
Dodo wondered if her daughter Georgie had begun looking at colleges yet. She was seventeen now and would be a senior in the fall. It was hard to imagine her on the cusp of adulthood.

She smiled, recalling one of their visits together when she was six years old. Georgie wanted to make brownies that day. Dodo had no cooking tools or even an appropriate baking dish at her drafty Cambridge loft. She knocked on her neighbor's door and asked to borrow a cookbook.

Mother and daughter walked to the corner store to buy ingredients. Dodo pointed to many boxed mixes with simple instructions to add water, oil, and eggs. Georgie refused to negotiate about her preference for homemade cooking. So, they bought flour, baking soda, baker's chocolate, and the rest of the brownie ingredients listed in the cookbook.

Later, at the kitchen counter, Dodo searched her drawers for a mixing spoon. "Do you think it's okay if we use a fork instead?" she asked Georgie.

"Dodo, you have to use a spoon."

"Don't forget to call me Mom," Dodo admonished.

"Ok. *Mom*, you have to use a spoon." Georgie looked over at her, raising her eyebrows in exasperation.

"Well, I'm sure I'll find one." Dodo finally pulled out two tablespoons. "Let's just use these."

Georgie looked doubtful but took one of the spoons from her mother.

"Now you put in the flour," Georgie said, pointing to the bag.

"But, how much?"

"You have to read the recipe, Dodo."

"*Mom*," Dodo reminded.

"Mom," Georgie sighed.

Dodo consulted the recipe, took a coffee cup out of the cabinet, and then filled it with flour. "This is probably about one cup."

"Okay. Just pour it in."

"I think we have to add some more dry stuff," Dodo said, consulting the cookbook.

"It's called bite-carbonny."

"Bite-carbonny?"

"Yes. You can never eat it plain or it will kill you." Georgie's affect was stern. "You should learn about this, Mom."

"Okay. Let's see. It says here, baking powder. We got baking soda."

"That's it. That's the bite-carbonny."

"Oh." Dodo took the tablespoon and filled it with baking soda, then added it to the bowl.

Georgie looked up at Dodo. "You have to stir it."

"That can be your job."

Dodo broke off four pieces of the Baker's Chocolate and tossed them into the bowl that Georgie stirred.

Her daughter was skeptical. "I don't think this is how you do it."

By this time, Dodo had lost interest in their activity. She added a cracked egg, a coffee cup of oil, and a little bit of water.

Georgie stopped stirring. "It doesn't usually look like this."

"Well, it's all going to melt together and it will look right after that."

She let Georgie pour the mess into the disposable foil pan, then put it into the oven.

"How long does it take to cook, Georgie?"

"A very long time."

"Okay, let's take some pictures of you while we're waiting."

"Daddy says I can't let you take pictures of me."

"Really."

"Yes. He says I'm way too pretty to be in your pictures and he thinks you will try to put me in a magazine or something."

Dodo gritted her teeth, then took a deep breath.

"It's true that you are pretty enough for a magazine but I just want to keep the pictures for myself."

"Daddy says no."

"All right. Let's go down to the park then."

They left the loft.

When they returned an hour later, the hallway was filled with the acrid smell of burned chocolate. Her neighbor stood next to the building superintendent who shook his keys at Dodo. Dodo rushed in, leaving Georgie behind to discuss her mother's incompetence with the responsible adults.

Q: How did the decision about family affect your goals?

Dodo should have added Georgie's name to her list of goals.

PAMELA CARDIN

Pamela closed her eyes and thought back to 1991.

"It's called, *What To Expect When You're Expecting*," she told the clerk at the book store.

"That's very popular. I think we have one copy left. Please follow me."

At the shelf, the clerk handed the book to Pamela, smiled and left. Pamela flipped through the pages, noting numerous suggestions and instructions to follow to achieve a healthy pregnancy. There were similar books on adjacent shelves. She selected *A Child Is Born*, then sat on the Danish design chair at the end of the aisle. On page eighty-nine, there was a photograph of a 5-6 week old fetus in utero. Its dark eyes looked at her. Tiny webbed fingers reached out.

Closing the cover, she returned both books to the shelf. It was probably better not to have copies at home.

Next door, at the upscale children's clothing store Little Ones, she lingered in the crowded aisles, fingering small shirts and pants and tiny dresses. On a table at the end of one aisle, she spotted some yellow satin booties. She caressed them in the palm of her hand, trying to imagine feet small enough to fit. Newborn $19.00, read the attached tag. Pamela took the weightless bundle to the counter and paid the cashier.

"Are congratulations in order?" the clerk asked, handing her the bag.

"Maybe," Pamela answered softly.

Bruce arrived home early. He had flowers in one arm and a small blue box from Tiffany's in other.

"Sorry about the other night," he started, moving close to her. "I don't know what got into me. Everyone at work was gushing about how beautiful you looked at the event. I promise not to get mad at you for stealing the spotlight again."

"Oh, Bruce, it's okay. I know you have so much stress at work. I should be more aware of that."

He set the flowers on the counter, then handed her the box.

Pamela knew what to do. She opened the box and said it was the most beautiful piece of jewelry she had ever seen, and that she was the luckiest woman in the world.

He always kept her on the edge. If he wasn't gushing, he was gnashing. Hopefully, this most recent apology was a new start for them. She would not lose hope.

Over a candlelit dinner, she told Bruce she was pregnant.

"How the *fuck* did that happen?"

"Maybe when I had that horrible cold and took antibiotics. They say that can interfere with the pill." She did not dare remind Bruce that he had insisted she take the drugs so she would be well enough to host an important business party.

"If you knew that already, why did you let it happen?"

"I was so congested. I guess I wasn't thinking clearly."

They both looked down at their plates.

Bruce finally spoke.

"Make the appointment."

"But, Bruce. This time—"

"You heard what I said."

"I—"

"Goddammit!" Bruce rose and Pamela instinctively turned away from him, leaning into the wooden arm of her chair. As he moved, he bumped her, perhaps unintentionally, but the hard wood pressed into her belly.

Q: Was your family supportive?

Pamela was certain they would have been.

HEIDI BELANGER

Heidi finished wrapping foil around the last sub, then added it to the eleven others already in the cooler. She always made extra food, anticipating her sons would unexpectedly invite friends to their family gatherings.

"Two bags of chips, pickles, cookies, napkins, dip..." Heidi was thinking out loud just as Jim walked into the kitchen.

"You're talking to yourself," he said, smiling.

"As long as I'm listening to myself, too," she responded.

Jim walked over to her and draped his big arm over her shoulder. "What's for lunch?"

"I made ham and Swiss subs and a few roast beef sandwiches."

"Sounds great. I'm going to pack the car. Did you get the beer?"

"It's already in the other cooler down by the door."

"Good job, Hon'." He kissed the top of her head and left the room.

Jim was an excellent husband; faithful and hardworking. He and Heidi had been married thirty-six years. They had been truly happy years and she did not wish to live them over in any other way. She enjoyed raising her sons and spending time with both sides of their extended families.

Today, Jim and sons Justin and Jordan were going to meet at their house at Island Pond in New Hampshire. She and Jim bought the house ten years ago, furnishing it in incremental spurts with yard sale finds. The boys spent a considerable amount of time there. The house was not theirs, but ownership of what belonged to whom seemed to be blurring as they progressed through young adulthood. Justin and Jordan both worked full time, but their salaries were meager. Because of that, Jim worried they would feel inferior. He wanted Heidi and him to continue to be generous with what they had.

Jim had saved his money, though. That's how he was able to buy the various snowmobiles, kayaks, and the small boat they kept at the pond. Their sons were more interested in spending. If there was any friction between Jim and Heidi, it usually involved the topic of giving too much to their boys.

Heidi loved being busy with family activities and waking up to tasks only she could accomplish well. For decades, she tended to the needs of their large circle of relatives. It was a boisterous and lively group and she found pleasure in their company. The rules were firm, however, and the pecking order was clear: husbands were in charge, children's priorities came next, and wives kept husbands and children fed and comfortable.

Jim returned to the kitchen.

"Are you ready?" he asked.

"Do I have a choice?"

"No," he said, smiling.

"Then, yes." Heidi smiled back.

TOPIC: FAMILY

Family was *always* the topic. She wondered if there was any room left for herself.

DARLY

"Hey."

She looked for the face to match the voice. Ian took a step closer and touched her elbow, distinguishing himself from the rest of the crowd waiting in line outside the movie theater.

"Oh, hi!" she responded.

"Which movie are you seeing?" he asked.

"Wavelength. How about you?"

"Same."

At that moment, a tall woman with long red hair sidled up to him. "Who's your friend, Ian?" she sang.

"Marla, this is Darly. Darly, Marla." Marla had green eyes and copper-hued skin. Three silver chains weighted with a collection of pendants nestled between her breasts.

"Nice to meet you," Darly offered. She heard her own group of friends call her toward the front of the line where they had progressed. "I guess I'd better buy my ticket. Enjoy the movie."

"You, too." Ian answered.

"Nice to meet you!" Marla called out.

When Darly reached her group, they walked together through the double doors.

Her friend and roommate Gracie looked back toward Ian. "What a hunk!" she said. "Who is that guy?"

"My academic adviser. He's with his girlfriend, I guess."

"That's the one you told me about? Too bad."

"Yeah. Too bad." Darly responded.

Gracie was one reason why the theater was crowded. As a freelance writer, she had submitted her movie review to DIG Boston, an alternative newspaper. After that, everyone their age wanted to see the film.

In the twilight interior, Darly watched Ian and Marla find two of the few empty seats several rows in front of where she sat with her friends.

Marla's red hair shimmered under the low light as she settled into her seat and pivoted her attention between Ian and the screen. Darly observed the back of their heads as they carried on animated conversation. Marla's infectious laugher during the movie was unmistakable.

The next day, Darly replayed the audio recording of the first study dinner. She wished she had directed it with more authority. A strong personality like Sherall would have to be tempered, while Kimberly would need to be drawn out. There was always the risk she could lose control of this group of disparate personalities as they became comfortable with one another. She vowed to keep the upper hand. Her undergraduate degree in psychology would be a real asset.

THE SECOND DINNER

Inside Vivere, gauzy curtains blew around the windows as heavy rain outside cooled the upstairs room. A pink damask cloth covered the round table. A square vase packed with white tulips was at its center.

The seated women turned their attention to Darly.

"I hope everyone had a good week," she began.

Their smiles relieved Darly. She hoped their lively rapport from their first dinner would continue. She had since listened to the recording of that night numerous times. Each time, her confidence diminished. She had not anticipated how much they seemed to play off of one another's comments. Her presence seemed secondary.

Darly continued, "Tonight's topic is Family. Does anyone want to begin?"

"I will," Heidi volunteered. "I think I probably have the biggest extended family!"

"Do you like that?" encouraged Darly.

"Pros and cons. There are always people I know around me. They drop by my house. I see them at the grocery. When I meet someone new, they know one of my relatives or in-laws. There's always a connection."

"So, you feel part of something bigger?" asked Darly.

"I guess you could put it that way."

"How many of you are there?" Pamela asked.

"We only have two sons but then there are my four sisters and two brothers, their husbands and wives and kids. So, that's, ah, thirty. Plus our two boys, my husband, and me makes thirty-four. Then there are my mom and dad, so add two more. My husband has five brothers, and they're all married, and they all have kids. I think there are twenty-four of them. No, wait, twenty-six. Then, there are my aunts and uncles and cousins and their kids, too. All local." Heidi shrugged her shoulders. "Honestly, I've lost count. If we all get together, it can easily be over a hundred."

"God, I'd need a matrix to remember that," Dodo laughed.

Darly consulted her computer screen. "Let's back up for a second. I forgot that I'm probably the only one who knows everyone's situation. Sherall has two kids; Dodo has one; Heidi has two; Kimberly has five; and Pamela is childless.

Pamela lowered her eyes.

Darly continued. "Let's move on to you, Kimberly. *Five* kids!"

The focus shifted to the other side of the table where Kimberly sat.

"Correct. There's Matt, Kurt, Brittney, Connor, and Meghan. Only Meghan is still at home, though." It was important to her that everyone knew her children's names.

Sherall stood. "I bow down to you, Earth Mother."

Everyone laughed.

"It's not that big of a deal. You take it one day at a time. Pretty soon, they become your life." Kimberly's smile was lopsided.

"And, then?" Pamela asked.

"Well, it's not what I expected. Things sort of fell apart."

"What do you mean?" Darly asked.

"One minute you're doing everything for everyone, and the next minute, they're all gone." Kimberly's eyes searched the others for confirmation.

"I was relieved when that happened to me," Heidi said.

"I suppose it's good if you have another plan." Kimberly's voice trailed off.

"What about when the kids were little?" Darly asked. "Did anyone feel they had made the wrong choice to have them?"

"That's a hell of a question, Darly," Sherall said.

"I suppose," she responded.

Dodo offered, "It didn't seem like the smart thing to do at the time, for sure. We all knew it would tax our ambition and energy. Daycare was supposed to be this straightforward thing we did with the kids while we worked but everyone learned how unreliable daycare actually was. It was theory versus reality. A grand experiment."

"It sounds like you might have had some bad experiences," Darly said.

"I don't know if you could say they were bad, but my ex and I were always arguing about who should be the one to take care of our daughter. With only one child, things never seemed to tilt in the direction of family. It was always two single lives with one kid between them." Dodo rubbed her temples, as if reliving the stress of the past.

"So, did you feel pressure to accept a traditional role for the sake of your daughter?" Darly asked.

"Yes!" Dodo answered. "And, I hated that feeling. It took me by surprise, too. I love my daughter but it didn't take long for me to resent all of the time I was supposed to devote to her. Things like taking a walk in the park together made me crazy. Instead of enjoying her playing on the swings, I just wanted to photograph what was going on around us."

"You could have taken pictures of *her*, right?" Kimberly asked. She had thousands of photos of her own kids.

"Yeah, but for some reason, I didn't find that inspiring. Sounds bad, I know. I wanted to do what I wanted to do.

It was a perpetual annoyance."

"Was your husband supportive?" Heidi asked.

"No. After the baby was born, he considered my work frivolous. To be fair, I really hadn't hit my professional stride. It was a double bind for me though. I felt I was on the cusp of something. I knew if I just gave it more effort, I'd break through artistically."

Darly jumped in. "All right. So, at least for DoDo, parenthood and professional achievement were incompatible. Anybody else?"

Sherall spoke next. "I totally get what you're saying, Dodo. Here's the thing, though. Women can't have it all. It really sucks to say that, but I think it's the truth. We set ourselves up to achieve in a singular field, but once we have kids, the whole scheme falls apart."

"Can you elaborate?" Darly asked.

"Nobody tells you that you have to put in the drudgery to get a kid to love you. They won't love you if you only show up for dessert."

The other women nodded.

"Fathers don't get the same treatment," Dodo added. "It also sucks when the kid seems to love the nanny more than you."

"Yes," Sherall responded. "That's the price you pay. You get a professional life served with a shitload of guilt."

"Do you still feel guilty, Sherall?" asked Kimberly.

"Sure do." Sherall pursed her lips.

Kimberly spoke again. "I don't know if this will help, but *I* feel guilty, too. And, I was almost always home for my kids. I basically have done everything for them and pretty much still do."

"What do you feel guilty about?" Darly asked.

"That I never left them. That I never explored myself."

"Hmm. That must be hard to live with," Darly said.

"It is. I'm kind of hoping it's not too late."

"It's definitely not too late, Kimberly!" Heidi offered. "I'm feeling the same way, too. It can't be too late. We still have so many years left."

Kimberly looked shyly at the group. "But, won't it seem silly to start something new at this stage?"

Dodo gave her a stern look. "It would be a crime if you didn't. It's still *your* life. It's always been your life. You just never gave yourself permission to live it."

Kimberly smiled. "Thank you. That really helps."

Darly took charge. "The only one I think we haven't heard from yet is you, Pamela. I know you don't have children, but what are your thoughts on this?"

Pamela shifted uncomfortably in her chair as five sets of eyes focused on her.

"I would have liked to have had children but my husband never wanted them. It's just one of those things I've tried to accept. There really is nothing I can do about it now. And also, he insisted I have my tubes tied." She lowered her eyes.

"How old were you when you did that?" Darly's tone was tender. It was hard to be otherwise when addressing Pamela.

"Thirty-eight. It was hardly worth the effort for just a few more years. My husband was persistent. A year after that, he had a vasectomy. I'm not really sure why."

"Well, duh. He must have been cheating," Sherall pointed out.

"Maybe."

"What do *you* think?" Sherall persisted.

"I don't know. I think he probably did. Maybe he still does."

With this comment, the room grew quiet. Pamela folded her napkin and looked like she would like to leave.

Darly swiftly changed the topic.

"The pill was still fairly new when you were teenagers. Did anyone want to take it?" Darly asked.

"Hell, yes! I got mine at Planned Parenthood," Sherall said. "That's where everyone I knew went. I think I was fifteen at the time." She chuckled. "I rode my bike there."

The other women chuckled at the image of a teen Sherall.

"No guys were looking at me when *I* was fifteen, that's for sure!" Dodo laughed.

"I might have started a little too early," Sherall admitted, grinning.

"My father would have killed me if he found out I tried the pill," Heidi said. "I'm not sure about my mother. She probably wished she could have used it. Honestly, can you imagine having seven kids in eight years?"

"What birth control do you think she used after that?" Dodo asked.

"I'm starting to think she was so busy that she and my dad rarely got together. Or, she was exhausted and became less fertile. Not really sure. I just knew that I would never let that happen to me."

"Having so many children?" Darly clarified.

"Yes," Heidi answered.

Kimberly cleared her throat, then spoke. "Well, this

may sound ridiculous, but I really enjoyed being pregnant and having my babies. They were so cute when they were little. Plus, when I was pregnant, people were extra nice to me and always asked how I was feeling." She looked around, apologetically.

"You really are an earth mother. Power to ya, babe," Sherall said.

"I think it sounds lovely, Kimberly," Pamela encouraged.

Dodo said, "I felt like I looked stupid when I was pregnant. Not just physically, but mentally."

"You probably didn't get fat, did you?" Heidi asked.

"No. I wore baggy shirts, too. No one could tell what was going on underneath them until the last month or so."

"What about abortion?" inquired Darly.

The women were silent.

"No one?" Darly urged.

Pamela looked down at her plate. "I had three."

"I'm so sorry. It looks like those are painful memories," Darly said.

Pamela nodded. "One was when I was twenty-nine; two in my thirties."

"But why?" Seated next to her, Heidi gently put her hand over Pamela's on the tabletop.

"Like I said, my husband never wanted kids. I thought things would change when he found out I was pregnant— but, no. He insisted."

Sympathetic eyes turned to Pamela.

"Why did you stay?" Dodo asked softly.

Pamela sighed. "Why do any of us? I believed in the dream, I guess. I thought I should keep holding onto it, just in case."

Darly asked, "Now that you're too old to have kids, does your husband regret it?" She missed how others winced at her phrasing.

Pamela answered, "I'm not sure. It's not something we talk about. Our lifestyle really never had room for kids. Plus, Bruce always said he didn't want to share me with anyone."

"So, he pampers you?" asked Dodo.

"No. Far from it. But, I don't want to get too personal." Pamela looked tense.

"Isn't that why we're here?" asked Sherall.

Dodo threw out a challenge. "Okay, then you go first."

Sherall turned to Darly. "What do you need to know?"

"What about you and abortion?" Darly responded.

"I had one. I was an undergraduate. I asked my roommate to come with me and wait while I had it. I think it got to her. She didn't want to talk about it later. I honestly don't know who the father was."

"Do you ever wonder about the baby?" Kimberly asked. She imagined being haunted by the experience.

Sherall turned toward her. "Well, it wasn't a baby; it was a fetus. And, yes, I sometimes do think about it. It would have had a horrible life with me as its mother. I definitely did it a favor."

"How can you say that, Sherall?" asked Heidi.

"I just said it."

For the second time, the women fell silent. Darly had not considered whether her own mother had ever had an abortion. She made a note to ask her father when they spoke next.

Dodo said, "You know, Darly, you should never take the right to choose for granted."

Darly was confident. "I don't think my generation has to worry about that."

The older women exchanged glances. They knew how naïve this assumption was. Politics could change everything.

"Let's move onto another perspective," Darly said. "If you don't mind being honest, I'd like to know whether having a family was worth it. Would you do it again?"

"Another big-ass question." Sherall inhaled deeply through her nose. "I'd have to say, no—and I can tell you why."

The other women watched intently.

"The thing that might surprise you, is not that I think having children is bad for everyone, it's just been bad for me. I'm not the nurturing, give-everything-away kind of person. Missing that trait can be a disaster if you're a mother."

"But, you do have two kids, right?" Pamela asked.

"Yes, except it seems like I barely know them. First, they had nannies, then they had boarding school. Then college. They're mostly on their own now. They don't need me. I think the nannies and their friends' parents raised them pretty well. I sent birthday presents and things to them at boarding school and at college. It's always been kind of polite. There's not a lot of affection in either direction." Sherall twisted her napkin, uncharacteristically lowering her guard. "I'm not particularly proud of this. You guys are really getting an earful."

"You shouldn't be too hard on yourself," Darly offered.

Sherall lowered her eyes for a moment. "I *should* have done better, and you all know it. I let them down."

"That *should* thing will kill you if you let it, you know," Kimberly's voice was barely audible.

"Maybe. I can't go back and do anything different now," Sherall countered. "That's the hard part."

"Have you ever considered starting over with them?" asked Heidi.

"What do you mean?"

Heidi continued. "How old is your daughter?"

"Twenty-six," Sherral answered.

"How about asking her to go on a trip with you this year?" Heidi offered.

"I doubt she'd want to do that."

"But, have you asked?" Heidi persisted.

"No."

"That would be great for you both," Dodo said.

"I have to go to Japan for work in November," Sherall said.

"Perfect! You could take her with you!" Heidi was not letting this go.

"I could show her around the places I know."

"There you go." Heidi sat back in her seat, satisfied. Sherall smiled at her. She was unaccustomed to this kind of compassionate attention. It made her feel a little shy.

Darly resumed questioning. "Kimberly, you're the one with the most kids. You told us a little about how you feel about parenting. Is there anything else you want to add?"

"I'm fine with the way things are, really. My kids are all happy and living their own lives. After they get married, I guess I'll have the grandkids." Kimberly put up a good front.

"So, it was all worth it?" asked Pamela.

"I guess so," Kimberly answered. "It's been my life. I don't know what else I might have done." Actually, she did know what else she might have done, but it was futile to consider that now.

"How old is your youngest child?" Darly asked.

"She just turned eighteen."

"So, she's graduating this year?"

"Yes. She's going to Brown University in Rhode Island."

"Wow." Dodo remarked. "Things are really going to change for you this fall."

Kimberly nodded. "I'll probably pick up some hours at my husband's accounting business to make up for the extra time." She knew this would be impossible since her husband had recently banned her from his office.

"Is that what you want to do?" Heidi asked.

"I guess. I haven't really thought about it much."

"Maybe *you're* the one who should go on a trip," Pamela said.

"My husband doesn't like to travel," Kimberly responded.

"Who said anything about your husband?" Sherall asked.

Kimberly's face gave it all away. It was clear she had never considered this. "I wouldn't know where to go by myself. I guess I could start thinking about it, though."

"Woo hoo!" Dodo clapped her hands and stomped her feet. "Way to rally, Kimberly!"

There was laughter around the table.

Darly looked down at her computer. "And, how about you, Dodo? We haven't heard much from you on this topic."

"Oh, god. Here we go," Dodo responded.

"You said you have one daughter. What's her name?" Darly continued.

"Georgie."

"That's so sweet," Pamela said.

"It's actually Georgia. After Georgia O'Keefe."

"Nice. How old is she?" Darly asked.

"Seventeen."

"I've heard that's a tough age," Pamela commented.

"It is for me, at least," Dodo said.

"Is she hard to live with?" Kimberly asked.

"She lives with her father." Dodo's voice was flat.

Kimberly was mortified to have inadvertently exposed a tender spot in this seemingly tough woman. "I'm sorry. That must be painful for you."

"I'm kind of used to it by now. She's been with him since she was three. After my divorce."

"Do they live in Boston?" Heidi asked.

"No. Connecticut. He's remarried and that's where his wife is from."

"So, you see Georgie on the weekends?" Darly asked.

"She doesn't want to see me."

The rain had stopped. In the quiet room, DoDo could hear the collective murmur of compassion.

"That sounds hard," Darly said. She had risen to the moment, but she felt over her head. The dinner had become more like a group counseling session, not the fact finding mission Darly had foreseen. She knew the next thing she should say. "Do you want to share any more about it?"

"I guess I might as well. It seems like we're all spilling our guts, right?"

"It's up to you," Darly responded. She reminded herself to keep breathing.

"Okay." Dodo paused to refill her wine glass. "Right after Georgie was born, I got my first big booking for a photo shoot. Dallas. I remember so well being torn by the excitement of it—and then realizing that I would have to wean my baby right away. I mean wean, like, over the weekend. It was horrible. She kept screaming and pushing the bottle away. Finally, I just handed her to her father and hid in another room. I knew she had to get used to Rolf feeding her. They were both unbelievably mad at me. But, I'd tried so long to get this kind of work. And then suddenly, there it was. Plus, we needed the money."

"So, you left for Texas?" Darly prompted.

Dodo nodded. "I was gone a week. Rolf's mother helped with the baby. Pretty much everyone was still angry with me when I got back."

"What else could you have done?" Sherall asked.

"I know. That's exactly how I felt. After that shoot, I kept getting better offers. I was pretty much gone two weeks out of every month. Starting out, it really helps to be able to drop other things when you're on assignment. I was either doing nothing, or crazy busy. I'd be with Georgie during the time I was home, then not even able to speak with her for the rest of the time. Sometimes, when I made it back home, I'm not sure she knew who I was."

"That stinks," Sherall said.

"It sure did. I was bringing in some pretty good money, so for a while, Rolf was fine with that. Then, he met someone who had kids and everything changed. We split, and he got custody. The judge didn't think very much of me. To be honest, at that point, I wasn't sure where Georgie would fit into my life, either. Maybe it was all for the best."

"She's going to get why you did this when she's older, Dodo," Darly said.

Five exasperated faces pivoted toward Darly. Clearly, there was something *she* did not understand about the conversation. Her heart beat a bit faster. Just as quickly, heads turned back to Dodo.

"Maybe." Dodo lifted her shoulders, halfheartedly.

Darly struggled to recover from her apparent faux pas, then asked, "There's one more thing I want to hear about. Maternity leave."

"Say what?" Sherall asked.

"Maternity leave. I'm curious about how much time women took off and what it was like returning to work."

"Darly, Darly, Darly," Sherall shook her head.

The other women smiled.

"I'm sorry. It looks like I'm out of the loop again. What's up?" Darly asked. She was grateful the dinner would soon be over. The information was excellent, but the process was exhausting and stressful.

"There was no such thing as maternity leave when we were your age," Dodo said.

"But, I thought—" Darly started.

Sherall revealed the facts. "It was totally at the

discretion of your employer, or sometimes the state where you lived. I basically used two weeks of sick time I'd accumulated, and then another week of vacation. I showed my face at the firm without the baby every few days just to bare my fangs at everyone so they knew I was still ferocious. I *never* talked about my children at work."

Dodo added, "Since I was self-employed, it was work or don't get paid. It was local gigs in the early weeks, but I don't really think I took a break. It's kind of a blur now."

Kimberly spoke next. "That must have been so hard for you both. I was only working at my husband's office, so I got to stay home until the kids were old enough for school. I do remember some of the women in his office quitting after they had kids, even though he gave them a little time off. He was angry when they said they would return but didn't. He didn't pay them for the time off, but he still counted on them to come back to their positions."

"That doesn't seem very professional of them," Darly ventured.

"Darly," Heidi said, "sometimes a woman is surprised at how she feels about leaving her baby. Before it's born, everything seems so organized. You think you can manage emotionally. Afterward, especially with sleep deprivation, things can look pretty different. I thought I'd go back after a few months, but I ended up waiting until my youngest was in kindergarten. I worked as a teacher's aide then. The hours were really good and the money helped us a lot. Plus, most of us there were women, so sometimes we covered for each other. We had to get sneaky if one of our kids was sick or daycare failed."

Although Darly didn't want to end the meeting on a

serious note, she realized their time had exceeded the allocated two hours. "I guess we'll need to wrap up with that. I really appreciate all of you being so candid with me. I hope I didn't step on any toes."

"Not mine," Dodo said.

"Don't worry about it, Darly," Heidi encouraged.

"It was like a little free group therapy," Pamela added, smiling.

"Okay. Good. And, thank you. Here are the handouts for next time."

It was just what was needed to change the tone. The group's laughter grew raucous as they read the topic.

"Pandora's box!" Sherall yelled out.

"She doesn't know what she's getting into," Heidi giggled.

"What?" Darly smiled, innocently.

"You'll see," Dodo said.

TOPIC: LOVE and SEXUALITY
Did the sexual revolution revolutionize your sex?
Have you found sexual fulfillment?
Is sex love?
How has your sexuality changed?
Is love enough?

DODO QUIMBY/PAMELA CARDIN

The meeting was over, but Dodo was in the mood for something sweet. She sprinted to catch up with Pamela who was walking toward the parking garage.

"Hey, you!" Dodo called out.

Pamela twirled around and smiled at her breathless new friend.

"Hi, Dodo. Do you need a ride?"

"Thanks, maybe later. I'm in the mood for dessert now. Want to check out Sweet Nothings with me? It's on Charles Street."

"You know, that sounds like fun. Bruce is still at his conference in Florida. For once, I'm not in a rush to get home."

Dodo looked down at Pamela's expensive shoes. "How are those for walking? It's not far, but there are bricks and cobblestones."

"I'll be fine. Just point me in the right direction."

The two tall women, one chic, the other scruffy, walked together down Charles Street as it cut through the Common, stepping around puddles and chatting amiably.

A rising moon glowed through the foggy air.

Dodo and Pamela found a corner booth in the empty bistro.

Pamela rarely indulged in anything sugary but because Dodo made it sound like so much fun, she ordered a chocolate volcano cake, just for the experience. She felt expansive after sharing quality time with a supportive group of women.

"Holy crap!" Dodo exclaimed as both desserts were simultaneously set on the table in front of them.

"Oh my goodness. What have I gotten myself into?" Pamela laughed.

Dodo opened her napkin and tucked an edge into the collar of her shirt. She picked up her spoon, looked at Pamela, grinned mischievously, and then dug into an enormous bite of chocolate caramel cheesecake trifle. Pamela's eyes widened and her mouth fell open in shock at Dodo's gusto.

Both women broke out laughing, which was especially difficult for Dodo with her mouth full of whipped cream.

"You are unbelievable!" Pamela laughed.

After she managed to swallow, Dodo responded. "I've been craving this for months. I swear it's the best thing on the planet."

"It sure looks good."

"Here, take a bite yourself." Dodo moved her bowl toward the center of the table so Pamela could reach it.

After a dainty bite, Pamela agreed. "Mmm."

"Yours good, too?" Dodo asked.

"Amazing. Would you like to try it?"

Dodo helped herself to a small bite.

"You can have a bigger bite. You've already proven you can do that," Pamela joked.

"Show me some mercy! I've got my hands full!"

After a few more bites, both women put their spoons down and relaxed back onto the upholstered booth.

"You just witnessed my feeding frenzy. That is a very private thing to see. Now, I will have to kill you," Dodo deadpanned.

Pamela giggled. "I never eat dessert. How did you get me to do this?"

"Well, sometimes a girl just has to let it all hang out."

"I think we did just that, didn't we?"

"After that downer discussion with the group, I needed a sugar high like nobody's business," said Dodo.

"Some of it was pretty hard. At least we're all being honest."

"You don't mind?"

"Being honest?" Pamela asked.

"Yeah. At this point in life, we all have our share of skeletons in the closet."

"You're probably right."

"Do you think it's possible to change at our age?" Dodo asked.

"In what way?"

"Become a better person. Or, I don't know, just make life richer?"

Pamela's smile was kind. "Is that what you want to do?"

"Pretty much. I want to make these last twenty or thirty years count more than ever."

"Where will you start?" Pamela leaned in for the answer.

"I don't know, but I could sure use some company as I try to figure it out," Dodo responded.

"Do you have good friends for that?" Pamela wanted her to be happy, but hoped the answer would be that she needed a new friend.

Dodo shrugged. "It's funny, but the people I used to hang with seem to be slowing down versus speeding up. Some of them are getting very set in their ways. No fun at all."

Pamela decided to be brave. "I could use a good friend."

Dodo's blue eyes twinkled as she responded with her best Humphrey Bogart impression, "Pamela, I think this is the beginning of a beautiful friendship."

They didn't leave the restaurant until it closed two hours later.

HEIDI BELANGER

Heidi stared out the window of MBTA Bus number 93 on her way home from Vivere. She enjoyed time away from her house and these pleasant forays that did not center on family related errands. Jim was easygoing about her absence. She sometimes wondered if he even registered that she was gone. Supper was prepared for him without exception; he had only to take the lid off the slow-cooker, or pop a homemade meal into the microwave oven. She knew he would happily set himself up in front of the TV and watch whatever sport was in season. Tonight would be baseball.

Arriving at Twenty Auburn Street, Heidi unlocked the door and entered her kitchen. Jim's big work boots were dumped on the linoleum floor. His shirt was tossed over the back of a wooden chair. The red light of the uncovered slow-cooker glowed. Its lid rested precariously on the counter's edge. Next to the butter dish, a ragged chunk of leftover Italian bread grew stale in exposed air.

"I'm home!" she called out, waiting for a response.

After a minute, Jim responded. "In here, hon'!"

Heidi knew that the delay was due to his attention to some riveting play. She would walk into the den and give him a kiss and he would make a supreme effort to focus on her for as long as he could manage until the announcer's droning tone turned urgent and said, "And it's a high fly!" Jim's eyes would plead with her and she would smile and kiss his forehead, signaling her forgiveness as he turned with relief back to the TV.

Not every woman would thrive in this marriage, but Heidi was content with her choice of a mate. True, he did not often surprise her, but it was his steadfastness that made her love him all the more. They had grown comfortable together over the years and their bond made her feel safe and grounded. Some might say they were in a rut, but Heidi knew she truly loved her husband. The longer they stayed together, the more her feelings were reinforced.

She cleaned up the mess in the kitchen. At the stair landing, she called out good night to him.

"I'll be up in a while!" he responded.

After the game, she knew Jim would wander back to the kitchen to see if he had to clean up his mess. He was always too late, though.

He was a big sloppy bear, but he was *her* bear.

Q: Did the sexual revolution revolutionize your sex?

Heidi chuckled. She had married a meat and potatoes kind of guy. Fortunately, those were her favorite foods. Her appetite was satisfied.

KIMBERLY DOLAN

Driving down Newton's woodsy Withrow Street, Kimberly admired the brightly lit houses on either side. There was a Tudor on the corner, then a saltbox, a contemporary, and a colonial. She knew all of the neighbors because their children were her children's friends. It had been an exceptional environment to raise a family. Crystal Lake, only a bike ride away, was where her children and their playmates spent many summer days swimming, boating, and fishing. The schools were excellent, too. Twice the national average was spent on each student; a wise investment validated by the high percentage of these same students who went onto college and pursued lucrative careers.

The fourteenth house on the left, number twenty-eight, was hers. Its expansive lawn hung on the cusp of its most green splendor. The automatic sprinkler system consistently watered the grass every morning at five, ensuring lush growth.

Their home, a Victorian replica with six bedrooms and five bathrooms, had perfectly accommodated the Dolan family since the children were little. It was all excess space now. Tonight, only one light was burning. It was the turret in Meghan's room.

Gary was in Philadelphia visiting a fraternity brother

from college. He almost always took time off following the busy tax season. He rarely invited his wife to accompany him on these post-season trips. They both knew someone had to stay home to take care of the details that kept their family stable.

Kimberly recognized the familiar pit in her stomach as she pulled into her winding driveway and accelerated up the incline. Once inside, she set her purse on the kitchen counter, walked up the stairs to Meghan's room, and softly knocked on the door.

"What?" Meghan yelled from inside.

"I just want to say hello," Kimberly responded. "Can you open the door, please?"

After almost a minute, the doorknob turned and a side of Meghan's face appeared between a sliver of light.

"What?" she asked again.

"I just want to say hi."

"You already told me that."

"Well, how was your day, then?"

"Shitty. Especially because I didn't have anything for supper."

"Meghan, it's in the refrigerator. I left you a note on the counter."

"Mom, I'm not eating that stuff. You know I hate Shepard's Pie."

"I'm sorry. I forgot. Would you like me to make you some French toast now?"

"Yes. Text me when it's ready." Meghan shut the door.

Kimberly was halfway down the stairs, when she heard the door open again.

"And, whatever you do," Meghan yelled, "don't

sprinkle powdered sugar on it. I hate it when you do that. It's disgusting." She shut and locked her door again.

Kimberly continued down the stairs and into the kitchen. She took out a frying pan, eggs, milk, and bread, then made her daughter's supper to her specifications. When it was done, she texted her that it was ready.

She had been warmed by the glow of possibility at Vivere. Opening up to a new group of women might be just what she needed right now. Perhaps she could risk some other small changes.

Before she set the French toast on the counter, she slid one slice onto another plate and covered it with powdered sugar. Her daughter's footsteps were on the stairs as she took her first bite. In that mouthful, Kimberly tasted a new flavor—the delicious idea that her life mattered, too.

SHERALL SAVARD

After leaving Vivere, Sherall walked through the Boston Common toward home. She maintained a punishing pace up the steep grade that began on Spruce Street, then continued onto Chestnut and Willow Streets. Just past the cobblestones of Acorn Street, she turned left. Magnificent homes on the famed Louisburg Square to her right were brightly lit. Only a short way beyond, she stopped at number Ninety-One Mount Vernon Street, tapped the key entry code, then turned the brass door knob. It had been several evenings since she had been home this early. There was nothing to come home to. Scott often worked late or traveled to exotic conference locales. When he was home, he was occupied by his own activities and interests. They no longer bothered to share their schedules.

She pushed the heavy door open, walked through the foyer and down the hall, flipping light switches on her way. The interior had the polish familiar to old money homes. This 1835 Beacon Hill brownstone had been carefully modernized to retain its charm. It had also been a valuable investment that impressed visitors.

Sherall reached the kitchen at the back of the house. Large black and white square tiles on the floor set off the warmth of a dozen cherry cabinets lining the walls. Edison bulbs suspended over the granite island. Her surroundings were sumptuous. Sherall hardly noticed.

She was thinking about Scott.

Theirs wasn't really a marriage. She couldn't fathom why she hung onto it. With Lina and Luke far away, it seemed more of a charade than ever. Their relationship— or lack of one—was draining. She sighed and shook her head. Their attraction to each other in the early days stemmed from mutual independence. Scott admired that about Sherall. He had said he didn't want anyone to drag him down. Indeed, she had not.

She took out a new bottle of Shiraz from the pantry, absently examining its label. On it was a drawing of a wild boar sitting under a eucalyptus tree. Below that, *McLaren Vale, South Australia*. She uncorked the bottle and poured the dark red wine into her glass. She swirled it, then deeply inhaled the aromatic bouquet building within. That full breath of something foreign unsettled her. For one long moment, Sherall squeezed her eyes shut. A strangled sob escaped from her throat.

She shut it down. Briskly grabbing both bottle and

glass, she moved to the den, kicked off her shoes, and settled onto the couch to watch the news.

DARLY

With a silent gesture, Ian offered Darly a seat in his office while he finished his phone call. She noted the novelty of his fresh shave, accustomed to seeing him with several day's growth. Ian's back was to the desk and his legs were extended toward her. There were not many places for Darly to look as she waited with him in the tiny room. Her eyes dropped to her lap, to her shoes, then eventually wandered the few inches to where Ian's feet rested on the floor. As usual, one pant leg remained rolled for his bike commute. She noted the tiny hairs on his slender toes where they jutted out of worn leather sandals. When Darly glanced at Ian's face, he rolled his eyes, silently mouthing the word, "Sorry" to her.

"It's okay," she whispered and nodded.

Seeing Ian at the movies with red-haired Marla had been a disappointment, but she reminded herself that his relationship with Marla was none of her business. Ian and Darly were student and adviser.

Finally, the phone call ended.

"Darly, I apologize. I probably shouldn't say this, but that department head can be such an ass," he laughed, hastily organizing the paperwork on his desk. "So much for my being a good role model."

Darly chuckled. "He's probably cranky because he has to work inside on such a nice day."

Ian cocked his head and pointed a finger at her. "You just gave me a great idea. *We* don't have to stay inside!

Let's take this baby out to the Charles. We can sit in the sun and talk about all of this stuff there by the river. Game?" he asked.

"Sure. Sounds nice."

Yes, it did. She checked her enthusiasm, given her sober assessment of his interest in her.

They walked along Silber Way and across the *T* tracks on Commonwealth Avenue. At Torpedoes, they ordered subs which Ian slipped into his messenger bag. They crossed the footbridge to arrive at the reservation next to the Charles River.

"Bench or grass?" Ian asked.

"Grass is fine with me," Darly answered.

"My kind of woman."

Darly smiled tentatively, then turned away, looking for a good place to sit.

"Let's eat lunch first. Are you in a rush?" he asked.

"Not really."

"That's the best thing about summer."

"It's not officially summer yet," Darly said.

"I know. I start my summer early, though. It's way too short, otherwise, don't you think?"

"I agree. Michigan is the same way."

"Do you miss it?"

"Not really. I like my life here. I have some nice friends and a good apartment."

"Lots of friends?" he asked, taking a bite of his sub.

"Just the right number," Darly answered.

"It seems like you can get comfortable with who you're always with. It's hard to fit someone new into your life."

"I've never thought of it that way, but that's pretty

true."

"So, how did you like the movie the other night?" Ian asked.

"Loved it. How about you?"

"It *looked* pretty good. Marla's a talker, so I missed some of the dialogue," he grinned, shaking his head.

"Maybe you can see it again."

"With you?" he asked.

Darly blinked. As friends, she reminded herself. "It would be my third time."

"That's crazy."

"I know. I just like it."

Ian pulled a laptop out of his bag. "Okay, let's get started with your old Guinea pigs."

PAMELA CARDIN/DODO QUIMBY

Pamela ended the phone call with a smile on her face. She and Dodo had spoken several times over the last few days. The countless stories and questions Dodo shared were both interesting and flattering. The warm attention was a salve to her hurting heart.

When Pamela mentioned that Bruce would participate in a golf tournament Saturday, Dodo proposed that the two women spend the day together. They would visit the Isabella Stuart Gardner Museum and grab a late lunch in the museum cafe. It had been almost a decade since Pamela had been to the museum. She looked forward to seeing it again.

Early Saturday morning, Pamela listened to Bruce outline his strategy to network with Boston notables and win the golf tournament at The Country Club in

Brookline. She offered her customary affirmations, then set his breakfast on the table. Bruce took one bite, dropped his fork, then pushed the plate away.

"These eggs are dry."

"I'm sorry. We ran out of cream."

"No, you ran out of cream. Not we. I can't eat this."

Bruce got up from the table and left the room. He called to her from the hallway where he stood near the garage entrance. "I won't be home until after midnight. Don't forget to take my shirts to the cleaners."

Pamela didn't immediately respond.

"Did you hear me?" He asked, annoyed.

"Yes. I won't forget. Have a good time, Bruce. I hope you win."

She heard the door close. Through the front window, she watched his silver Lexus roar down the street.

Pamela took a deep breath. The breakfast dishes sat on the table next to her husband's pushed out chair. She would walk away from this mess, for now.

After stopping at the cleaners, Pamela drove toward Boston. At the Museum Road parking garage, she left her Jaguar with the valet and walked the short distance to where she and Dodo agreed to rendezvous.

Dodo had already arrived and was leaning against the museum's wrought iron gate, observing passers-by as they enjoyed the revitalized Emerald Necklace section. Pamela made her way down the street, framed by an arc of bursting cherry blossoms. She wore fitted black pants and flats, a crisp white shirt, and turquoise cardigan. A bright scarf was artfully draped over one shoulder. As soon as she spotted Dodo, she removed her large sunglasses and waved. Dodo swelled with admiration. She noted that others around her paused to watch this woman glide gracefully across the street. Toward her.

"Morning!" Dodo said, grinning.

"Good morning! What a beautiful day we picked."

"I agree. I've been walking around the Fens for about an hour, just to take it all in. Nothing like spring in Boston."

"So true." Pamela agreed.

"Had breakfast?" Dodo asked.

"Yes. All set. You?"

"Croissant and latte."

"Sounds yummy."

"I should mix it up. I have the same thing every day."

"You could eat at Cafe Pamela. Our breakfast menu is ever changing." Her perfect bow lips formed a shy smile.

"Love to. Ready to go in?" Dodo gestured toward the entrance.

By design, the museum resembled a fifteenth century Venetian palace. Lighting at the admission desk was dim, but steps away was the dazzling interior courtyard. In that bright light, fine lines around Pamela's eyes were like etchings on a porcelain cup. Dodo thought she looked as beautiful as one of the statues in front of them.

"Oh! I forgot how gorgeous this is!" Pamela looked up as she twirled around on the marble floor.

They made their way up the shallow steps of the worn marble staircase. At the top, a long row of glass cases ran alongside the wall. They removed the protective velvet covers and studied the historic letters inside.

Dodo paused to read to Pamela from the brochure. "*Isabella inherited $1.6 million from her father in 1891.*"

"How nice for her," Pamela murmured.

Dodo read on. "Oh god, her baby son died from pneumonia when he was two."

They exchanged horrified looks.

"*She had a zest for life, an energetic curiosity...*"

"I love that!" Pamela said.

"*She lived an engaging, exuberant life including much travel, entertaining and adventure.* It says there was lots of gossip about her because of this lifestyle. Know what she said about that?" Dodo asked.

"What?"

"*Don't spoil a good story by telling the truth!*"

Dodo and Pamela explored the rest of the second floor. When they walked through the Dutch Room, they saw the empty frames there. The infamous Gardner heist had yet to be solved.

The massive Rape of Europa painting hung in the third floor Titian Room.

"It's so lush," Pamela whispered inside the empty gallery.

"But, incongruous, in this place."

"What do you mean?"

"The way women are portrayed in these rape and pillage paintings. This is a woman's house, after all," Dodo said.

They studied the painting.

Pamela leaned over to whisper to Dodo, "She looks almost willingly helpless. Like she's resigned to her fate."

"Exactly. But what could she do?"

"It seems like she should put up a fight, but the oceans and the sea monsters are the alternative," Pamela answered.

Dodo reopened the brochure. "Here's what Isabella said about waiting to buy this painting: *I am drinking myself drunk with Europa and then sitting for hours... thinking and dreaming about her. Every inch of paint in the picture seems full of joy.*"

Dodo looked up from the brochure. "I wonder if she was referring to the bigger picture. The story behind the story."

"Which is?"

"Well, it says here that the bull is supposed to be Jupiter. Europa was raped by him and this marked the beginning of civilization."

They stared at it a bit longer, then Dodo said, "Sex with a man is always a little violent, even if it's consensual."

A docent entered the room. He announced an imminent string quartet performance of Vivaldi in the second floor Tapestry Room. Dodo and Pamela followed him there. It was a magical interlude in a superb acoustic environment. They toured the rest of the museum and had lunch at the museum cafe.

Outside again in the brilliant sunshine, a fresh breeze whipped through the budding trees.

"How much time do we have?" Dodo asked.

"I'm totally free."

You're not afraid of water, are you?" Dodo said, walking briskly toward the Green Line train stop.

"No. Why?"

"Stay tuned," Dodo answered.

After a short ride, they exited the *T* at Arlington station, then walked toward the Common.

"Are we swimming in the lagoon?" Pamela joked.

"No. Much better. And you won't get wet."

Dodo linked arms with Pamela again as they walked across the Arthur Fiedler Bridge and down the Esplanade toward the Community Boating Dock.

"Sailing?" Pamela was incredulous.

"Yup. I'll take the helm."

"Good, because I don't know the front from the back."

"The bow is the front and the stern is the back. Just remember that bow is spelled like bow and you wear a bow on your head."

"Isn't the head another name for a boat bathroom?"

"Clever you!" Dodo laughed.

Because it was late afternoon, a daysailer soon became available. After securing their life vests, the women pushed off from the dock. Dodo trimmed the sail, then shifted her weight from one side of the boat to the other.

"This is wonderful," Pamela called out into the wind. She tied her colorful scarf over her hair. The pointed loose ends flapped around her shoulders.

"My favorite way to spend an afternoon!" Dodo yelled back. "I volunteer to take a ton of their event pictures, so they let me use a boat as often as I want!"

After about 30 minutes, the wind shifted and calmed considerably. At last they could speak at a normal volume.

Dodo propped her foot on the bench where Pamela's thigh rested.

"I feel like I've known you forever, Pamela."

"I was just going to say the same thing!"

"Should I have said that?"

Pamela patted Dodo's foot. "Why not?"

"You're so beautiful, and kind, and...well, just look at me."

"Look at you? What I see is a kind and beautiful woman, DoDo. You are all I am not. You seem so brave and daring. You're the best possible opposite of me."

"We make quite a pair!"

Both women sensed the shifting dynamic.

Dodo had been in love with a few females, but she never had courage to act on her desire. She felt like a teenager with Pamela. Butterflies in her gut were relentless and her emotions felt beyond her control. She worried she would scare Pamela away.

Pamela had not taken the next step in her mind. She knew only that she had begun to treasure her relationship with Dodo. Because of her beauty, sex in a heterosexual relationship almost always presented early, and in her estimation, prematurely. Even in her own marriage, consent was not something she considered an option. Sometimes, it was easier to simply give in and go along, regardless of her wishes.

"I'm not used to being part of a healthy pair," Pamela offered.

"Because of your husband?"

"Yes."

"What's it like?"

"He tries to control me."

"Does he succeed?" Dodo asked.

Pamela lowered her hand over the side of the boat to

test the cold water. "So far, he has. Maybe it's time that stopped."

The marina was about to close for the evening.

"We have to head back now. Do you want to see my studio before you go home?" Dodo asked. "I can show you some of my work."

"I'd love to." Pamela couldn't recall the last time she had felt so relaxed.

Waning sunlight poured through the side window of Dodo's starkly furnished apartment. It lit up the metal kitchen countertop where a chipped latte cup had been left. Pamela peered into it. The forlorn aspect made her wonder if the cup's owner was more vulnerable than she revealed.

They sat on the couch, thighs touching, and leafed through the studio look-book left out for clients to peruse. Pamela was astounded by the breadth of Dodo's talent, evident on each page.

"These images are remarkable, Dodo."

"You're very sweet to say so." Dodo took Pamela's hand and kissed it.

Later, Dodo pointed out cameras and other tools of the trade stored on the various shelves. She explained the story behind the numerous prints on the walls, then continued the tour down the narrow hallway toward the back of the studio. Turning at the end, they found themselves only inches apart. Skin, lips, and necks burned to connect.

Dodo moved the small distance to kiss Pamela.

"I've never—" Pamela whispered.

"Me, neither."

One kiss became another, until they found themselves moving together toward the bed, giggling, and breathing hard with a new mixture of familiar and unfamiliar sensations.

Dodo tore off her shirt. She had managed the perfect disguise. Once naked, her angles no longer looked ragged. Pamela touched Dodo's braid, then loosened the plait to watch long, gray hair cascade around her shoulders.

"You *are* beautiful," Pamela said.

Dodo turned serious. She gently pulled on Pamela's scarf, bringing her closer, kissing her again. Taking extra care with the silk fabric, she unbuttoned the other woman's blouse until it fell open. Voluptuous breasts were collected in the lace of a pale lavender-colored bra.

"Can I take it off you?" Dodo asked.

"Yes." Pamela turned around to make it easier. With the bra off, she faced Dodo again.

Goosebumps rose on the surface of Pamela's skin. Dodo leaned over and kissed her breasts, then her stomach, then back up to her neck and mouth. Embracing, they fell back onto the bed, where they remained entwined, talking softly, and exploring each other.

At 11:30 pm, Pamela returned to reality.

"Dodo! I need to get home!"

"You could stay."

"No, I can't. What would I tell Bruce?"

Dodo sighed. "I almost forgot about him."

"I'm sorry. I have to go now." She sat on the side of the bed, collecting her wrinkled clothes, tears welling in her eyes.

"I'll order you a ride," Dodo said.

"Thank you. I'm so confused." Pamela searched around for her purse.

"Don't worry. Things will be okay. Can I call you tomorrow?" Dodo asked.

"Bruce will be home all day."

"Monday?"

"Yes. Let's definitely talk Monday. And, we'll see each other at Tuesday's dinner meeting."

They kissed once more before leaving the studio. Arm in arm, they walked down the empty street to meet Pamela's ride back to the museum parking garage.

Q: How has your sexuality changed?
Dodo didn't feel she had changed. She felt society had.

Pamela raced back to Weston. When the automatic garage door rolled open, Pamela was relieved to see that she had arrived before her husband. Quickly, she tidied up the kitchen that had been left in disarray that morning, then went straight to bed. Almost immediately afterward came the sound of her husband downstairs. Pamela closed her eyes to recapture her encounter with Dodo, struggling to comprehend its new significance in her life.

Q: Is sex love?
Before today, Pamela had never connected the two.

SHERALL SAVARD

Sherall's dress hiked up around her waist. The man's pants were at his ankles; his shirt and tie were crumpled on the floor next to her shoes.

"You are so hot," he said, breathless.

"I bet you say that to all of the girls," she joked.

"Only the ones who really are," the man answered.

Sherall focused her eyes to better assess her partner. She hadn't asked how old he was. Maybe thirty? The thirty-year-olds were easy. They didn't want the entanglement of women their own age. They liked the fact that Sherral wanted only one thing and wanted that thing only once. Well, maybe twice, but at least confined to one night.

Sex was simple for her now. No concern about pregnancy. The threat of STD remained, but these young guys were accustomed to wearing condoms. She had tried every texture and flavor on the planet, courtesy of the internet.

Sherall ran her finger down the young man's waxed chest.

"Hey love, go get me some champagne from the mini-bar."

She watched him step completely out of his pants, then walk toward the credenza. This one knew how good he looked and it was her fortune to observe. She sat up in bed, unzipped the back of her dress, then tossed it onto the floor.

The young man poured two glasses of champagne. Sherall could see it wouldn't be long before he was ready again. She looked at the clock. 10:45 PM. Plenty of time, she thought, falling back onto the pillows. She took a glass from his hand and tilted it over her breasts, allowing a few drops to spill and dribble down the chasm between them.

"Tsk. Oh, look what happened," she said.

He grabbed the champagne flute, placed it on the bedside table, then licked the drips off. Stuffing one of the firm pillows under her bottom, she arched her back and moaned.

Q: Have you found sexual fulfillment?
Sherall considered. Fulfillment, yes. Satisfaction, no.

HEIDI BELANGER

Heidi and Jim loved this special time when they could sit out on their deck on Island Pond and watch twilight turn the water black. Bats appeared in the sky, flitting up and across; their erratic flight pattern distinguishing them from birds.

"Did you see that fish jump?" Jim asked her.

"No. Where?"

"Just beyond the raft."

"I'll keep looking."

They each nursed a beer. Every once in a while, Jim would reach over and squeeze Heidi's hand and smile at her, saying nothing.

Steady conversation and laughter from inside the house drifted out the window behind the bench where they sat. Justin and Jordan had invited two friends up to the pond, and four additional friends of the younger group arrived late in the afternoon. Heidi wasn't sure how many would spend the night, but she was glad she had honored her hunch, stopping at the grocery on the drive up to buy two crowd-sized packages of chicken breasts. The salad she made earlier was chilling in the refrigerator. Jim had already started the grill. They made a good team.

Jordan's girlfriend finally arrived, carrying a large pan of Seven Layer Bars for dessert. Heidi liked that girl. Once the food was ready and the table set, all ten of them sat down to dinner.

After a long night of drinking and card games, no one was in shape to drive home. Jim helped the boys inflate the camping mattresses kept in the shed. Meanwhile, Heidi finished cleaning the kitchen and searched the pantry for pancake breakfast ingredients. She filled and set the automatic coffee maker, positioned the griddle on the counter, said good night to everyone, then retreated to the tiny master bedroom.

After about an hour, she felt Jim's presence as he gently slid across the mattress. He was a big man but knew how to be considerate. Heidi moved her foot over the sheets and rubbed his calf. Jim put his arm around her waist and kissed her. Years of practice had taught them how to make love quietly.

KIMBERLY DOLAN

Propped up against two pillows on the king-sized bed, Kimberly turned the page of the magazine she was reading.

"It says here that people should create a digital will, or at least a will that talks about your digital stuff. Did you know that?" she asked Gary, who was leafing through an issue of Accounting Today.

"Yup."

"Apparently, when something happens to someone, all of these loose ends are left open and no one can get the person's passwords or anything like that. It's a real problem."

"Uh huh." Gary kept reading.

"Do you think we should do something with our passwords? Places like Google and Facebook?"

"That's nice."

"Are you even listening to what I'm saying?"

"Sure thing."

"Gary, this is serious."

Exasperated, Gary tossed his magazine onto the floor and looked over at Kimberly.

"Kimberly, you don't have a clue what you're talking about. You wouldn't even know the first thing about how to navigate the web. Let it go and stop worrying about things that don't affect you." He turned away from her, pulled the blanket over his shoulder, and was soon snoring.

Kimberly put her magazine aside and turned off the light. She wasn't tired, just polite. As her eyes grew accustomed to the surrounding darkness, she found the familiar comfort of the black void. It enveloped and accepted her. Tonight felt different, though. Instead of growing tired, she became more alert. Into the nothingness, she dared to test a whispered phrase. "This is my house and my life, too."

Q: Is love enough?

Kimberly felt she did not have enough experience to answer the question.

THE THIRD DINNER

The evening was damp. It felt like a tropical storm. Lights flickered, and a few seconds later, a thunderclap shook the room. Even waiter Marco jumped at the sound as he made his way out the door. The women laughed from where they stood chatting in one corner of the room, holding stems of wine glasses like high society dames.

Clearly, they enjoyed the company of one another. Darly felt like a housemother breaking up a sorority party. She had strategized about how to finesse this very scenario. She sat at the table. She opened her laptop. She cleared her throat. No one noticed. Subtlety failed.

"Okay, everyone! Can we get started?" She said loudly.

"I propose a toast before we begin," Sherall said.

"All right. To what?" Darly asked, hiding her exasperation.

"To the gathering of the Cougar Club!"

The women laughed and clinked glasses.

Kimberly was skeptical. "I'm not sure I could pass as a cougar."

"I know *I* look like a cougar!" Everyone laughed as Heidi draped a napkin over her face like a woman in a harem.

Dodo suggested, "What about Marvelous Mavens?"

"That's cute!" Heidi said.

Darly used her laptop to inch the discussion forward. "Here it is. Maven. It's Yiddish. One who is experienced or knowledgeable." She looked back at the group.

"I'm experienced, that's for sure," Sherall winked.

"It also means expert," Darly added.

"We are experts about our own lives," said Dodo. "Experts at screwing up, maybe? Or, experts at doing it right, if we're lucky."

"I think everyone here has done it right," Kimberly offered. "Well, you *have*. You're all unique and original. Who wouldn't be impressed by you?"

"Then, I propose a new toast," Sherall laughed, raising her glass again. "To the Marvelous Mavens!"

Darly took a sip of water, striving to maintain a professional distance from the enthusiasm. After the women settled down and took their seats, she cleared her throat and started again. "Our topic today is Love and Sex with the question, *Did the Sexual Revolution Revolutionize Your Sex?* Who wants to go first?"

To no one's surprise, Sherall began. "Personally, I feel like my sexual revolution didn't start until I was in my early forties. I mean, what does an eighteen-year-old really know about sex?" Sherall was pleased to recollect the pleasure of past liaisons.

Pamela added, "When I was younger, I felt like sex was mostly for the guy. I thought my job was to look good while he was doing it to me." She glanced at Dodo, who winked at her.

"God, that's spot on. Who hasn't faked orgasm just to keep the mood together?" Sherall said.

"I've done it a few times, I'll admit that." Heidi surprised herself by releasing such a personal detail. Her strawberry-blonde complexion betrayed her. She could feel a blush spreading, but also a growing sense of self.

"I *never* do it now, though. It's either there, or it's not. No gray area anymore." Sherall was defiant.

"How does your husband react?" Darly asked.

"Who said I was talking about my husband?" she shot back. "I got tired of holding my appetite back. There's love-sex and then there's sex-sex. I've had both. Women don't always give themselves that option." Sherall looked around the table. "Well, have any of you?"

"I think I'd be afraid to," Kimberly said. She wondered if the women could tell how she had fantasized about making love to her husband's colleague, not so long ago.

"Why is that?" Darly asked.

"What if it was better than being with my husband?" she answered.

"Bingo!" Sherall shouted.

Although unsettled by the prospect, Kimberly continued. "What would happen when the new guy got sick of me?"

"Why would any man get sick of you, Kimberly?" Heidi said.

Kimberly smiled. She felt like she could be friends with this woman.

Sherall added, "That's the whole problem. We always think they'll find something lacking in *us*. Maybe we need to get what *we* want."

"Do you think your husband knows about your affairs, Sherall?" Darly asked.

"Maybe. I think he plays around, too." She paused and scrutinized the other faces. "You've got to be kidding if I'm the only one in this room who's stepped out by this age."

"I'm divorced," Dodo declared, "so it's a non-issue for me." It had been a long time since she had sex with anyone. Being with Pamela had reawakened a tenderness that she thought she had lost.

"If my husband ever found out..." Pamela's voice grew soft.

"What would happen?" Dodo asked. Her brow furrowed.

"I can't even imagine how angry he'd be." Pamela looked down at her half-empty wine glass.

"But, he's had affairs!" Dodo argued.

The other women snapped to attention. It became clear to them that Dodo and Pamela were on more familiar terms than others in the group.

Darly was oblivious. She was too busy trying to direct the group. She fired up another question. "What do you all think about living together before marriage? It started with your generation. Now everyone does."

"The difference between then and now, Darly," Heidi answered, "is that more of us actually got married after we lived together."

"You don't think they do now?" Darly asked.

"I'm not sure of the statistics," she answered, "but I think more women have babies now without being married." The prospect of unwed fatherhood was always a danger for her sons, as far as she was concerned. She and Jim had worked hard to be good examples for them to emulate.

Sherall said, "It cracks me up when a women has three kids with the same guy, and she calls him her fiancé."

"That's really sad," commented Kimberly.

"Why?" asked Darly.

"Because," Heidi spoke slowly to Darly, "kids won't have the security of knowing their parents took charge of their lives. I can't understand a woman who would do that to herself, and to her kids."

"Maybe the guy won't marry her," Sherall said. She had been with many younger men who revealed similar tales to her about their girlfriends.

Dodo added, "I think, just as often, it's the woman who won't marry the man."

"Why do you think that happens?" Darly encouraged. So far, she had not found herself in a situation like that. She wondered what she would do.

"All I know," Sherall responded, "is that when I first got married, I felt like it was such a demotion. It was a real shock. People started calling me Mrs. Scott Green. It made me crazy. I didn't even change my name, so there was no reason for them to do that. To this day, I still get mail for Sherall Green. Can you believe it? I can't blame a young woman today for bucking that."

"That's pretty bad," Heidi said. "I got married really young. My parents would have killed me if I tried to live with Jim before we got married. My father always said to me and my sisters, 'Why buy the cow, if you can get the milk for free?'" She shook her head. "A cow."

Darly drilled deeper. "What do all of you tell your kids to do?"

"With my boys," Heidi said, "I tell them to be good to their girlfriends. I say, don't lead them on. It seems like it's the girls who usually dump them, though. They're both really nice guys."

Sherall took her turn. "I'm not an advice giver. I doubt my kids would listen to me, anyway."

"Seriously?" Heidi responded. "You seem like the kind

of person someone younger would think understood them."

"Thanks for the confidence. We all know how different things are when it comes to your own kids."

"Where are your two, Sherall?" Darly asked, reviewing her notes.

"Lina is in California, and Luke is in New York."

"You must miss them," Kimberly said.

Sherall shrugged. For the first time, she seemed to have nothing more to say.

Dodo broke the silence. "You all know I'm not close to my daughter, either, but I really wish I was."

Across the table, Pamela's face changed. She fought the urge to rush to Dodo's side to comfort her.

"I'm sorry you feel that way," said Darly. "It must be painful."

Dodo shrugged and offered an upside down smile.

"It's not easy being a parent," began Kimberly. "My five kids don't seem too happy about me even bringing them into the world. I don't know what I did wrong." She sighed.

"I'm sure you've been a wonderful parent, Kimberly," Pamela offered. "I can't tell you how much I admire all of you."

"Every one of us has had such different journeys," Heidi said.

The energy in the room had plummeted.

"Hey, Marvelous Mavens!" Sherall laughed, "Let's get back to talking about sex!"

Darly waited for someone to respond to Sherall's overture. For once, she was grateful for her. She felt like she walked a tightrope between orchestration and organization.

"What kind of vibrator do you ladies use?" Sherall asked, matter-of-factly, leaning in onto the table.

Heidi's mouth fell open. Kimberly pursed her lips. Pamela held her breath, waiting for someone else to answer.

Dodo threw the question right back at Sherall. "Why don't you tell us what kind we *should* use?"

"Ha! Am I really the expert?" Sherall looked around the room. "God, I am, aren't I? Are you seriously telling me that none of you use one?"

"Are we supposed to?" asked Kimberly. She hung on the answer. If she bought one, she could hide it from Gary. But, she could never risk the kids finding it!

"Well, if you want to get what you need, yes," Sherall responded.

"With a penis shape?" asked Dodo.

"Duh," Sherral responded.

"Okay, here goes," Heidi began. "I can't believe I'm telling you guys this, but I do have one. I discovered it by accident. Jim bought a flat kind of thing for his back injury and I just decided to try it out once. It was pretty intense. It's sort of noisy though." She giggled.

"Does he know you tried it?" Pamela asked.

"Are you kidding? No!" Heidi laughed.

"Would that be bad?" Darly asked.

"It would be embarrassing for me, that's for sure," she answered. Could she ever find the courage to tell Jim? What would happen then?

"Why?" Darly continued.

"Well, I guess it would mean that there was something the matter with me. That I wasn't enough of a woman to get my pleasure from a man. Plus, it would hurt Jim's feelings." Heidi looked around for understanding. She and Jim had grown up together in every way. Could they grow further?

"Maybe there is something wrong with Jim, not you," Sherall said.

Heidi shot a hard look at her. "No. Jim is really good to me. He's still in great shape, too."

Dodo asked, "How about the fact that most women don't climax with penetration only? It's just a male fantasy."

"Really?" Kimberly asked.

"You've never heard that? Why do you think foreplay is so important?" Dodo answered. It was hard for her to believe Kimberly's sense of sexual understanding was as arrested as it seemed. She couldn't help thinking of her as a bit naïve. Maybe there was more to her than she let them see, though.

"But, the penetration seems like the cherry on top, at the end," Pamela blurted out.

"That's a good way of putting it!" Sherall laughed.

"Maybe we've just trained ourselves to think that," Dodo continued.

"Meaning?" Heidi asked.

"Well, do you remember what it was like when you were a girl, before you ever even thought about men? When you did it to yourself, it still worked pretty good. Right?" Dodo added.

"I'm getting hot," Sherall breathed. She wasn't lying.

She wondered who she could call after the dinner had ended.

There was laughter around the table.

"So, you're just supposed to be secretive about using one?" asked Kimberly.

"No! Find somebody who gets it, for god's sake," Sherall answered.

"I don't think that would be very easy, Sherall," Heidi said.

"Younger men love it. I've been with some older guys who think it's great, too."

"Because they can't keep it up?" Dodo asked.

"Sometimes. But usually, that's a real buzz kill," she responded.

"How old are they when that starts to happen?" Kimberly asked.

Sherall had sharp radar. "It's already happening to your husband, right?"

Kimberly did not respond, appalled by Sherall's lack of tact. Even if it was the truth.

Dodo broke in. "Maybe you're getting too personal, Sherall."

"I'm just trying to help her," she answered.

"Maybe she could help you with the fidelity part," Dodo said.

Darly cleared her throat, preparing to intervene, but Kimberly came back to life.

"No, she's right. When it happens, he usually says it's my fault, though. Like it took me too long to warm up, or something like that. Do you think I should say something to him?" She looked around the table.

"What would happen if you did?" Heidi asked.

"I don't know. He'd probably get upset." It would definitely ruin their night, she thought.

"As in, angry?" Pamela asked.

"No. Gary would probably get sad."

"Then what?" Darly asked.

"Then, he'd roll over and go to sleep."

When she saw the sympathetic expressions, Kimberly was encouraged to continue.

"I guess I *could* try talking about it. Maybe when we're not in bed, right?" She asked the group.

"They say that's best. Not in bed," Heidi said.

"Tell him to get some Viagra," Sherall added.

"But then *he'll* be the one who can't get enough!" Heidi argued.

"Tough. Let him see how it feels." Sherall was adamant.

Kimberly crossed her arms over her chest and slipped down in her chair.

"Sorry, Kimberly. I didn't mean to pick on you," Sherall said.

"That's okay. I guess I'm the one who needs the most work."

"Anybody else?" Darly asked.

Kimberly rallied and put herself in the spotlight again. "What about us getting older?"

"You mean menopause?" Darly asked.

"Yes, that, but what about how sex is as *we* age?" Kimberly clarified.

Sherall did not need to be prodded. "The only thing I notice is that I need more lube."

"Your level of desire has not diminished?" Darly asked.

143

"Sure it has. But not enough to keep me home. The thing is to keep up the variety. So much of all of this is in our heads. You take away the spice and nothing is tempting. You need more than salt and pepper, too."

"Does anyone else share that opinion?"

"I guess I'm content to just cuddle a bit more these days," Heidi offered.

"Does your husband mind that?" Darly asked.

"Sometime. But sometimes he's pretty tired, too." She smiled as she recalled the recent weekend with Jim at the lake, which was not just a cuddle.

"Honestly, I hope it's not over for me yet," Dodo said. "I've been single such a long time."

"Well, being married doesn't mean it's all pleasure," Pamela reminded her.

The two women smiled at each other.

"Well, if we are really being honest here," Sherall offered, "I have to admit, I sometimes feel a little self-conscious about my body when I'm in bed with a guy. There's only so much a woman can do."

"But Sherall, you're in such good shape!" Kimberly said.

"Thanks. It's not just the outside that's sagging though, if you know what I mean."

"That is supposed to be a common malady." Darly continued, "You know, prolapse and other complication of childbirth and aging, I mean."

"Shit happens," Dodo said.

"I almost feel like giving my body a break," Kimberly began. "It's done what it's supposed to do. Reproduction and everything. Sex just really doesn't seem to be on my

mind lately. I'm not sure I'm going to miss it, either."
Especially with Gary, she thought.

"Everyone has different levels of desire, even when they're young," Darly added.

"But, society makes us feel as though we're almost dead if we're not thinking about sex all of the time," Pamela said.

"And how about derogatory comments about older women?" Sherall asked. "As if we are crypt keepers instead of human beings."

Darly wanted to learn more. "Can you give specifics, Sherall?"

"It's not so much that we're criticized openly, it's more that older woman just drop out of the picture. They become invisible. First we're portrayed as sexy young women, and then as mothers. Then the images pretty much stop for about 30 years, until we show up again in nursing homes. They make fun of us. It pisses me off."

"So," Darly encouraged, "you'd like to see more images of thriving older women in the media?"

"Hell, yes!" Sherall answered. "I want to see women in their fifties, sixties, and seventies buying cars and going on vacation and running companies. What's so scary about showing that?"

Dodo said, "Well, for starters, they'd have to be honest about what a woman looks like when she ages. The sagging neck, the puffy eyes, etcetera."

Sherall continued. "You're right. Everyone needs to get over their inability to come to grips with our *realistic* appearance. Men are never treated like that. So many look like crap and no one seems to notice. Women are supposed to feel shame about aging—like we're letting everyone down by not beautifying the planet. Then we hide to avoid being ridiculed when we can't keep up. If we look like we're trying too hard to stay young, people are embarrassed to be with us. It's so ironic. They want us to cooperate and dress our age, then they ridicule us for that pastel cruise ship style. We were taught to feel shame about our adolescent bodies, remember? If your curves weren't developing the way you thought was the right way, you felt defective. Now, here we are again at the other end of life, feeling ashamed about our bodies deteriorating." Sherall shook her head, disgusted.

Pamela nodded. "That is so true. My least favorite term is *aging gracefully*. What does that even mean?"

"You," Dodo said, "are an example of aging gracefully, though. You still look beautiful. Even the little wrinkling you have just artistically accentuates your appearance. Not everyone ages so well. Some women just look tired and angry."

Pamela looked uncomfortably apologetic. She knew Dodo spoke the truth.

Kimberly said "I don't like the phrase, *You get the face you deserve*. As if you have control over the hardships in your life that make you get worry lines instead of laugh lines. Men are considered distinguished if they have serious folds in their faces. It's not fair."

"It isn't fair," Dodo said. "But, if we're not playing along—not worrying about how we're viewed—then we're free. I stopped thinking about my appearance a long time ago. It was a conscious decision. I stay clean and groomed, but other than that, I don't give a damn. All I care about is seeing, not being seen. When I finally let go, both men and women stopped responding to me in terms of my appearance. No more comments about my clothes, my earrings, or my hair. It's the way men are treated. Like they're human beings. It's incredibly freeing."

"That's admirable," said Sherall. "I don't know how it would fly in my field, though. I'm envious. It would be good to try. I think some women dress for comfort eventually, just because of physical maladies like bunions and expanding waistlines. It's difficult to present the illusion of effortless beauty. Beauty actually takes a shitload of work."

"This gives me a lot to think about," Heidi said.

Others nodded.

"Well, it's getting late, so let's wrap up for tonight." Darly logged off her tablet, then took five sheets of paper out of the messenger bag stowed under her chair. She handed them to Dodo, who took one and passed on the remainder.

"You can see the next topic. Is everyone good for that date, too?" Darly asked.

"Looking forward to it." Sherall said.

They settled the bill and left the restaurant.

TOPIC: ANOTHER CHANCE
Did you squander opportunity?
Are you satisfied?
If you could not fail, what would you do?
What are your regrets?
Would you accept advice?

DODO QUIMBY/PAMELA CARDIN
Dodo walked Pamela to her car.

"I have a shoot in DC over the Fourth of July weekend," Dodo said.

"Congratulations! I bet you'll do a fabulous job," Pamela responded.

"I'd do a better job if you could come with me. What do you think? My treat all around."

Dodo watched Pamela's expression evolve as she contemplated the possibility of doing something daring. She rarely left town without her husband.

"Dodo, I really want to try to do this. I'm ninety-nine percent sure that Bruce is going away that weekend. I'll check again and tell you soon. It would be so nice to get away with you."

"Let's keep our fingers crossed that it works," Dodo said. She wished Pamela did not have to work around her husband. She would have to learn more about their marriage dynamic. Most of all, she wanted to make Pamela happy. If that meant sharing her with Bruce, that is what she would do—despite the pain it caused her.

HEIDI BELANGER

Jim sat at the oak table in their sunny kitchen with the Sunday Globe sports section splayed in front of him. "After I finish the lawn, George and I are going to the driving range," Jim told Heidi.

"Sounds fun. Just you and George?"

"Carl and Derrick, too. If they can get out of their Honey-Do lists."

Heidi wanted to tell Jim something she had been thinking about. It looked like this would be her last opportunity for a while. She stopped unloading the dishwasher to blurt out what she had wanted to say for weeks. "I want to go to college and get my degree."

"God, Heidi. Not this again." Jim shot her an uncharacteristically irritated look. "What do you want a degree for? It's just a waste of money at our age."

"You have one."

"Yeah, but an Associate degree is important for moving up in the maintenance business. You know that. All you do now is volunteer."

This hit a sore spot. The flip side of Jim being a good provider and protector was that he was also paternalistic. Her father had treated her mother similarly. Over the last few weeks, Heidi worried she had sold herself short. Maybe she had not taken herself seriously. Even her youngest sister Elaine had a degree and was employed as a nurse. It was a field that her father had approved, but Elaine had made it happen and paid for her education.

"I'm determined," Heidi answered.

"You'll get over it," Jim chuckled. "You sure are a funny little girl." He smiled at her and returned to the newspaper.

Heidi would not get over it. Not this time. Maybe he was right about the degree, but he was wrong about her determination. She would make a mark that was uniquely her own. The idea of family would be the springboard.

Later that afternoon, Heidi sat at the computer and clicked on the University of Massachusetts at Boston page she had bookmarked. She wanted to learn more about a campus organization chartered to nurture female entrepreneurs. There was a business idea percolating in her mind.

The concept occurred to her after a family poker night when she noticed her loyal brother-in-law wearing yet another of the annual family picnic shirts she had designed. If she could convince other families to let her personalize items for their gatherings, she would have a business. She could hire people to help with what she did not know, such as accounting and advertising. A college degree might not be necessary, after all.

Women Entrepreneurs lit up the screen.

On the side bar:

Volunteers from the entrepreneurial community are available to answer your questions.

Tuesday - 10 am

Drop-ins welcome

Free

Heidi ran upstairs, gathered all ten shirts she had designed, then spread them out over the floor in Justin's old room. This view of her handiwork proved inspiring. Her heart raced. Maybe she could really do this. Maybe she could make something spectacular of her life after all. If she did not believe in herself, who would?

Q: Would you accept advice?
Heidi was all ears.

SHERALL SAVARD
Because Sherall hated losing, she strategically whacked the handball just inside the line to score the winning point.

"Good game," said the other woman. "One of these days, I'm gonna beat you."

"Not. A. Chance." Sherall milked her dominance.

Her opponent tonight was MetaBase client Alison Baer. Their two year business relationship blossomed after connecting through Boston Racquet's handball matchmaking league. Although they were both strong and equally skilled, Sherall's long arms and legs gave her an advantage.

Later, in the locker room, she invited Alison to get a drink next door at Inspire.

"Sure," she answered. They had never socialized other than for sports or networking. "Is everything okay?"

Sherall laughed. "I just don't feel like heading home yet."

The lights at the bar were low, but not dim enough to hide what the male patrons turned to see: confidence, curves, and legs. The two women made their way to the bar and slipped onto high stools.

"God, Sherall, they're panting for you," said Alison.

"Just ignore the beasts," she laughed.

"What can I get for you ladies?" asked the bartender, sliding napkin squares across the dark wood of the bar.

"I'll have a Rob Roy," Sherall responded.

"Same," said Alison.

Their drinks arrived and easy conversation followed. Sherall brought up the "Marvelous Mavens."

"They're *all* over fifty?" Alison was incredulous.

"Is that so unbelievable?" Sherall asked. She had forgotten how young Alison was.

"I never think of older women as that interesting." Alison added quickly, "Except you!"

She knit her brows, realizing she had only worsened her comment.

"How old are you, Alison?"

"Thirty-seven."

"A baby."

"Oh come on. How old are you, Sherall?" Alison prodded.

"I'm fifty-nine. I usually don't tell my age, but lately, I'm starting to feel proud of it."

"Really?"

"Yeah. I'm starting to want to say, *this* will happen to you," she gestured broadly toward her body, "if you are really, really lucky."

"Growing older?"

"Growing older, getting wrinkles, having stories, battle scars, and the rest of it."

"I guess I never thought about it that way."

They absently watched the bartender tidy his station.

"It's weird," Sherall mused. "For most of my life, I focused on the outside of aging. Now, I'm starting to look at the inside. Pretty amazing."

"Well, you must be doing something right. I know my mother doesn't look anything like you, and she's only three years older."

Sherall rolled her eyes. "Forget what I just said."

Driving home, Sherall considered being thirty-seven again. Would she do things differently? Lina and Luke were mere babies when Sherall was in her late thirties. Mrs. Velasquez lived in the den they had converted to a bedroom. From the time the children were newborns, this capable nanny woke them, fed them, took them to the park, arranged play dates and lessons or activities, and changed an equally endless number of diapers. Because Mrs. Velasquez immersed herself so deeply into their lives, Sherall quickly re-established her preferred routine: an early morning run followed by breakfast in the financial district with clients or associates. If a trial was in progress, her day would end late. By the time she arrived home, Mrs. Velasquez would have already bathed and fed the children a nutritious supper. She kept them awake as long as prudent, hoping the children would have an opportunity to kiss their mother good night. Sherall remembered the sight of her children in their footie pajamas, their wet hair neatly combed back, a menagerie of favorite stuffed animals nestled between the two of them where they sat waiting together on the leather couch.

It was especially important to Mrs. Velasquez that the children connect with their mother daily. Unfortunately, this did not always occur. If the nanny knew Sherall would be particularly late and would miss Lina and Luke, she had both children draw pictures of the day's activities. Sherall glanced at their drawings when she got home, then left them on the counter. In the morning, Mrs. Velasquez collected the two sheets of paper and put them in the expanding folder she kept in her own room.

Sherall did not pretend that her parenting was anything but abysmal. She knew she did not spend enough time with her kids, but neither did Scott, she rationalized. Lina and Luke were a shared responsibility and she aimed for an equitable division of labor. If she embraced the role of primary parent, she worried she would carry that burden for decades. Mothering at that level was incompatible with her professional life.

Sherall's concern about appearing less than fully committed to her career was valid. Even a hint of conflict of interest between work and family meant professional suicide. A woman's best strategy was to not reference her family. Ever. Because Sherall withdrew from mentioning her children while she was away, she eventually stopped thinking of them at work as well. They were in capable hands, after all.

Over the next decade, her attention was consumed with positioning herself for a future as a Suffolk County judge. This pursuit required calculated energy, shoulder-rubbing with powerful and influential Bostonians, and wooing those who sat on the Governor's nominating commission. There was mounting interest from others for her to run for Congress, too.

Those were heady days. An attractive and intelligent woman with an ambitious agenda garnered considerable rewards in the 1990s. There were newspaper articles in which Sherall was quoted, radio talk shows on which she was a guest, too many cocktail party invitations to possibly attend, and people clamoring for her attention. She soon secured her place in the Massachusetts pantheon of the powerful.

No one could have predicted that all of this would eventually leave her unsatisfied and yearning for change. This restless nature pushed her to pursue a dramatic career swap from law to sales. She decided to prove to herself that she was more than the sum of her connections. From scratch, she built a fresh network in an entirely new and formidably competitive field. She seized the opportunity, tackled the challenge, and rose to the top. Again.

Sherall parked in the narrow garage behind her Beacon Hill home, then made her way up the old staircase. At the landing, she set down her bag and briefcase, and flicked on the light. Her somber reflection in the foyer mirror startled her. Could it be she was bored again, already? Or, was it something else? This felt like a different energy. More accurately, a lack of energy. Rekindling the desire to *fight* for something—a philosophy once deeply ingrained into her personality—now felt like a chore. If she was no longer that woman, who would she be?

Q: Are you satisfied?
Define satisfaction, thought Sherall.

PAMELA CARDIN

Pamela pressed down on the spine of her journal so it lay flat, then picked up her pen to write from memory:

> The difference between Despair
> And Fear—is like the One
> Between the instant of a Wreck—
> And when the Wreck has been—
>
> The Mind is smooth—no Motion—
> Contented as the Eye
> Upon the Forehead of a Bust—
> That knows—it cannot see—
> Emily Dickinson

Dickinson was her favorite poet. She felt she understood that kind of suffering. They shared a resignation about fitting into one's surroundings. Circumstances were something to endure, versus change. That mindset resonated with Pamela. Dickinson could not shift her own surroundings. It was nearly impossible for a woman of that era. Could Pamela do it now? She felt herself teetering on a precipice. Step back or fall.

Dodo brought this tension to the fore. Since Pamela met her, a new universe had appeared. She struggled with her churning emotions. Did this mean they were lesbians? Their encounter seemed a dichotomy of titillation and innocence. Maybe what she was feeling was love.

Before Bruce entered her life, Pamela's relationships with men had been overwhelmingly superficial.

Invariably, she attracted the kind of male who wanted to have her on his arm, if not in his heart. She was uncomfortable with attention she received from men who sought to conquer her, and saddened by the lack of attention from sensitive men afraid to approach her.

To her great relief, Bruce acted unimpressed by her beauty from the start. He told her she was not especially pretty. He said he found many women more beautiful. When this matter-of-fact opinion proved oddly comforting, she persuaded herself that this was a man who had discovered her essence, looking beyond her exterior to love what was beneath. Then he said no one else could possibly love her if they really knew her like he did. Intellectually, she knew this was irrational, but emotionally, she feared it was true.

One night, while Bruce and Pamela were entertaining his business colleagues at their home, she left the room to give instructions to the kitchen help. Before rounding the corner to join them again, she overheard Bruce say, "It helps business that she's beautiful. You wouldn't believe how many deals I make while my competition is momentarily bewitched by my wife. She's incredibly high maintenance, though."

She turned her journal to a new page and took up her pen.

Whether taken or left behind,
Nothing settles
While the fox hunts.
He will find what he can.
Its origin, inconsequential.

If nothing else,
Garbage will do.
With no conscience, he is easily satisfied.

She had always found solace in reading and writing poetry. As a child, Pamela hid the paper evidence of her heart so deeply between her mattress and box spring that her little arm strained to retrieve them. Later, at Smith College, Pamela impressed professors with her expository submissions but revealed her poetry talent only if required for an assignment. Her collected journals were her greatest treasure because they spanned her lifetime. Bruce had no interest in a single stanza of her poetry. No interest in *her*.

Despite the volatility of her marriage, Pamela was terrified of being alone. Out of respect for her long-deceased foster parents, she had never investigated her birth origins. Other women could tap sisters, mothers, cousins, or close friends for support. Without them, Pamela felt the pain of being a family of one. She soldiered on. She always had. She knew she must. Who would care for her other than herself?

Having never learned to bond with family, she struggled to maintain a bond with friends. To avoid seeming odd, she crafted an appearance of normalcy. Observing others, she learned to speak of her foster parents as her "folks," and how to look up and off to the side and smile subtly when recounting a childhood memory. An astute onlooker would not detect how Pamela felt suspended in a bubble, invisibly estranged from those around her. She kept this unsociable secret close, fearing that if her solitude was revealed, others would treat her as a pariah—the unloved one.

When she was with Dodo, Pamela felt accepted and freed from her past. Circumstances that transpired in a previous life now seemed irrelevant. She eagerly anticipated their next conversation when Dodo would listen intently or make her laugh. Pamela knew she was free to phone her whenever she pleased, but didn't want to interrupt Dodo's work.

Instead, she picked up her pen and jotted down another verse:

The vixen is contrastive.
She must discriminate
Between what is good and what is bad.
The pups grow inside her.
Soon, she will need to feed them, too.

That evening, after Bruce returned home, they sat in their customary seats in front of the TV. Tonight, she was grateful for his inattention. They would watch his favorite shows for a few hours, then turn it off and head upstairs. They would almost certainly have sex. Bruce's good mood was the best predictor of this occurring. He'd expect his wife to fully participate. Bruce was an adept lover, and Pamela's body rarely failed to respond in the anonymity of darkness. Bruce had been everything to her. But now there was Dodo as well.

During a commercial, she subtly explored Bruce's schedule.

"Do we have any new plans for Fourth of July weekend?" Pamela asked.

"I do."

"Of course. Will you still be golfing?"

"Greg and the guys are going up to the lake for the weekend. I told you that."

"I'm sorry, I forgot. That sounds really nice."

"No wives are going."

"I didn't think so. Will you leave on Friday or Saturday?"

"Friday night. Pack my bag for all of the days."

"I will."

Q: What would you do, if you could not fail?

This was a question Pamela had never asked herself. She would start now.

KIMBERLY DOLAN

On Kimberly's left side was a fresh sheet of vellum paper and the designated fountain pen. Before she composed another draft, she promised herself she would finish the enrollment details surrounding her daughter's intention to attend Brown University. Meghan's fall departure would mark the first time in decades that she and her husband would be alone for an extended period. A wave of nausea passed through her body. It was not the empty nest that caused alarm. It was the empty marriage.

Kimberly considered the blank suicide letter at her side. The refuge of this ultimate escape would have to wait. She felt strongly that she should not leave her family in this definitive way before Meghan completed college. It would be unfair to her daughter. If she left prior to then, it would confirm that she had been a bad mother.

When she finally returned her focus to the computer

screen, a pop-up ad caught her eye.

Cruise With Class!

She clicked, then watched a colorful page fill the monitor. A cruise ship with a pristine deck floated in the middle of a brilliant blue ocean.

Join other adult learners on a round-the-world-cruise while continuing your education. Study at Sea. Classes daily. Complete the Accelerated Master's Degree program in International Relations. Guest experts provide customized tutorials before arrival at each port. Independent individual/group excursions included.

Itinerary: Morocco Ghana Namibia South Africa Mauritius India Myanmar Singapore Vietnam China Japan Australia Fiji Tahiti Ecuador Costa Rica Panama Cuba

Kimberly's breath grew shallow. Travel on her own had become an abandoned dream, but now this opportunity glowed on her monitor. Could she possibly consider it? Money was not an issue, thanks to her late Aunt Muriel. She left trust funds for each of her nieces, stipulating the sums were for personal use only. Kimberly had intended to violate the terms by disbursing this inheritance to her children through her will.

She knew a bit about travel logistics. Whenever she traveled with Gary on business and family vacations, it was Kimberly who made the arrangements. Her husband took charge again once they left home. She felt she was a capable planner, but was no longer confident about traveling alone.

She wouldn't exactly be alone on this cruise ship, though. According to the website, there would be two hundred adult students. Half of the students would have single rooms. She could join groups of others on their excursions. She could also earn her Master's degree.

Kimberly twisted a strand of hair around her finger, twirling an endless loop. She scrolled to the end of the page. A midsummer deadline left only weeks to decide.

She saved the link into her favorites and printed the main page. The fountain pen and blank sheet of paper went back into the drawer.

Q: What are your regrets?
There was not enough time to list them all.

DODO QUIMBY
"Chin down," Dodo commanded the young model over the clicking sound of her camera. "And please fix the left side of her shirt," she said to the wardrobe stylist, who quickly tiptoed over the white floor to where the model stood.

The model whispered to the stylist, "I'm not sure what she wants me to do."

The stylist repositioned her shirt, then gave the model a stern look.

Dodo shot a few more images, but again stopped suddenly.

"Shine!" she yelled.

Dodo lowered her camera. A shoeless makeup artist rushed across the white floor until she reached the model. The artist pulled a brush and container of powder from her waist pack and dusted the young woman's forehead and nose. Wild-eyed, the model frantically searched the makeup artist's face for affirmation of her beauty. Now, the hairstylist joined them on the pristine floor. He fluffed the model's hair and used the tail end of his teasing comb to correct a limp curl. Both stylists exchanged concerned looks.

Dodo checked her phone while she waited. Scrolling through messages, she noted that final arrangements for the Washington, DC trip were complete. She quickly composed a text to Pamela.

DC trip all set! Depart Logan Friday @ 2. Return Monday morning Logan @10ish. Will stay @ Fairview on Embassy Row. Been there often. You'll love it. Really can't wait to see you Saturday.

She sent the text.

"Whenever you're ready, Dodo," the artistic director said quietly from where he stood a few feet behind her.

"Ok, let's see how this goes now. Please put some discipline into it this time, Dameron," Dodo said to the model.

Dameron turned her head and jutted out her hip. In a few seconds, she bent down and leaned forward. After another interval, she held her left leg out at an angle.

"Much better," Dodo said, moving with as much agility as the model. "Let's use the ladder now."

Immediately two young men carried a ladder onto the set, awaiting the photographer's instructions regarding its placement.

This is how the morning photo shoot progressed. It was a typical day. When Dodo was on set, talent and crew were anxious to please. Her reputation for excellence caused all involved to devote extreme attention to detail.

Detail, after all, was her trademark. When Dodo was booked as a photographer, the client knew shots from the session would be golden. Dolores Quimby saw what everyone missed. Although the hairstylist, makeup artist, wardrobe stylist, lighting crew, set designer, and even artistic director scrutinized their own categories of responsibility, Dodo would be the one to uncover a flaw that could potentially make the image unusable. Even more valuable was her ability to suggest a small change that would result in a picture that would sell a million dollars' worth of product.

She had reached the pinnacle of her career.

Q: Did you squander opportunity?

How ironic, Dodo thought. I create perfect visions for a living, but my own life is blurry mess.

DARLY

"Are you talking about Marla?" Ian asked Darly.

She nodded. They sat next to each other, cross-legged under a tree on the bank of the Charles River, eating lunch.

Ian threw his head back and laughed. "She's my sister's lover! The three of us were going to meet up at the movie but Claudia got paged at the last minute. She's a resident at Mass General. I can't believe you thought we were together *that* way."

Darly adjusted the beads on her bracelet.

"It sort of looked like you were."

"Is that why you've been a little aloof?"

"Have I?" She looked up at him.

"Yeah."

"Well, I'm trying to be respectful. You are my adviser."

Ian sighed. "You know it's only temporary. I'm not the one who will be assessing you anyway. Look at it this way: I'm your adviser while we're sitting in my office; when we're not, I'm not."

"How can you switch on and off like that?"

"Darly, have you looked in the mirror lately?"

"What do you mean?" She grabbed her napkin and dabbed at the corners of her mouth.

"You don't get it, do you?"

"Sorry. I guess not." She looked befuddled.

"You are easily the most beautiful woman in this entire university," he answered, smiling.

Stunned, Darly stared at him for a moment, then looked down at her lap, blushing.

"Thank you," she answered.

He laid his hand on her knee where it was close to him, then leaned toward her. "May I kiss you?"

She looked back up at him and nodded.

It was a brief kiss, but long enough for Darly to imprint the sensation deep in her mind. His smell, his taste, the soft texture of his lips. She was sure she would remember this kiss.

Ian pulled his head back and smiled.

"Nice," he said. "I knew it would be."

The Marsh Chapel bell in the building behind them rang two times.

"Oh, shit!" Ian grabbed around for his messenger bag. "I forgot about the staff meeting. I apologize for leaving you like this, Darly. Dinner Friday night?"

A mute Darly nodded up and down too many times, then watched Ian sprint off over the grass and across the footbridge. She brought both hands up to her face and pressed her fingers over her cheeks, her mouth, and eyes. She could feel her hands. She must not be dreaming.

PAMELA CARDIN/DODO QUIMBY

Bruce was at another Saturday golf tournament. His frenetic summer recreation schedule had begun. Pamela eagerly anticipated this season. It meant she would rarely see her husband, and when she did, he would invariably be in good spirits.

It was easy to make plans with Dodo for a day like today. She drove down Route 60 until she reached Arlington Catholic High School, then parked in the empty lot and wrestled her bicycle out of the car trunk.

Down the street, Dodo hopped off the bus at the intersection of Massachusetts Avenue and Route 3.

They arrived at their designated meeting spot within minutes of each other.

"I'm so glad we could do this," Dodo said, lightly touching Pamela on the shoulder.

"Me, too. I've been looking forward to it all week."

The tall women stood eye-to-eye.

In Pamela's bike basket was a bag containing a water bottle, sunscreen, journal, and a pen—all her essential items.

In the early morning quiet, they spun side by side on the Minuteman trail, encountering little traffic from other bikers. As they rode down the paved railroad bed, sunlight pierced the thick weave of leafy branches and left a mottled pattern on the asphalt. The only sound was the whoosh of air as they made their way across the land.

When the trail ended in Bedford, they dismounted to drink water.

"Should we turn back?" Pamela asked.

"Maybe. Let me check something first." Dodo consulted her phone. "If we ride up here a bit, we'll be on the road to Walden Pond. Have you ever been there?"

"No. Never." Bruce disliked any local places frequented by tourists.

"It's probably another ten miles or so. On our way back, we can catch a bus just past the bridge over the highway. Do you think you'll get too tired?" Dodo asked.

Pamela shook her head. "I can definitely do that. It sounds fun."

They stopped first at the market to select a picnic lunch, then put everything inside the soft cooler Dodo had strapped onto the rack over her rear tire. Opposite that was the rigid box where she stored her camera.

"Thoreau, here we come!" Dodo called out as they pushed off again.

At the entrance to the pond, they locked their bikes.

"There's a path around the entire pond. Let's head that way until we find a good place to eat," Dodo said, slinging the strap of the cooler over one shoulder and her camera over the other. "It's still pretty early in the season so there's no crowd. Sometimes there are so many people, they won't even let you in."

"Do you come here a lot?" Pamela asked as they made their way down the path that hugged the perimeter of the pond.

"Not lately. I took Georgie a few times, when she was just a baby. She was so cute in the water. She turned out to be a pretty good swimmer."

After a while, Dodo stopped at a large rock, then motioned for Pamela to follow.

"Hardly anybody knows about this place," she whispered. "You're not supposed to stray off the trail, but I'm always careful. They don't want the banks to erode from traffic."

Pamela followed Dodo down the steep path until they reached the water in a secluded miniature cove. Hot sun beat down on the surface of the pond.

Dodo slid the soft pack off her shoulder and opened it. "Are you as starved as I am?"

"After all that exercise? Yes!"

"Did I push you too much?" Dodo said, handing her a sandwich.

"No, not at all. I used to ride everywhere when I was younger. Plus, I take a spinning class."

The two enjoyed lunch, then lay back onto the grass in the midday sun.

"I wish I brought my bathing suit. This looks like a nice place to swim," Pamela said.

Dodo propped herself up on one elbow. "You don't have to wear a suit unless you're swimming at the beach near the parking lot. Wait until you feel the water. It's going to be pretty cold but it's rejuvenating."

Dodo pulled her shirt over her head, then stood and stepped out of her shorts. She wore neither bra nor underpants.

Pamela rose from the ground and looked around, uneasily. "Shouldn't I keep my underwear on at least?"

"Come on, Pamela. Don't be shy."

The beautiful woman removed her clothes, folded them carefully, and placed them on a rock. Dodo took her hand and led Pamela into the water.

"The only thing you have to watch out for is the giant snapping turtle."

"Snapping turtle!" Pamela turned to rush out of the water, but Dodo kept a firm grip on her hand.

"Don't worry. I'll protect you," she laughed.

Dodo pulled her down into the dark water, but both shot up quickly in reaction to the cool temperature. They found their footing and eventually acclimated to the chill.

Rivulets of mascara ran down Pamela's cheeks and her hair hung slick from her face. The surface water was warmer, so she let her feet float up and felt the heat of the sun on her chest. Dodo soon floated beside her and reached out to hold her hand. The shadow of a bird flying over them momentarily blocked the sun. Occasionally, a breeze blew over their skin. Water lapped gently against the twisted tree trunks at the shoreline.

On the computer screen that evening, Pamela viewed a soft focus picture of herself floating on the surface of the smooth pond. In the accompanying email, Dodo wrote that this was the favorite picture she had taken of their day together. In it, water sparkled all around the outline of Pamela's body. Dodo had cleverly used the sun as back light to allow only a suggestion of nudity.

When Pamela heard Bruce at the side door, she quickly

shut down the computer, then left the room to greet her husband.

"Did you have a good time?" she called out to him on her way to the kitchen.

"Yeah. We played cards afterward. I won about three hundred dollars." Bruce was in a good mood.

"That's great! You love playing cards."

"Sure do." He sat on the couch and kicked off his shoes.

Pamela sat down next to him. He stroked her hair, then moved her feet to his lap so he could massage them. He was being sweet, but Bruce's mercurial temperament always kept her wary.

They spent a few more minutes talking about the day.

"Get me a drink, would you?" Bruce said.

"Scotch?"

He nodded.

Pamela moved to the wet bar where she dropped exactly four ice cubes into a highball glass then covered them with scotch. She poured herself a glass of Pinot Grigio. She carried both drinks over to the couch where Bruce relaxed, his feet propped on the ottoman.

"Thanks," he said, taking the drink from her. He took a sip, then made a face. "What's this?"

"Berman's had some kind of run on Glenfiddich."

"I can't believe how lazy you are sometime. Why didn't you just get some at Arbundale's?"

Pamela was silent, having learned years ago that no response was her best response to avoid escalating Bruce's temper.

"I give you everything and this is what I get in return." Bruce shook his head. He moved the TV remote control proprietarily next to his leg.

"So, what did *you* do all day?" he asked after a few minutes.

"I went for a bike ride on the Minuteman Trail. It was so beautiful. Then, I actually went swimming in Walden Pond."

Bruce looked at her, his face blank. "Are you serious?" he asked.

"Yeah."

"Why did you go all that way for a bike ride?"

"Because I've never been there before."

He shook his head, then grabbed the TV remote control. "Anything good on tonight?"

THE FOURTH DINNER

At four o'clock, Darly replied, "Namaste," to her instructor and left the refuge of the peaceful studio. Yoga offered the serenity she had come to need. Unfortunately, anxiety about tonight's meeting resurfaced the minute the yoga class ended. She tucked her mat under her arm and jogged back to her apartment, dodging others along the crowded Allston sidewalk.

She had spent the earlier part of the day assessing the study participants' breadth of perspective. Darly reviewed her notes and listened to the dinner audio tapes. She sought to understand the historical significance of the participants' experience. She wanted to collect specifics so she could create a consensus about what they had lived through, and bring it all together in a cohesive and coherent report. She was determined to give the women a sense of direction and structure during their gatherings.

Darly had not expected the study group to take on a life of its own. If she threw a topic into the circle of these women, they tore into it with alarming gusto. Although she searched for themes to organize the information they revealed, she was invariably left with more questions than answers. She felt her leadership status diminish and her ability to harness the energy of the group slipping away. Because it reflected poorly on her management skills, she was embarrassed to consult Ian about this issue. It was an obstacle she would have to overcome on her own.

In truth, she had been withholding much more from Ian. How could she explain her desire to support the camaraderie and warmth that this group found together, and also her dismay about the information they revealed? Weeks of listening to discontent about their lives left her anxious about the way her own future might play out. It seemed every choice made by these diverse women had an unsettling outcome. They were always in upheaval!

Once Ian no longer held official responsibility for her, she would be free to be completely honest with him. She needed his support and wanted to vent, but now Darly worried about how Ian would react to these women's stories. They seemed critical of men of all generations. Would she become that kind of woman? Was Ian the sort of man they disdained?

The Mavens were a powerful force. Kimberly, Pamela, Heidi, Dodo, and Sherall—all contrasting personalities. Darly staggered under the challenge of mining their cumulative life experiences. How could she have been so naïve to think that a twenty-four year old woman like herself could possibly hope to understand the over three-hundred years of life these women embodied?

Darly's mother would have been the same age as the Mavens if she had lived. Perhaps she would have joined them in drinking the wine that Darly regularly declined.

Too soon for her emotional comfort, Darly arrived at Vivere. She pulled open the restaurant door, walked through the bustling crowd, then made her way up the back stairs.

Clustered at the other side of the room, the Mavens were already having another of their grand moments. To them, there was always much to say, much to ask, and much to learn from one another. It was an electric atmosphere and Darly had grown to dread its wattage.

Kimberly was the first to notice her arrival.

"Darly! We were worried about you," she said, walking over and laying a hand on her shoulder.

"I just got stuck in T traffic. You know how it gets this time of day," Darly answered.

One by one, the other women disengaged from conversation and made their way to the table to take their seats. They were expectant; bright eyed; jubilant. Their moods were in stark contrast to Darly's.

After the food was served, Darly spoke. "Okay, let's get started." She managed a weak smile as she turned on her tablet. "The last time we met, you were going to consider the prospect of Another Chance. Kind of a do-over. Can you please tell me your thoughts about that?" Darly looked up from the screen.

"There are no do-overs," said Sherall.

"I know. But just give it a try, okay?" Darly realized she sounded a little testy.

"All right, I'll go first," Heidi said. "I have to admit, I really thought about this since our last meeting. It's not like I've really done anything spectacular in my life so far. I think I've done the right things for the right reasons, though. I had a job as a teacher's aide while my kids were small, and that was really helpful financially. It was also good because I could spend time at my sons' school while they were there. The only thing I regret is that I wish some of it was more about *me*."

"Can you elaborate on that?" Darly asked.

"I wish I'd made a little bit of a stamp on the world. You know, just something that only Heidi Belanger could do."

"Did you ever have an idea about what that might be?" asked Dodo.

"Not really. That was a big part of why it never happened. That, and not having much quiet time to myself to think of something, I guess."

"Thank you for sharing that, Heidi," Darly said. "Anybody else?"

Sherall went next. "I don't think I'd actually want to do things over, and also, as I said before, it's pretty futile to look back. If I could *add* something though, I'd try to be a big fish in a big pond instead of hanging around Boston all of these years."

"Some people think Boston is pretty big," Dodo commented.

"You know what I mean, Dodo. You've traveled."

"Point taken," Dodo responded. "But, sometimes the

hardest and most rewarding work happens right in your own neighborhood. It's crazy but the more I travel, the more I think a place like Boston is just the micro version of the macro world. It's all here—good, bad, beautiful, ugly— at your doorstep."

"Interesting perspective," Darly said.

"I don't know how I could have done things differently, but I definitely would have," Pamela said. "I wasn't brave enough." She shrugged her shoulders.

"Would you like to add anything to that?" Darly asked.

"Not right now, I guess," Pamela said.

Kimberly looked around at the other women then lowered her eyes. "I guess, if I *could* do it over, I'd get my Master's degree." She looked up to gauge reaction to her declaration.

"Kimberly," Heidi said, "you can still go back to school! I might."

"That would be great for you, Heidi," Kimberly responded. "I hope you can do it. I don't think Gary would want me to, though. Then, there are the kids. They still need me to be available."

DoDo leaned onto the table, across from where Kimberly sat. "But what about *you*? You're important, too. You always do everything for everyone else. Why not do something for yourself?"

Kimberly assessed faces. Finally, she said, "I'm afraid."

"For God's sake, Kimberly, afraid of what?" Sherall asked.

"Sherall, go easy," said Dodo.

Kimberly continued. "It's a long story but I sort of have this thing about trying not to be better than the people I love."

"Why?" Darly asked. "Can you tell us?"

"I don't want to take up everyone's time."

"Kimberly, we have time and you're worth it," Pamela told her.

"Thank you."

The room went silent, anticipating Kimberly's explanation.

She began. "Remember when I said my mother died when I was 21?"

"Yes?" Darly had not forgotten.

"Well, she committed suicide."

Each woman's face reflected Kimberly's pain.

"Oh, you poor thing. You must have been so sad," said Pamela.

"That's not the worst part." Kimberly's eyes grew moist.

Heidi got up and stood next to her, rubbing her gently on the back.

"I'm okay." Kimberly looked up at her gratefully. Heidi handed her a tissue.

"I know why she killed herself." Kimberly finally said. "She killed herself because of me."

"But, why do you think that?" Darly's voice was soft.

"Because she was disappointed in her own life and she couldn't bear to see me do more than she had."

"How do you know?" asked Darly.

Kimberly sighed deeply, then continued. "She left me a letter. Everything was clearly spelled out. It was hard to understand when I was young. I thought I had come to terms with it. Now that my own daughters are grown, I'm starting to feel the same way I think my mother did."

"But, you have a beautiful family, a wonderful home, and a great husband!" Darly said.

Five sets of eyes turned to Darly. She stared back at them.

"Sometimes, that's just not enough, Darly," Heidi said.

They rose as one and embraced Kimberly, their tears mingling with hers.

"We're here for you, Kimberly," Pamela whispered.

Darly hoped these women would give her another chance. She had never imagined that her study would turn into something so emotional for the participants. Were they okay with that? Would they want to continue or would they decide they had had enough of the heart-rending ups and downs? As for herself, Darly wanted desperately to be a part of it all and share that she had lost her own mother. She wanted to rush to Kimberly's side and cling to her and tell her how much she understood that loss, too. When she felt tears welling, she jutted her jaw forward—a trick learned long ago as a way to stop crying. It would be imprudent to lose composure in front of these women and in this atmosphere of sympathy for another. The trigger was real though.

Seeing Kimberly still upset at her age told Darly she would never process her own mother's death. She had assumed the pain would become less acute.

These women were beginning to feel like surrogate mothers. It was an inappropriate projection on her part. She was the one in charge! *She* led the study, guided the discussion, and selected the topics. She had knowledge. The Mavens had life. But Darly knew she was ignorant in many ways. The Mavens were indulging her. They cared enough about her to nurture her research endeavor to a successful outcome. They did not have to continue participating for the small stipend B.U. offered. This study was bigger than that for them. But where was it going and where did she fit?

The women continued murmuring their comfort to Kimberly.

Darly decided to cut the dinner short. She would have to collect the rest of the evening's information another way.

TOPIC: FRIENDSHIP
How did the feminist movement change your
friendships?
Do you feel competitive toward other women?
Do females who are not your age understand you?
Did parenthood impact your friendships?
Is your significant other your best friend?

DODO QUIMBY

At her studio, Dodo draped the backdrop for
Wednesday's fashion shoot. From the rungs of a ladder,
she arranged multi-colored lights so tiny beams would
bounce off the canvas and backlight wisps of the model's
curly hair. It was a technique she discovered last year at a
shoot in Italy. She would test the display tonight by
experimenting with a mannequin. Stepping off the ladder,
she smiled with satisfaction. Progressive clients who gave
creative free rein brought out the best in her.

From a young age, she had the same photographer's
eye and mind that made her so successful today.
Unfortunately, this quirky trait did not attract friends.
Finally, someone took pity on her and told her that she
was too aloof. She needed to make more of an effort to
interact if she wanted female friends.

Dodo was also particular. It was hard to find a good
match. She liked women with character. She also did not
like to waste time. Before social media, it was a challenge

to connect with like minds. Male friendships were easier. Rarely romantic, but always fun.

She was an affable woman, but she was also a loner. Dodo liked the ease of an unencumbered lifestyle. Her associations generally revolved around professional colleagues, domestic and international. She had some local friends—all single. Although she was still invited to her married friends' parties, it was more of a strain the older she got. It felt like the glue was missing. The bond could not hold. As their families grew and they became more insular, Dodo started to feel like an intruder. It was her own bias. Everyone was welcoming and kind but she didn't feel like she fit in anymore.

She would see some familiar faces at the upcoming Washington, DC shoot. Dodo was pleased that Pamela would join her. She was also anxious to learn more about her husband, Bruce. She had gathered only fragments of information about him and she liked none of it. Most alarming was that he was a volatile man, stopping short of physical abuse, at least so far. Despite that threat, she was perplexed that Pamela seemed oddly protective of her husband. Even so, she intended to support her, not push, because pressing for more information might jeopardize their own budding relationship.

Dodo grappled with these new sensations, feelings, and trepidation about performance with Pamela. She had no idea what she was supposed to do next. The only thing she knew for sure is that she wanted more.

Q: Is your significant other your best friend?

Dodo was eager to find out. A best friend slot had been empty for a long time.

SHERALL SAVARD
 "I excel at my work.
 I understand my customers.
 I am strong.
 I enjoy challenge.
 I consistently exceed my monthly sales quota.
 I will *win* today."

Sherall stopped speaking to the image of herself in the bathroom mirror. She took a deep breath, then studied the second index card in her hand. Toward her reflection, she whispered the additional phrases.

 "I am lovable and worthy of friendship.
 I deserve to be happy and fulfilled.
 I am a warm and kind person.
 I forgive myself."

She forced a broad smile then put the cards back into the vanity drawer.

Sherall attributed her excellent sales record to the first affirmations, read out loud morning and night. The phrases about friendship were new. Although she was socially active, her acquaintances were professional colleagues, not friends. These interactions were more like competitive jockeying, and they tested her. Her single-minded approach to the world had proved financially lucrative, but personally unsatisfying.

Late Saturday afternoon, Sherall popped a fresh piece

of NicAway into her mouth, then leaned back in her chair. She looked out the window of her 4th floor office. Only one month earlier, trees lining the street below were covered with delicate white blossoms. Since then, light green leaves had given way to dark green. In the fall, they would turn yellow. In the winter, tiny white electric lights wound around those bare tree branches would twinkle and sparkle in the cold wind. Life moved forward but inevitably returned to the same circle where it began.

Perhaps some doubted Sherall noticed such things. In truth, she noticed a lot that she hid from others. Outside the Newbury Street window, walking into various stores and restaurants together, were the *others*. She never felt close to them—or anyone.

Next Saturday, she and Scott would see each other for the first time in two weeks when he was honored at a Massachusetts General Hospital gala. His groundbreaking research on myelodysplastic syndromes had an enormous impact on the international medical community. The Boston Globe ran a spring series about him and his associates on four consecutive Thursdays. He was in demand as a speaker all over the world. No wonder he had no time for Sherall. Frankly, she had no time for him either. By silent and mutual consent, they allowed their marriage to atrophy to the point where it was not recognizable as any form of union.

Her emotional life was wretched.

Q: Do you feel competitive toward other women?
Sherall knew the affirmation by heart: I forgive myself.

HEIDI BELANGER

"She wants to get married," Justin explained to his parents.

Jim and Heidi exchanged glances.

"And what do you want to do, Justin?" Jim asked his son.

"I'm not sure. I don't really feel old enough to get married."

"But, you felt old enough to be a father," Heidi said.

"Don't lecture me, Mom. I know I screwed up."

"So, it looks like she's going to have the baby then," Jim said.

"She doesn't think it will be a problem." Justin walked over to the refrigerator and opened the door, surveying its contents. He returned with a beer and flipped off the cap.

"You know that this baby will be your responsibility, right?" Heidi asked.

"Well, not all mine. Her parents said they'll help."

"What kind of help are they going to give you?" Jim asked.

"Just buying stuff, you know, like a crib and whatever junk a baby needs."

"Justin Belanger." Heidi waited until her son put down his beer and gave her his full attention. "This is a very serious situation that is going to change your life forever. Do you understand that?"

"Shit, Mom. You think I'm happy about this?"

"Don't swear around your mother, Justin."

Justin brought the bottle to his mouth and took a long swig. Jim and Heidi remained silent.

"Her parents said we could move into their house and live there."

"They don't mind that you won't be married? I thought they were extremely conservative," Jim said.

"Well, they are kind of the ones who want us to get married, but Courtney said they'd be cool either way. Plus, her dad said he could get me a job at Somerville Public Works. He knows lots of people there. I guess he's lightened up a little since you knew him through your work, Dad."

Jim shrugged and looked doubtful.

"What about school?" Heidi asked. "You were almost finished."

"None of them went to college and they seem to have done all right," he responded. "Look, I don't want to sound like a jerk, but the whole thing is really not your problem now. Her parents are going to help take care of us, so that's where I'm going."

Justin grabbed his car keys and left.

Heidi immediately began to cry. "God, I never thought things would turn out this way."

Jim walked over to her and took her into his arms.

"I know. I know," he said, rubbing her back with his hands.

The comfort Jim offered was almost enough. She felt so secure in his arms; so complete. This joining together had always made their troubles seem halved.

"He has no idea," Heidi sobbed.

"Honey, I was his age when he was born," Jim reminded her.

"But you had me!"

Jim looked down at her with immeasurable love in his eyes.

"Yes. I had you. And, I still do. We'll get through it together, just like we always do."

They embraced until Heidi felt strong enough to stand alone.

Lying on the couch later, Heidi adjusted the bag of frozen peas she rested over her eyes.

"Everyone will know I was crying."

"They won't be able to tell," Jim replied. "Plus these are our friends."

"They are our family. And, the others are your friends."

"It's our regular Friday night. Do you want me to cancel?"

"No, of course not. I just don't want to talk about this to anyone. Will you promise not to? You tell your brothers everything."

"I promise."

After a pause, Jim continued. "Will you tell your sisters?"

"Absolutely not!"

"You'll have to eventually, you know."

Heidi sighed. "This is when it all feels too incestuous. We spend all of our time with family and sometimes I want some privacy."

"They are always there for us."

"You're right. They are. And I love them for that."

"We'll get through this thing with Justin. The baby will have us all. It will be okay." He rubbed her ankle. His calm demeanor always comforted her.

"I'll be ready to go in a few minutes. Life must go on,"

Heidi said.

The weather on Saturday morning was beautiful, so Heidi decided to go for a run on a trail she had heard about in Newton. She could take the T. She wanted to clear her head and try to think through her family's new reality.

The trail snaked through the woods and then opened to a loop around a pond. It was there that she saw an athletic woman running toward her. She recognized her face.

"Kimberly!"

"Oh my, gosh. Heidi!"

The women embraced.

"I've never seen you running here before," said Kimberly.

"It's my first time. So beautiful," she panted. "Do you come here often?"

"I do. It's part of my usual route. I live just a few miles away."

"Lucky you!"

"I'm almost done. Just 10 minutes more," Kimberly huffed. "How about you?"

"I don't have much of a plan. Do you want some company?"

The women set off together, pleased about their surprise encounter. They reached a fork in the trail.

"I usually walk for a while here. Would that work for you?" Kimberly asked.

"That sounds great. I could really use a tranquil walk through the woods today."

"Did you have a hard week?"

"Yes. It's been a week from hell."

Kimberly touched Heidi's elbow. "Do you want to talk about it?"

Heidi looked up at the tall woman. They didn't know each other well, but Kimberly represented the circle of trust she always felt when she was with the Marvelous Mavens. After only a moment of hesitation, she decided her family secret would be safe with this new friend.

"My son got a girl pregnant."

"His girlfriend?"

"I guess so. They haven't been together that long. We've never even met her." Heidi looked down at the ground. She could feel tears of shame coming to her eyes.

"I guess this is not happy news for you, then." Kimberly said.

"He's just not ready. He has no concept of what being a father will do to his life. I can't believe this is happening to our family."

"Do you know if the girlfriend wants the baby?"

"It seems like she is all in. Her parents are fine with it. My husband knows the family and thinks they are pretty rough."

"Oh, my. What does your son say?"

"I think he was pretty surprised. The sad thing is that he's a good guy, so he's ready to step up and shoulder his responsibility."

"Will they get married?"

Heidi dried her eyes. "I'm not sure. The whole thing makes me angry and sad at the same time."

"I can see how it would. How old is your son?"

Kimberly asked.

"Justin is 24."

"That's my son Kurt's age, too."

"Maybe they know each other. Boston can be such a small town sometimes."

"Yes."

The two women walked silently together in the tranquil woods.

Finally, Kimberly said, "I have an idea. I'm seeing the kids tomorrow. How about if I ask them if they know her?"

"The girlfriend?"

"Yes. I could just toss it out there. My kids love to gossip. They won't even think anything is weird about it. Maybe I can learn a bit more about her that will help you move forward."

Q: Did parenthood affect your friendships?

Heidi's friends were her family. She and her sisters and sisters-in-law had been there for one another. It was expedient and safe. And suffocating.

KIMBERLY DOLAN

Gary's birthday was always a big occasion at the Dolan household. The children adored their father. He spoiled them and indulged them in ways that Kimberly did not find helpful. Her attitude about family was more traditional. She wanted their kids to think of them as parents. Gary wanted them to be his friends. She knew their kids liked a partying lifestyle, but she thought it was inappropriate for her husband to join into the mindset as much as he did.

As was typical, the kids recounted their exploits in great detail. Gary was egging them on to share even more about their nightlife. This was a new behavior. Kimberly imagined that doing so made him feel he had a social life as well. It was a perfect time for Kimberly to ask about Heidi's problem.

"Does anyone know Candace Holebrook from Dorchester?" Kimberly practically yelled to get their attention.

Her family paused to look up at their mother. Kimberly thought it was because she had been so loud. But, once they looked back at each other and burst out laughing, she was forgotten.

"The Holes?" Kyle was hysterical. He could barely manage to get the words out of his mouth.

And, they were off. Her words were interpreted as a new topic, instead of a question to be answered. For once, this was exactly the response Kimberly needed. She listened carefully as they traded raunchy stories about the twin Holebrook sisters who reportedly had spent several years competing with each other to see who could have the most partners.

Once Kimberly felt satisfied that no additional details about Candace were forthcoming, she turned to go back inside. She was already near the kitchen when she heard, "Mom, we need more wine!"

She didn't bother to answer her daughter. No one could hear her out on the deck anyway. Kimberly had gone inside to get another bag of tortilla chips and a second bottle of salsa for her family. She opened the wine cooler and pulled two bottles of Chardonnay off the rack.

She paused to consider her own situation. Gary never taught them to think of her on her special day, so they never did. In the Dolan family, if Kimberly didn't organize it, it didn't happen. Perhaps she would arrange something for her own birthday this year.

With a bottle of wine tucked under each arm, salsa in one hand and chips in another, she pushed the door open with her hip and walked out onto the deck. Gary was positioned at the grill, one job he considered too important to entrust to her.

Before Kimberly could set down the food, Matt grabbed the bag of chips, Kurt took the salsa, and Brittney swiped the two bottles of wine. She handed one of them to Connor.

As she stood there empty handed, Kimberly had an epiphany. *This* was all her doing. She was the one who should have taught her children to respect her, instead of waiting for them to figure it out, or for Gary to coach them.

She turned and walked back into the kitchen.

The counter was full of all she had prepared for her family's day together. There were hamburger rolls, garden salad, freshly made potato salad, baked beans, condiments, utensils and napkins. Warm brownies were cooling in a pan next to the oven. And, of course, Gary's homemade birthday cake.

Her work here was done.

Kimberly took off her apron and left the kitchen.

In the study, she walked right to the bookshelf. She removed the dictionary from the shelf, opened it to page 1249 *subtrahend—sulforaphane*, and removed the nineteen sheets of paper stored there. She knelt on the floor next to the shredder and fed them into it one by one.

Q: How did the feminist movement change your friendships?

She may be a little late, but Kimberly was ready to find out.

DODO QUIMBY

Dodo stared at the digits she had entered onto her phone. Rolf had given her Georgie's cell phone number to use in case of emergency. Dodo was beginning to feel as if her estranged relationship with her daughter qualified as an emergency. She knew the longer she kept silent, the harder it would be to reconnect.

But what to say? And when? Fairfield, Connecticut was not a long distance from Boston. Dodo could be there in two hours. She could slip down to watch one of Georgie's swim meets. Maybe she would hang back so her daughter would not know she was there. Later, she could tell her, demonstrating her good-faith desire to get reacquainted.

The phone was still in her hand. She confirmed the number one more time, then pressed the call button. Dodo's leg jiggled nervously while she listened for an answer.

"Hey." It was the voice of a young woman, not a girl anymore.

Dodo's identity had not appeared on Georgie's screen. She felt certain her daughter would otherwise have left her call unanswered.

"Georgie, it's your mom." Dodo was trembling.

There was a long silence.

"What do you want?"

"It's been so long since we talked, I just thought we'd try."

Georgie sighed. "I don't really have anything to say to you, but I'll listen if you want to talk."

"That's a good start. I appreciate it."

Dodo took a deep breath, then continued, "How's school going?"

"I told you I don't have anything to say."

"It's almost the end of your junior year. Are you excited to be a senior?"

"Sort of, yeah," she answered, in spite of herself. "I'm pretty sick of high school, though."

"What's your favorite class?"

"You're not going to believe this," Georgie replied.

"Try me."

"Photography."

Dodo did her best to control her enthusiasm. She wanted to keep her daughter talking.

"That *is* surprising. What do you like best about it?"

The conversation lasted about fifteen minutes, which was fifteen minutes longer than they had spoken in the last three years. Toward the end, Dodo asked if she could come down for a visit.

"That wouldn't be very interesting," she replied.

"I'm sorry." Dodo was taken aback. She thought things were going so well. "Why is that?"

"Well, I think it would be better if I came to see you, so I could look at your studio and stuff."

DARLY

Beyond her reflection in the dresser mirror, Darly observed the pile of rejected clothing strewn over her bed and dresser. She wanted to select an attractive, yet not overly eager style for her first date with Ian. Finally, she chose a black and rose mini-print dress with a moderate neckline, paired with black wedge sandals, good for walking.

There was little she could do to dress up her short hair except run her fingers back and upwards to add some drama to her features. Extra eye-liner and lip gloss, drop earrings, and multiple bangles on her wrist accentuated her look.

She was pleasantly surprised when Ian suggested they meet at Hamilton's. It was the same restaurant where she dined with her father during his March visit. Located on Columbus Street, it was renowned for fresh seafood. After dinner, if the date was going well, they could turn the corner and walk down Berkeley Street for a drink at Ransom. She hoped this would be the case. She also hoped Ian would not sense her romantic rustiness.

Ian waited at the restaurant entrance, partially hidden by an expansive potted plant on the massive granite landing. When he saw Darly walking down the street, he bounded down the steps to greet her. Darly had never seen him dressed so well.

"God, Darly, you look gorgeous!" Ian seemed truly stunned.

"Thank you." Darly could feel the heat of her blush.

"Are you ready to go in?"

She smiled as he held open the door for her to walk

across the threshold.

After they were seated and placed their orders, the conversation flowed.

"So, what happened after that?" Ian asked her over his appetizer.

"Well, my dad was dead set against Boston because he wanted me to stay closer to home, but the stipend made the point moot."

"It is a cool place. I don't miss home at all," Ian said.

"At least Vermont is not too far of a drive."

"Have you been there?" Ian asked.

"Not yet."

"It's beautiful. I grew up on a semi-working farm. We have animals but my parents also have regular jobs."

"What was it like growing up? Did you have to wake up early to milk cows?" Darly asked.

"I did for a couple of years, until we sold them. Mostly we just use the land to graze goats and sheep. My mom is a weaver and has a shop. My dad is an engineer. He loves to tinker with all of the farm equipment on weekends."

The waiter arrived and set two plates on the table.

"Wow," Darly said. "This sure looks rich."

"Like you," said Ian.

"I'm so far from being rich, you can't imagine," she giggled.

"And I'm not suave," Ian laughed.

That was one of the things Darly liked about Ian. He was polished enough to fit in wherever he needed, but he was also authentic. In some ways, he was similar to her father. Both loved the countryside and being self-sufficient. She wasn't looking for anyone to take care of her, but she felt as if Ian would be capable of it.

"What will you do after my permanent advisor Simon Grady returns?" Darly asked.

"Go back to what I was doing before. Post-doc research on class and conflict. I'll hopefully be able to teach full time. Some old guys need to retire first though!"

Darly smiled. "An important detail."

"It seems like research can swallow up your life," Ian continued. "I always fight against that. I bet you're more organized than me. What else do you like to do?"

"Promise not to laugh?" Darly asked. "I like to go antiquing."

Ian's face lit up. "Are you serious? I'm so into that! You should see my parents' house. All my finds are stored there. Someday, I'll have a big old house for them."

A fresh glow infused the young couple.

After dessert, Ian said, "How about we head over to Ransom and see what's up? I know the band playing tonight."

Ian and Darly walked a short distance down Columbus Avenue, turned onto Berkeley, and then took another left into the club.

Ransom was packed. The band's fusion playlist had the appreciative crowd dancing. Ian cocked his head at Darly, tilting it suggestively toward the dance floor. She took his warm hand as they made their way into the center of the crowd. Darly loved feeling Ian close to her. She hadn't been in a serious relationship for a long time. There was something about Ian that made her feel she had arrived home. They didn't consider leaving the floor until the band took a break.

That's when the drummer stepped down from the stage and approached Ian and Darly.

"How you doing, Ian? Looks like you're moving up in the world," he said, sizing up Darly.

"Rick, this is Darly. Darly, Rick." Ian squeezed Darly's hand.

"My pleasure," he said to Darly.

She smiled at him.

"So, where've you been? We never see you anymore," Rick asked Ian.

"Things have changed."

"I saw her last night at our gig in the North End."

Darly looked at Ian for an explanation.

Instead, he said, "Let's get a drink, Darly."

"She didn't ask about you, Ian!" Rick yelled after them.

"Who is he talking about?" Darly asked.

"My ex-girlfriend. She was his ex before she was mine, so that's why he's acting like that."

"Oh. Drama."

"Darly, seriously, just look at me for a second." He took both her hands in his and held them to his heart. "I am completely over her. I honestly can't think of anyone but you. Day and night. It's making me a little crazy. I don't want to scare you off, but it's true." Ian looked sheepish. He had not planned to give that speech.

Darly looked down at his hands holding hers, then up at his face again. She was happy. There was really nothing to say—except that—so she did. "I'm so happy. Let's get that drink."

The next day, they sat in his office, having previously

promised each other never to discuss school outside of it. Darly was amazed at how easily Ian switched between romancer and academic adviser. She found it more difficult. Earlier that morning, in her apartment, they had made love and she had cooked him a big breakfast. It had all seemed so natural to her. Fortunately, both of her roommates were away.

"So, what's the latest on the study time frame?" Ian asked.

"I'm up to date with the compilation, so I think I'll probably need two more meetings to round out the collection of information."

"Simon Grady will probably be swamped when he gets back," he reminded her. "He'll need at least a week to take a look at it after you're done."

"I'll try to get it to him a little early."

"Are you happy with the way things are going? You seem like you're not sharing many details lately."

"These are complicated women, Ian. I guess I underestimated them. They know so much more than I do."

"You're no slouch, Darly."

"Thanks. It's not book learning, though. The five of them together cover just about every life situation. It's like they see the future."

"Theirs?"

"No. Mine."

Darly spent the next rainy week immersing herself in the history of the women's movement. She pored over all of the information she could find. There were videos of marches to watch, speeches to listen to and read, declarations, resolutions, and books to devour. It was possible to do much of it in her apartment, so she did. She was in deep. She didn't even want to break for showers. On the third day, she came across a video. At first she did not recognize the woman, but she was drawn to her shouting voice. She then realized it was her own mother. Nora Brumm-Lane stood on the steps of the University of Michigan library in the pouring rain—her long hair plastered to her scalp, her tee shirt soaking wet. Under those conditions, her breasts and nipples were the prominent visual. Someone had zoomed in on her and made a secondary video clip that ran in a loop. Every time Nora pumped her fist and yelled, her breasts moved up and down. Up and down. And up and down.

Darly was enraged. How dare someone use her mother's image this way! Nora was at a National Organization for Women rally championing the Equal Rights Amendment. She was doing serious work. Darly watched the original video over and over, yearning to stand next to her mother and support her effort. She felt as if she belonged there in that time, with her mother and her righteous contemporaries. The women around Nora were sisters in solidarity. How could Darly be so complacent about the state of women's rights in her own time? Why had she never realized that the Equal Rights Amendment had not been ratified?

She printed the selection:

SECTION 1. Equality of rights under the law shall not be denied or abridged by the United States or by any State on account of sex.

SECTION 2. The Congress shall have the power to enforce, by appropriate legislation, the provisions of this article.

SECTION 3. This amendment shall take effect two years after the date of ratification.

Darly grabbed the sheet from her printer and ran into the kitchen where roommates Gracie and Sari were snacking.

"Did you know that the ERA never passed?" Darly demanded.

"The what?" Gracie answered. Sari licked almond butter off her fingers.

"The Equal Rights Amendment!" Darly replied, waving the paper.

"I think that's pretty old. It's probably irrelevant now," Sari said.

"NO. It's still very important," Darly argued. "Women aren't protected by the constitution. All of the stuff we take for granted can be taken away."

"You can't be serious, Darly." Gracie looked concerned. "Are you getting enough sleep? You've been spending all week binging on this stuff."

Sari glanced at Gracie. "Maybe the old ladies in her study are making her crazy."

Darly looked at both of them and shook her head. "You have no idea." She left the room to get back to her research.

Q: Do female friends who are not your age understand you?

Darly was sure no one of any age understood her right now.

THE FIFTH DINNER

"Today's topic is friendship." Darly looked up from her computer. "I'm curious how patterns of friendships have changed for you over the years."

Dodo spoke first. "I don't know about everyone else, but I'm getting very selective about who I allow into my life these days."

Around the table, heads nodded.

"It looks like most of you agree." Darly hoped to nurture the topic.

Heidi said, "Well, being selective would be nice. I have so many family members in my life that I don't really have that option. Some of them are more pleasant than others." She rolled her eyes.

"Can you confide in any of them?" Sherall asked. "It seems like that would be tricky. You know, if they're married to your husband's brother or something like that."

"Actually, my husband is my best friend. I've always felt that way," Heidi replied. "I wouldn't want to hurt his feelings by talking about him to any of our relatives."

"And you still feel romantic toward him?" asked Pamela.

"Well, not always in the same way, but usually I do, yes."

Dodo smiled. "I'd say you're a very lucky woman."

"I guess I am. But, girlfriends are special, too. It's just hard to find time to be with them."

"Friendship does take time," Darly said. "So, does anyone still have a friend from childhood?"

Kimberly and Heidi nodded.

"Kimberly, let's hear from you," Darly said.

"There is one friend who is always in my heart, but we've lost touch."

"Why?" Darly encouraged.

"She was my college roommate. For about ten years, she lived in Newton, too. We used to be so close. When our kids were small, we did everything together. Our husbands even liked each other."

"Then what happened?" Darly asked.

"She divorced her husband. All of the sudden, her life was dramatically different. I don't know if she was envious that my life was still the same, or if she was happy that her life was changing. She got busy with work and we just were never able to talk about it. After a while, we drifted apart. I heard she moved to North Carolina."

"You can probably find her on Facebook, you know," Sherall offered.

"I don't even know how to do that. It's sort of embarrassing to admit."

"Just log onto the site and sign up. It's really easy, Kimberly. I bet you can do it tonight with no problem at all," said Heidi.

Kimberly's face brightened. "Maybe."

Darly shifted the focus to Heidi. "What's the story behind your childhood friend?"

"I still live in the same town I grew up in, so I run into

my old gang pretty often. Like I said before, it's hard to find time to fit them in between all of my extended family activities, but lately I've been thinking of making it happen."

"Can you still relate to any of them?" Darly asked.

"Not all of them but I don't want to shut them out. I admit it can feel kind of strained sometime. Like we know each other, but we really don't. Mostly, we're gentle with each other when we talk, but there's some bitterness. You can just tell. It's hard to hide your mistakes when you all live in Charlestown."

Darly asked, "Why do you think they're bitter?"

"I can't speak for everyone, but I guess it has to do with the choices we've made. It's a bummer when you look back and realize, it really was *all* up to you. Even though everyone in our group grew up in different families with different values, we had to decide what to do once we came of age. Sometimes I wonder about the women who moved away and stayed away. Maybe they've had more interesting lives."

"Isn't that the big question?" Sherall asked. "Whether it really makes a difference to your happiness if you do things that seem extraordinary to others? I know someone who swam in the Olympics, got her PhD, then married a wealthy Argentinian rancher. She's miserable."

"I guess I'm the extreme opposite of that as far as achievements, but I can't say I'm even close to miserable," Heidi said.

"Meeting with us must be such a change for you. We're all new in your life. Not like family, or your old friends," Pamela said.

Heidi nodded. "I was really glad when I found out I'd get to participate in the study. Even though I'm not unhappy, I've been searching for a way to bring something fresh to my life. I'm definitely getting it here."

Darly continued questioning. "Dodo, you said you've become more discriminating about who you choose for friends."

"Well, I've always been snobby about who I hang out with," she laughed. "It's true that I meet tons of people through work—but even though we share interests, I don't always relate to them as friends. Once in a while, I come across someone I adore and then pull out all of the stops."

"Don't you worry that you'll overwhelm them?" Sherall asked.

"Hopefully not." Dodo smiled over at Pamela, who blushed at the attention.

"Wait. What's happening here?" Sherall asked.

"What do you mean?" Darly was confused.

Sherall ignored her and focused instead on Pamela. "Do I detect some combustion?"

"Leave her alone," Dodo said.

"I knew it." Sherall raised her eyebrows at Dodo.

Darly said, "I'm not sure what's happening between you three, but could we please try to stay on topic?"

"No, wait," Pamela's voice was barely audible. "I want to say something." She looked over at Dodo before continuing. "Are you okay with this?"

Dodo nodded.

Pamela took a deep breath, then slowly exhaled. "My relationship with my husband is—difficult. For a long time, I believed our problems were my fault. He definitely had me convinced of that. Dodo and I have been talking a lot and she's helped me see things from another perspective." Pamela looked at Dodo and continued. "She's been very kind. And a good friend."

"So, you're *special* friends now?" Sherall would not let go.

Pamela looked at Sherall and then back over at an agitated Dodo. With a delicate smile, she answered her inquisitor. "Yes. I guess we are."

Sherall's grin widened. Darly sat at the other end of the table, blinking with newfound comprehension. Heidi fiddled with her napkin. Kimberly examined everyone's faces for clues.

"This is an interesting turn," Darly finally said.

"I'm sorry," Kimberly began, still perplexed. "I don't understand what's happening."

"Kimbo, these two are lovers," Sherall explained.

A tiny gasp escaped from Kimberly. "Oh, please excuse me. I didn't mean to pry."

Dodo looked over at Sherall. "Well, that's out in the open now, whether we were ready or not."

"Do you want to talk about it anymore?" Darly asked Pamela.

She shook her head sideways.

"Dodo?" asked Darly.

"Not especially."

HEIDI BELANGER/KIMBERLY DOLAN

The other women left Kimberly and Heidi chatting in front of Vivere.

"I think your son Justin should ask her to take a

paternity test," Kimberly said.

"Justin would be so mad at me if I told him to do that."

"I'm sorry to have to say this, but from the way my kids talked about her, the baby might not belong to anyone in particular."

"She's that bad, huh?" Heidi asked.

Kimberly nodded her head as she touched her friend's arm. "It's probably the safe thing to do."

After she returned home, Kimberly went to her computer and typed FACEBOOK in search bar. To create her page, she typed Kimberly Wincroft Dolan. If she wanted anyone from her past to be able to contact her, she would have to include her maiden name. Her page looked bare, but she was now officially on FACEBOOK. She next typed Sandra Steinmetz in the search bar. Several photos appeared alongside a list of women named Sandra Steinmetz. Kimberly scrolled through them until she found Sandy's picture and next to it, Austin, TX. Her friend looked much older. And, why was she in Texas? She clicked on her name, then quickly discovered how to send a message.

Dear Sandy. I found you on a FACEBOOK search and I'm glad I did. I've been thinking about you a lot and I want you to know that I miss our friendship. I hope you will write back to me and tell me all about what you are doing. Everything is good here. Love, Kimberly. p.s. I don't have a picture on here yet because I am still figuring it out. Your picture looks great!

Kimberly twisted her hands together on her lap for several minutes, then finally pressed *enter* and watched the screen confirm that her message had been sent.

She was about to turn off the computer when a new message appeared.

Hello Kimmy!!! I am so happy to hear from you! I think it's been over 10 years. I hardly ever go on Facebook and just happened to tonight. Wonderful timing! Here is my email address: cmg1@gmail.com. What is yours? I can't wait to tell you everything!

Love, S

With a light heart, Kimberly immediately wrote back to her friend. Gary and Meghan were not expected home for quite some time, so it was a perfect evening to spend on the computer. The two women found email easier so they sent a few back and forth. In the space of a few hours, Kimberly rekindled her old friendship.

SHERALL SAVARD

Sitting at the Four Seasons bar, Sherall stared at ice cubes melting on the bottom of leaded glass. She regretted the way she had treated Pamela and Dodo earlier. Their personal lives were none of her business. Unfortunately, that line of reasoning never stopped her from creating divisions between herself and others. She was alienating herself again. As always, she had only herself to blame.

At ten, the bar was still half full. The downtown finance crowd was celebrating the market upturn and they would linger for another hour.

"What are you drinking tonight?" an Australian baritone inquired of her.

"Kool-Aid," she replied sarcastically, not bothering to look up to connect the voice with a face.

"I see. I hope that's working for you."

"Never does."

Long jean-covered legs slid onto the bar stool next to her. "I'll have a seltzer with lime," he told the bartender.

Sherall broke her downward cast to peer at the man with the accent. He was looking at her. His unruly salt and pepper hair showed evidence of otherwise regular maintenance. A navy blazer over a crisp white shirt draped elegantly from his lanky shoulders.

Neither of them spoke. Sherall was torn between annoyance and attraction. The man's kind eyes met hers in a non-confrontational way. He smiled with lips closed.

"Hello," she finally said. Sherall was in no mood for sparring. Even if she was, she already had the impression she would lose a match against this man.

"Hello," he replied.

They nursed their drinks.

Without looking at him again, Sherall said, "I apologize for being rude."

"No worries." The bartender wiped the counter in front of them with his white cloth, then set about tidying the sink below. "It's been a long day," the man said.

"You, too?" Sherall said.

"You first," he replied.

"I hurt two really great women."

"I'm sorry to hear that."

"Your turn."

"My mother died."

Sherall whipped her head around to look him more squarely in the face. "I'm so sorry! Please accept my sympathy."

"Thank you. She was ninety-seven and had a stellar life." He sighed. "Still, it's sad and there are lots of details to sort."

She extended her hand. "I'm Sherall."

"Pleasure. Brooks Wilder."

They talked for another hour. Brooks let her lead the conversation, but not because he had nothing to offer. Sherall very much liked the feeling she got with him. He acted like a peer, matching her mood and words effortlessly. She felt in tandem; not competition. This was a new experience for her.

At the end of the night, they exchanged cards.

"May I call you?" he asked.

"I'm married."

"Then let's be friends."

EMPIRICAL DATA

DARLY

"Whoa. Awkward," Ian reacted to Darly's revelation.

"Tell me about it. I mean, who am I to lead a discussion of women who are worlds ahead of me in experience?"

"You mean you've never had a lesbian affair?" he joked.

"Oh, stop it. You know that's not what I'm talking about. It's just that each of them is so complex. There is almost 300 hundred years of experience between them! I bet they're barely tolerating me."

"Why?"

"Why are they tolerating me?" Darly asked.

"No, why do you think they have 300 years of experience?"

"Ian, it's because they're so old."

"I disagree."

"What are you talking about?"

Ian leaned back into his chair and put his feet up on the desk in his favorite position.

"You are mistaking quantity with quality. Time on earth doesn't necessarily correspond to quality or even quantity of experience."

"I never thought about it that way."

"Consider Tired Cheerleader. She has experience with family and local community but not life outside her home turf. Sad Beauty has no clue about real love. Attention Addict doesn't understand how to be gentle. Do you get my point?"

"I think you're a little hard on them, but yeah, I see where you're going."

"Darly, you're not supposed to teach them anything. They will learn from you eventually because you brought them together."

"I'll keep that in mind. You've really helped me today."

Ian smiled and winked at her. "Let's get out of here, then."

Being with Ian was a novel experience to Darly. She marveled at the intensity of her feelings and the giddy way she felt whenever they were together. True to his word, Ian continued to separate the professional and personal whenever they were together. It was much harder for Darly.

Although she wanted to impress him, there were areas where she needed advice. Unfortunately, it looked unlikely he could give it. Ian had dismissed the challenges she expressed about wrangling the Mavens into a coherent group. He short-circuited her insecurities about her leadership skills. It was as if he had already made up his mind about the outcome of the study. She dreaded the return of Simon Grady but eagerly anticipated not having to hold information back from Ian. She wanted to be all in with him and share everything. There was a nagging sensation that he was not ready to hear her full story, though. She wanted Ian to know that the Mavens were more complex than she had previously believed.

She wished she could agree that the Mavens would learn from her. Every week, her confidence in their opinion of her eroded. There were small things, like not understanding a comment that they all understood. It left her feeling alienated from the group. It wasn't as if they were critical of her. They didn't seem to be judging her. She was judging herself. How could she have been so arrogant about these women?

For another string of days, she further immersed herself in women's movement research, projecting herself back to the era with gusto. In spirit, she found herself there with her mother, fighting together. Sisters in solidarity. She wanted to feel the passion.

At a vintage clothing store in Cambridge, she pawed through the collection of 1970s era garments— Huckapoo shirts, Landlubber bellbottoms, leotard tops, macramé belts, and Bort Carlton sandals. She imagined that her mother was the same size as her. When she looked at her reflection in the dressing room, she saw her mother's face.

Darly stopped shaving her legs and underarms. She would shave before she had sex with Ian again. Unless she decided not to.

Her office was crowded by a stack of poster boards lined up against the wall, one per study participant. A box of colored sticky notes sat on her desk—a different color for each woman. Her plan was to identify the individual themes of each participant's life, list the themes that they shared with one another, and then show how those common themes intersected with the goals of the women's movement. Weeks ago, she felt confident that these details would be expediently revealed to her. That did not turn out to be the case. There were too many moving parts. The Mavens continually changed the subject, confounding her and making it difficult to keep track of her intended academic destination.

Even more exasperating, the women did not seem like *they* knew where they were going. Darly had expected them to be more confident; more organized in their demeanors and aspirations. More *finished*. After all, they were mature women. Darly had anticipated that her study conclusions would be obvious. But she was more confused than ever. The more she heard, the less she knew.

Would her mother have been like these women? In her journals, she seemed more certain about her life than the Mavens were about theirs. Was it because the Mavens were older? They seemed to change their colors with each meeting. Darly was afraid of falling behind her research schedule. She was doing all she could to keep up. She needed help. Who could she ask?

PAMELA CARDIN

Pamela could tell by the way Bruce bounded in from the garage that he was in another good mood. If he was mad, he would have pushed the door open with his fist and let it bang hard against the wall. She had replaced that door stopper numerous times. Tonight, he held onto the door and closed it quietly. Not too quietly, though. That would mean he was distracted by something and would not talk to her at all.

"Welcome home, Bruce!"

"Thanks."

"How was your day?"

"Pretty good. Franco Brothers put in a big bid."

"That's terrific! All of your hard work paid off."

"True. What's for dinner?"

"Scallops and asparagus. Does that sound good?"

"I had asparagus for lunch. You'll have to make something different."

"Okay. A nice big salad?"

Bruce loosened his tie as he walked past her, not bothering to answer. Pamela returned to the kitchen to put away the asparagus and prepare a salad.

Bruce was immensely successful. Friends and associates gushed over him, and even their wives told Pamela she was fortunate to be married to someone so charismatic. They knew nothing of his threatening rage, or of her finely honed self-preservation skills.

The first time she experienced his volatility was on their honeymoon in Las Vegas. Bruce had been drinking too much and so had she. Her new husband had lost thousands of dollars at the Blackjack table that evening, so when they returned to their hotel room, Pamela quietly suggested he not gamble for the rest of their trip. At that comment, his expression devolved into a twisting crimson pulse. He pushed her onto the wall, held her by the shoulders and told her she should never, *never* tell him what he could and could not do. He ripped through her dress and reminded her who held authority. Pamela told herself that what followed was not rape, because they were a married couple. She looked at the episode differently now, but never again told him what to do, or not to do.

Tonight, Bruce returned to the room dressed in jeans and a tee shirt. He turned on the TV. In his home, only he chose what lit up the screen.

"Dinner is ready, Bruce," Pamela said.

They sat down together and ate. There was always conversation during their meals but it consisted of Pamela asking about his day and Bruce asking if Pamela had done the things he had asked her to do. Pamela finally worked in a way to confirm what she needed to know about his Fourth of July plans.

"Have you definitely decided when you'll be home this weekend?"

"Why do you need to know?"

"I want to make sure I have supper ready."

"I'm driving directly to work from there on Tuesday morning, so press and pack a suit in my bag."

"Of course." When Pamela finished cleaning the kitchen, she grabbed her phone to text Dodo with the final update. Their weekend away was free and clear.

HEIDI BELANGER

Heidi packed one more submarine sandwich into the cooler and closed the lid. Jim came around the corner into the kitchen.

"You're the best little girl! How long have you been awake, anyway?"

"Oh, since around six. I wanted to make sure everything was ready."

"Thanks for doing that. Everybody loves your picnics." He looked around the room. "What's for breakfast?"

"There are some scrambled eggs and hash browns in the oven."

Jim kissed the top of Heidi's head, then took the plate out of the oven and sat down to eat. After he finished, he stood and began to circle his right arm round and round in the air.

"I hope I don't injure myself today."

"I hope you don't either. At least you've been visiting the indoor batting cages all winter."

"It's not the same, though."

"I'll bring an ice pack, just in case."

"The boys will be there, right?"

"Remember I told you that Justin said he would be in Revere, and Jordan has to work?"

"Oh, yeah. Too bad."

"They'll be there next week for sure," she said.

When Jim glanced back at the table and noticed his empty breakfast plate and mug still sitting there, he carried them over to the counter and handed them to Heidi.

"Thanks, Hon'," Jim said, then left the room.

Heidi looked down at the dish, wondering how a grown man could always manage to deliver his plate to his wife's hands, but never into the dishwasher.

Jim returned a moment later. "I'm sorry," he said, and put the dishes where they belonged.

Heidi stood on tip-toe to kiss him. "Thanks, Sweetie."

Jim faced her, looking pained. "Heidi, I know I can be kind of a block head. Especially the other day when you said you wanted to go to school. I want you to do whatever you want. You've always been there for me and the boys. I'll try to be more supportive."

"Oh, Jim! How could I ever be mad at you?"

"I know you're not exactly mad. It's just that you seem like you want to do so many new things without me now. I'm not used to it." He turned away to put on his baseball hat. "I don't want to lose you." His eyes were moist.

"Lose me?" Heidi reached up to tenderly touch her husband's scruffy face. "Jim, I love you! There is no one I'd rather be with. Please don't worry."

He lifted her off the floor to hug her, the way he always did. "You're going to have to teach me how to help you."

She held his gaze. "I will, Jim. As soon as I figure it out myself."

DARLY

Ian had been good to Darly from the start—kind, considerate, attentive, nurturing. Although they had been dating for several weeks, tonight had the markings of something special. Inviting her for dinner at his place was unusual because his cooking skills were minimal. They most often went out to eat, but Ian joked that he had learned enough and was ready to take a big leap and play host. She decided to surprise him by wearing a sexy cocktail dress and precariously high heels, versus the casual uniform she customarily wore when hanging out at his apartment.

Darly knew Ian would be early, as usual. As soon as he called to let her know he was out front waiting for her, she wobbled down the stairs to the lobby. Meeting him at the street level was the arrangement they had settled upon. It was much easier than subjecting him to a stressful search for a parking spot, simply so he could come up to get her at the apartment.

On the stoop, some of her neighbors had gathered and were chatting together, enjoying the warm evening.

"Big date, Darly?" Carlos, an elderly man, asked as she let the massive old door close behind her.

She smiled back and nodded her head, a little embarrassed about the contrast of her outfit and the modest apartment house they all shared in Allston.

"Sure makes me wish I was young again," said Dexter, sitting next to him.

"She'd never look at you anyway, Peaches," his wife said, winking at Darly.

Darly looked around for Ian's battered silver car. She figured he must be circling the block.

A black limousine stopped at the sidewalk in front of the end of their steps. The neighbors exchanged glances. The door opened and a uniformed chauffeur looked up at her.

"Ms. Lane?"

"Yes?" She eyed him, uncomprehending.

"Mr. Brown has asked me to drive you to his home. May I help you down the steps?"

"Nice," Carlos breathed.

"Um, just a minute, please." Darly took her phone out of her purse to text Ian. Instead, she found a text from him that had just arrived. *"Really."*

Darly sheepishly took the chauffer's gloved hand, self-conscious about this ostentatious display in front of her frugal neighbors.

Inside the cool and clean limo, a freshly opened bottle

of champagne chilled in an ice bucket.

She enjoyed the now familiar route in this different way. Outside her window, she watched as Commonwealth Avenue became more narrow and gentrified. Well-dressed people walked their dogs on the grassy median and gave covert attention to the limo. Most were too proud to reveal curiosity about the identity of the passenger behind the tinted windows. Darly took another sip of champagne.

The driver turned left onto Fairfield Street, then right onto Marlborough. He stopped in front of Number 258. It was an imposing brownstone owned by one of Ian's much older colleagues. Ian paid him reduced rent for the basement apartment in exchange for regular pet sitting. Ian's private entrance had a posh address but the lifestyle between upstairs and downstairs occupants was dramatic.

The chauffeur double parked, then quickly hurried around the vehicle to open the door for Darly. He helped her over the uneven brick sidewalk and down the stairs leading to the apartment. As they navigated the steps together, they took care not to crush the different color roses that rested on each slab. Faint music emanating from Ian's apartment grew louder. Frank Sinatra sang *The Way You Look Tonight*. The chauffeur pressed the buzzer at Ian's entry. Once the lock was released, he opened it and let her in.

Ian stood before her in a suit and tie, a rose between his teeth.

"Welcome to Chez Brown's," he said, swooping into a bow.

"Ian! This is great! What you are up to?" Darly giggled.

"Well, I figured we should celebrate. I have been promoted to an exclusive role as your full time boyfriend. I am no longer your adviser." His grin was wide.

Darly raised her arms. "Simon Grady is back?"

"Yes!"

Ian swept Darly into a tight embrace. "If it wasn't for him, I'd never have met you."

"We were so lucky," Darly cooed.

She helped herself to hors d'oeuvres Ian had prepared, while he got them something to drink.

"Ian, that limo ride was fabulous. I was so surprised! You should have seen my expression when I figured out it was for me. My neighbors were even clapping when I drove away."

"I wish I could pamper you like that all of the time."

"And roses on the steps, too! I feel very special. I always feel special with you."

Ian handed her a glass of wine. "To us," he toasted.

Ian had watched enough videos to become a competent cook. He had roasted two chicken breasts with baby potatoes and onions. Their salads were already on the table.

After they finished, Darly told Ian about the Brimfield Antique Flea Market in September. "I've been told it's huge!"

"Then let's make a weekend out of it. I think we can manage a two day escape that early in the semester," Ian said.

"It'll be fun to see everything. I might get something

small. I have to grow my collection. And catch up to you," Darly teased.

"What a relief! Valuable antiques instead of decrepit old women." Ian laughed as he poured them both more wine.

Darly stiffened.

"Did you just call them decrepit?" she asked.

"Darly. They're a bunch of crones. You're a luscious young woman. It was a bit tedious, don't you think?"

"Actually, Ian, I find them fascinating."

He leaned back in his chair.

"But, the stuff they talk about is so depressing."

"In what way?" Darly asked, slightly slurring.

"It seems like they're bitter about one thing or another. They're not like women our age who at least try to get their acts together."

Darly got up from the table and took her dish to the sink. Ian followed with his.

"Is that what you really think?" She asked, scraping her dish.

"What do you mean?" Ian put his free arm around her.

"That women have a hard time getting themselves together? That we're basically incompetent?"

"Darly, what's going on? I didn't say that. It's just that those five women have their share of problems and you were starting to think they were important. You're way smarter than any of them."

Ian smiled at his compliment and moved to embrace her.

Darly shrugged off his arms.

"I think the one who doesn't get it, is you." she said.

"This is exactly what the Women's Liberation Movement was about. Raising consciousness." She stared at Ian for a moment. "Actually, you'll probably never get it because you're just a man."

"What the fuck? What are you talking about? I'm one of the good guys, remember?"

"This is just what the Marvelous Mavens said. Men can never understand all of the choices women have to make. All the sacrifices. If we focus on making ourselves happy, then we're selfish. If we make everyone else happy, then we're loser doormats. There's no happy medium. You have no idea how complicated it is, Ian. These women I've been listening to have walked point for our generation and they are *still* paving the way. I respect them for that, and you should, too."

Darly sat down in her chair, folded her arms and scowled at Ian.

"Are you done?" he asked.

"I don't know."

"Well, let it out. You obviously have been holding back from me. I can see it's important to you and that I missed the point entirely."

Ian stood in front of her with his arms hanging at his side. He looked defenseless. He looked hurt.

"I'm sorry," Darly started, before tears began to fall.

Ian took a tentative step forward. When Darly looked up at him, he dropped to his knees next to where she sat.

"It's okay. Lots of men are jerks, I agree," he began.

"Oh, Ian, it's not about men, really. I'm just so confused about the choices I'll have to make in my own life."

"Like which ones?" he asked, stroking her hair now.

"Marriage and babies and work and family and friendship and—I just never considered the big picture before!"

SHERALL SAVARD

Inside the garage behind the brownstone, Sherall and Scott closed both car doors simultaneously. The humid evening was uncomfortably sticky but the BMW's air conditioning quickly cooled the car's interior. Dressed for a gala, Scott wore a navy tuxedo with a black bow tie. Sherall adjusted the length of her magenta sequined gown over her legs so the long split of fabric did not fall between the seat and the door. She liked how the halter neckline set off her toned arms and ample cleavage. Scott had not commented on her appearance.

"Who are we sitting with?" Sherall asked.

"Brandt, Lawrence, Crowley, and Tan."

"Franz won't be there?"

"No, he's in Switzerland, delivering a paper."

"We knew these guys back when they were nobodies," Sherall said.

"Only you thought they were nobodies."

"Don't start. I mean that they weren't practicing yet. They were still in school."

Scott turned up the music. Sherall looked out the window.

They soon arrived at the Parker House hotel where the valet opened the car door for Sherall. As she prepared to step out, the heavy sequined fabric of her dress fell to one side, exposing her long legs. The valet looked down in admiration, then quickly away. She and Scott walked through the lobby and into the elevator. They rode to the fifteenth floor to join others in the pre-function area outside the Rooftop Ballroom.

"Dr. Green!" a young woman called out. She and her date rushed up to Scott the minute he crossed the threshold.

"I'm Ashley Crandon and this is my fiancé Brett Wood. We are so honored to have you join us tonight."

Scott shook hands with them both and introduced Sherall.

"Ashley organized this entire event," he explained.

"Can I have the waiter get you both something to drink?" Ashley asked.

"Scotch. Oban 18," Scott answered, then looked over at Sherall.

"I'll have champagne."

Ashley signaled to the waiter and whispered the order to him.

She turned back to Scott.

"My father is a big supporter of your research. He asked me to apologize for being unable to attend tonight. He's in Dubai."

"Please thank him for me," Scott responded.

Their drinks arrived and others began to approach them. Soon, Scott was surrounded by admirers. Sherall slipped off to the restroom to touch up her lipstick. She'd meet him back at their table. He wouldn't be looking for her anyway.

All afternoon, Sherall had been deliberating about what to do in response to the text her racquetball partner, Alison had sent her. Alison wanted some informal legal advice for a friend. Sherall was happy to give it until she asked who the offender was: it was Gary Dolan, Kimberly's husband! He had been sexting Alison's friend whose husband worked for Gary. Sherall wanted to give Kimberly a chance to confront her husband before she advised Alison to tell her friend to look into a restraining order. She thought it best to let Kimberly know in person. She could do so after the next dinner.

Sherall left the restroom and returned to the gala.

Inside the ballroom were notables from the medical and research communities, and the donors who made so much of it possible. Sherall nodded here and there to those she knew, then quickly matched her place card to the head table and took her seat. Tonight she was playing the role of supportive wife of a renowned physician and medical researcher.

Over the loudspeaker, a deep voice requested that everyone make their way into the ballroom for the beginning of the program. As Sherall checked her phone one final time to engage the vibrate-only setting, a new text appeared.

How nice to see you. Table #23, next to the bar.

Sherall placed her phone on her lap and discreetly swiveled her head to see who sent the text.

Brooks Wilder stood and tipped his head toward her in greeting. The man she had met at the bar. Sherall was surprised to feel her heart flutter. She returned his gesture with her own slight nod. In her lap, the phone vibrated again.

Sorry not to have been in touch. So many details with the estate. Are you here alone?

The room was filling up. Soon Scott would take his place next to her.

No, my husband is one of the honorees.

She could see Scott and his entourage making their way to the table.

Congratulations to him. Look forward to learning about his work.

Thnx, she responded.

Sherall put her phone in her purse, looked up and smiled at those approaching her table. It had been twenty years since she had seen LiMing Chen because he had returned to Hong Kong to practice medicine following his residency in Boston. LiMing kissed her on the cheek and said, "Your husband has become *Daifu*—a great man. You must be very proud of him tonight, Sherall."

She smiled at him and nodded.

The others—Charlie Brandt, Ed Lawrence, and Norman Crowley—had all settled in New England. Even so, it was a bit of a homecoming because they rarely found themselves in the same room. Guests were seated and the program commenced.

"Welcome Ladies and Gentlemen, Mayor, and other honored guests." At the podium, the Master of Ceremonies paused for a moment, waiting for the crowd to settle. "We are pleased tonight to have among us some of the best minds in medicine. I ask our honorees to stand and be recognized so we can officially welcome them home. Doctors?"

The men at Sherall's table and the men and women at the two tables on alternate sides stood to great applause.

"Thank you. I invite you to enjoy your dinner and

watch this video highlighting the advances made by our honored guests over the last decade."

The evening continued in its predictable fashion. Sherall had accompanied Scott to many similar fetes. Finally, it was her husband's turn to accept his award at the podium.

"I'd like to thank my colleagues at Kanto Labs," he addressed the audience, "the staff at Mass General Hospital, Mark Goldberg at Rand Associates, and last but not least, my personal assistant Candace Moore who helps me keep it all straight!"

Holding his plaque, Scott remained on the stage with the other honorees as the Master of Ceremonies closed the formal program. Photographers crowded the platform to get the best photos of the notable men and women.

Sherall looked down at her coffee cup and untouched dessert. It was no surprise that her husband did not mention her in his acceptance speech, but it was humiliating in contrast to the other honorees who gushed about the significance of their spouses and families. She glanced at Table Number Twenty-three. Brooks raised his glass to her.

What the hell, she thought.

Sherall left her table and walked over to the bar to order another glass of champagne.

Brooks wasted no time arriving at her side. "Impressive career. You should be proud."

"Thank you. He worked hard for it."

"I'm glad we ran into each other."

"What brings you here tonight?" Sherall asked.

"My mother was a big supporter of the BLC fund, so

the board invited me to come. I've met lots of interesting people."

"How are you holding up otherwise?"

"Pretty well. I'm staying at my mother's place in the Back Bay and will probably remain here another month or two, just to finish up."

"Then back home?"

"Yes."

"Australia?"

"No, I haven't lived there for about twenty years. I'm based in Miami. I do get Down Under once or twice a year."

"I've never been there."

"You should. It's a great place."

Sherall took a sip of her champagne. Brooks looked around the room.

Both spoke at the same time.

"Are you—" Brooks started.

"I'm not—" Sherall began.

"Please, you first," Brooks said.

Sherall looked out into the crowd, then back at Brooks.

"I'm not happily married."

"I see."

"As a matter of fact, I do believe my marriage is over. Just formalities remain."

"I'm sorry to learn that."

"Really?" Sherall searched his eyes.

"No. Selfishly, I'm ecstatic."

"Now what?" Sherall smiled.

"Is it too soon?"

"No, it's been a long time coming. He won't be

surprised."

"Lunch tomorrow?"

"Noon at Priscilla's on Newbury. Let's eat outside."

"I'm sure I'll find it," Brooks said.

"It's the place to see and be seen and that's what I feel like right now."

"We're blasting off."

"I know. I'm ready."

"Until tomorrow, then." Brooks raised his glass and they clinked them together in a toast.

TOPIC: SELF ACTUALIZATION
Have you self-actualized?
At what age should a woman achieve self-
actualization?
What obstacles prevented you from achieving self-
actualization?
Is it important to help younger women achieve their
goals?
How did the Women's Liberation Movement position
you for self-actualization?

KIMBERLY DOLAN

Kimberly logged onto her email. As expected, there was a new post from Sandy. She read it, then let her fingers fly over the keyboard in response.

Hi Sandy! I was just thinking the same thing! Of course I'd love to have you join me!! Study at Sea would be much, much more fun if we went together. Up until recently, I wasn't sure I'd be brave enough to do this but something made me change my mind. I know it's the right thing for me, and doing it with you would make it even better.

We have lots to get ready. Only 2 months left! I'm so excited!

Love, Kimmy

Kimberly could barely hold the mouse steady as she reread updated reviews for the Study at Sea program. Comments like: *Life changing; Rewarding; Nothing like it; Once in a lifetime; Best decision I ever made; You will NEVER be the same,* left her alternating between anxiety and exhilaration.

She had already submitted her passport renewal with an expedited processing alert. It would arrive in two weeks. Next, she and Sandy would select the activities they preferred to do while visiting each country. She had to schedule immunizations. She also had to request her transcript from Sarah Lawrence College where she had majored in Art History. Although Kimberly had been an excellent and conscientious student, that was a lifetime ago. During the last few years, she had begun to doubt her intellectual capabilities. Not challenging herself for decades had been a big mistake. If Sandy would study with her, she felt sure they could get through it together, just as they had mastered their most difficult classes at Sarah Lawrence.

There was much to think about. Consumed by the numerous planning details, Kimberly had little time to fret about what her family would think of her trip. She loved them but had finally convinced herself that they would be fine without her. Gary would have to take care of Meghan during her freshman year at Brown University. For the first time in over thirty years, she realized she was expendable to her family.

During the course of the afternoon, she completed and submitted her online application to Study at Sea, grateful to have found enough fortitude to make a decision. When the Marvelous Mavens encouraged her to do something for herself, they could never have known how seriously she would consider their advice. Until recently, she believed she had reached her potential, but now she was struck with how little time she had left to accomplish more things than she could count. Kimberly shuddered to think she might have missed all the splendor that awaited.

DODO QUIMBY/PAMELA CARDIN

DoDo watched Pamela exit the elevator and walk through the crowded terminal. When Pamela saw her, she smiled. She held Dodo in her focus as she continued making her way. Men glanced at her and turned to look again as she passed them, but Pamela ignored their attention.

"We're really doing it," said DoDo once Pamela was near.

"I know," Pamela said. "I'm so excited. It's a perfect day in every way."

"No problem getting here?"

"No, he left for work and confirmed he wasn't coming back home until Tuesday night. I even packed him a suit."

Once they arrived at the Washington, DC National Mall, the women walked arm in arm in the spectacular early dusk. Dodo grasped her camera from where it hung around her neck.

"Let me take a few pictures of you next to the reflecting pool."

"What do you want me to do? I'm not a model, you know."

"You might surprise yourself. Just sit next to the edge and talk to me about Walden Pond," Dodo instructed.

"That was such a nice day."

"Let me see it in your face. Just let go of yourself and be there."

"I remember how clean the water was. It was as if we had stepped back in time." Pamela's expression was soft and reflective.

Dodo clicked away, then after a few minutes said, "And, do you remember that snapping turtle?"

Pamela's face lit up and she burst into a laugh. Dodo kept clicking.

"I think you're going to like these, Sweet Pea."

After dinner, Pamela and Dodo decided to soak in the hotel hot tub. They shared the tub with another couple who soon left. Once the jets timed out, the room was warm and quiet. Dodo decided to ask Pamela to tell her more about her husband.

"What would you like to know?" Pamela asked.

"Whatever you feel like telling me."

"I forget what I was like before him."

"Did he change you or did you change yourself?" Dodo asked.

"I definitely adapted to suit him and his demands. It didn't bother me as much when I was younger, but now I'm starting to chafe at it. I want to find out who I really am."

"What is he like?" Dodo did not really want to hear more about this man who held Pamela hostage but she felt she must learn about him if she was going to be sharing her.

"He's very charismatic. He's good looking. He's successful. Most people think he is the life of the party."

"And, you?"

"What do I think?" Pamela asked.

"Yes. How would you describe him?"

Pamela looked toward the door to check that no one would enter.

"He's controlling. He's cruel. He's selfish."

"Wow. Anything else?"

"He's a good lover." Pamela cringed as she said it.

Dodo raised her eyebrows.

"That's not why I stay," she assured Dodo.

"Then, why?"

"I'm not sure. As bad as it is, I have a home of my own. I have furniture and a refrigerator and a car. I have a garden and a pool."

"So, you want those material things? Are they important to you?" Dodo tried to hide her disappointment. She had not thought of Pamela that way.

"No, no, no. It's not the *things*. It's the feeling that I am anchored. That I'm not adrift. That my life is solid because those things surround me."

Dodo found Pamela's hand under the water and rubbed her foot with hers. "I think I understand. I can't blame you for feeling that way, given how hard your childhood was."

Pamela squeezed Dodo's hand.

"What if you had somewhere safe to go?" Dodo asked.

Q: At what age should a woman achieve self-actualization?

Pamela knew the answer immediately: at birth.

HEIDI BELANGER

The Red Line train was hot and stuffy but Heidi hardly noticed. She was on her way to the University of Massachusetts Women's Entrepreneur Network and Support group. To get there, she'd have to take a ten minute bus after the train. Fortunately, she had allotted plenty of time. Next to her on the seat was a satchel full of the family shirts she had designed. She hoped to get advice about how to create and sell other tee shirts.

Heidi had expected Jim to laugh this morning when she told him where she was going, but he was true to his promise, and instead held her close and told her how proud he was. She was proud, too, but nervous as well, especially when she noted how young her fellow passengers destined for UMass/Boston were. She clutched the campus map in her hand. If she didn't do this now, when would she?

The shuttle bus rounded the circle and stopped. Heidi got off and stood in the sun, consulting her map. Wheatley Hall appeared to be only a short walk from where she stood.

"Need some help with directions?" a woman asked.

"Um, I think I'm all set. I'm trying to get to Wheatley Hall. It's that way, right?" Heidi pointed to the brick building.

"Sure is. I'm headed there, too. Why don't we walk together?"

The other woman carried a briefcase and looked sophisticated in her well-tailored clothes. Although she was a contemporary in age, Heidi felt immature next to her because of the contrast in their wardrobe and demeanor.

"I'm Carol Wright. I teach here." She extended her hand to Heidi.

"I'm Heidi Belanger. I'm just visiting."

"What do you hope to find in Wheatley Hall?"

"A group called Women's Entrepreneur and Support."

"What a coincidence! That's where I'm going, too."

They fell into a brisk pace.

"I'm the group facilitator, Heidi. What is your business?"

"I don't have a business yet. I'm hoping to get advice about how to start one."

"You'll be in good company with our group. I think the majority of the women are still contemplating how to actually begin."

"Really?" Heidi sounded relieved. She had been concerned about participating in a group with members above her expertise.

"Yes, really. The goal of the group is to give each other support. My role is to give you advice when you feel brave enough to begin." Carol's smile was kind.

"How long does it usually take someone to get to the point where they actually start something?"

"That depends," Carol chuckled. "Some women launch right away, and some—well, let's just say they find the water too cold and won't even get their feet wet."

"Oh, my. Do they pressure each other?"

"I wouldn't call it pressure, but they do encourage each other if it seems like someone is falling off track."

"I hope I can handle that," Heidi worried.

"You'll be fine. What's your idea?"

"It'll probably sound silly to you."

Carol abruptly stopped walking. "I'm going to interrupt you right there. There are no silly ideas. Having an idea means you're alive and kicking! Just think of all of the women who are too afraid to put themselves out there. Now, please continue."

"Okay," Heidi said. "I want to start a custom personalization business for family and work gatherings, starting with tee shirt designs."

"Excellent summary. I like the idea!"

"You do?" Heidi said.

"Yes, I do indeed. The next step is to develop a business plan. I'll help you, Heidi," Carol said. "Here's the entrance."

She held the door open for Heidi and the two women walked through the foyer together.

DARLY

Darly sat at attention on an uncomfortable wooden chair. She was inside the dim cavern of dusty books and papers that was Professor Simon Grady's office. Her academic advisor's massive desk established a firm barrier between them. Although Darly had left her study summary documents at Grady's office several days prior, it was clear that he had failed to view them until now. She watched as he laboriously opened the manila envelope with his letter knife, then fiddled with the ends of his white mustache while he read her submission.

Dust particles in a ray of sunlight sailed through the air between them.

"Hmm," he said.

The clock on the wall ticked.

"Humph." He raised his eyebrows and turned the page.

Darly waited fifteen minutes. Finally, Grady cleared his throat and began.

"Very interesting, Ms. Lane. I think you have chosen a topic a bit over your head, though."

"I'm sorry, but I'm not sure I understand. The topic was previously approved."

"Not by me. I see the study is anecdotal, but what are you trying to achieve with your research?" His condescending affect set Darly on edge.

"The stated goals are indicated here." She reached over to the folder on his desk and pointed to the second page. "I agree that the collection is anecdotal but I followed protocol on each of the modalities. As my research progressed, it became more apparent that there would be no definitive conclusion to my thesis question."

"Therefore?" he asked.

"Therefore?" she asked back.

Grady scowled, then spoke slowly to her as if she would not understand. "What should you have done at the point you realized the participants you selected were flawed?"

"I wouldn't exactly call them flawed. They—"

He cut her off. "Of course they are flawed. These women do not have an adequate grasp of the goals of the Women's Liberation Movement. It looks like the majority of them were not bona fide feminists. With that criteria, it would be impossible to judge whether or not they personally benefited from the movement."

Heidi spoke up. "All of them had peripheral participation in the movement. They weren't working with Gloria Steinem or other luminaries, but in their own ways, they were making paths for women who followed."

"By marrying and having five kids? By playing around with sex toys? It looks like you chose very immature subjects for a serious study and then you were unable to mine what limited depth they had for the required data. Their answers are miasmic. There is no way to categorize them and they have no boundaries. I'm not sure how five grown women managed to arrive at a point in their lives where there is no 'there' there." His pale fingers punctuated air quotes.

"Professor Grady, I respect your opinion and your knowledge of study modalities, but I have to disagree with the way you have characterized these women."

"Go on. I am curious to hear your argument." His expression belied his words.

"The fact that this particular group includes both highly accomplished women and those with traditional female accomplishments does not diminish their contribution to society. Each of them struggles with the same issues. They all worry about how they raised their kids. They all wonder if marriage was the right course to have taken. They all contemplate how their jobs would have changed if they had given more or less attention to their families. These are the basic themes of a woman's life." Darly's heart was racing.

"That doesn't sound very original at all, Ms. Lane." He put the study documents back into the envelope and handed it to her.

"But, don't you see?" Darly pursued. "Nothing has really changed! Nothing will ever change! As long as a woman has the capacity to give birth and the hormones to make her care about others and feel so acutely responsible for them, she is almost imprisoned. It's something men will probably never be able to understand. It's totally unfair in so many regards because no matter which path a woman takes, she feels she ultimately shortchanges herself *or* others."

Grady put his elbows on his desk and lined up his fingers into a steeple pattern. His eyes narrowed. He leaned toward her and spoke very quietly.

"Why don't you take a little breather, young lady? Give yourself a chance to calm down. Go home, read it over again, and let's regroup next week at this same time. I am sure, with some distance, you will be better able to comprehend my critique of your work."

"But—"

"Thank you, Ms. Lane." He lowered his head and directed his attention to the piles of paper scattered over his desk.

Darly quietly left his office, but once outside on Sherborne Street, she broke into a run and didn't stop until she reached the Charles River bank. She heaved her bag onto the grass, then dropped to her knees. Catching her breath, she took out her phone and found Ian's number, eager to share her indignation about how disrespectfully Grady had treated both her and her thesis.

She stared down at the phone for a minute. Maybe Ian had been humoring her all along. He had confessed that he found the Marvelous Mavens' laments insufferably boring. She put the phone back into her bag. Neither Ian nor Grady could ever fathom the depth of the Marvelous Mavens' experiences.

SHERALL SAVARD

On the corner of Newbury and Exeter Streets, Brooks observed the sidewalk crowd at Priscilla's restaurant. It was familiar from nightly walks around the neighborhood he routinely took to escape the oppressive confines of his late mother's rambling Back Bay residence. Compared to the heat of Miami, he found a Boston summer stroll refreshing. Although the city was growing on him, Florida was where his business contacts were, and he would soon return.

Brooks blended well into the upscale crowd. From a distance, his navy linen jacket and pale yellow shirt made him look similar to those in proximity, but on closer inspection, the weave and cut of his clothing was far superior.

Brooks was not an impulsive or reckless man. He was grounded in who he was, in the facts of his life, his finances, the realities of business, and in his relationships with others. Confident sophistication served him well. Although pragmatic in his actions, he still allowed himself to dream.

He knew it was premature to speculate, but Brooks could not resist wondering if Sherall would consider visiting him at his Florida home. He longed for a courtship shortcut because he had grown tired of banter, innuendo, and flirting. He knew what he liked and had no interest in taking things slowly, either. There was no point in wasting a day of opportunity. His emotional struggles had long ago been conquered. He saw before him life to savor. It would be nice to share it with someone who felt similarly.

Brooks arrived at Priscilla's entrance and walked slowly up to the hostess podium to take his place in line. Unspoken protocol at this restaurant did not require such an impressive looking man to queue for a table. Two couples who had been waiting longer humbly stood aside as the hostess deferentially escorted Brooks to a table for two at the coveted outer edge of the sidewalk. As he made his way between the jumble of patrons, he carried his height with elegant grace. Once seated, he politely returned the warm smiles of several women seated at neighboring tables. Because Priscilla's was situated on the shady side of Newbury Street, there was no need for cafe umbrellas. This allowed unobstructed views between lunch patrons and passers-by, all eager to see and be seen by others.

Sherall left her office and strode down Newbury Street. She always walked with purpose. She was someone important with somewhere to go. On the sidewalk, pedestrians gave way as she approached. But today, there was a new lilt in her step. There was a hint of possibility in the breeze that reached her nostrils and lifted her hair. Her sleeveless dress floated as she walked; the fabric swirled in the warm air and caressed her bare legs, reacquainting her with a long dormant sense of femininity. Its presence elicited butterflies and euphoria, and she was grateful for their return.

When she saw Brooks already seated at the sidewalk perimeter of Priscilla's, she blushed to realize he had been watching her walk toward him. He stood as she smiled and walked past him so she could enter at the break in the gate surrounding the diners.

When Sherral arrived at his table, Brooks kissed her on the cheek. The women seated nearby quickly looked down or away, disappointed.

"You look lovely, Sherall."

"Thank you."

Brooks pushed her chair in for her as she sat.

"Well, here we are." She smiled at him.

"What do we have?"

"I'm not sure. But, I like it."

"Me, too," he said.

Brooks had ample time to review the menu and Sherall knew it by heart, so when the waitress arrived, they placed their orders.

"Do you have a schedule to keep?" he asked.

"I cleared the afternoon."

"Good," he said, and took her hand in his.

"Where should we start?" she asked.

"You first," he said.

"I'm lost."

"I'm found." He smiled.

"It's not a bad feeling I'm having right now, but it sure as hell is not one I'm accustomed to," Sherall said.

"Can anyone ride an earthquake?"

"It's not just me, then?" she asked, smiling.

"No. I'm right there with you."

"Okay. Let's rumble," Sherall said.

After lunch, they made their way to Fairfield Street, crossed the pedestrian bridge spanning busy Storrow Drive, and arrived at the peaceful Esplanade. Students who crowded this area with their frenetic running and bicycling had long since returned to their parents' homes for the summer. Sherall and Brooks strolled the perimeter of the lagoon, hand in hand. A few single scull rowers glided by them on the river. Sherall felt the familiar surroundings of the Charles become new again—through Brooks' eyes.

Q: What obstacles prevented you from achieving self-actualization?

In the case of Self v. Others, Self had prevailed. But, had Sherall won? It was time to risk a loss. What stands in the way, becomes the way.

KIMBERLY DOLAN

"Yes, it's for one year." Kimberly's voice quivered.

Exasperated by the audacity of her plan, Gary said, "You can't just leave like this, Kimberly. What is the matter with you? Are you on drugs or something?"

"I'm going to do it, Gary. I've already made up my mind."

"But you didn't ask me and you didn't ask the kids. You're supposed to be here for them. Plus, I count on you to get everything done around the house. What the hell am I supposed to do?"

"I'm sorry, but I think you can figure that out. Also, I have considered the kids and we both know that four of them are already over twenty-one. They don't really need me. They just like to have me around to help. You'll still be here for them." Kimberly held onto the side of the counter, worried her legs would buckle.

"This is insane. You're being so selfish! I can't take care of the kids, and I don't want to take care of this house.

What the hell are you thinking? Can't you even consider what the rest of us need?" Gary yelled.

Kimberly sat down in a chair. She had thought through this moment but even with preparation, it was difficult to bear.

"Gary, I'm done with my job here. I'm done with working for everyone and never getting paid in money or praise. I can't keep this up. It's killing me and I don't want to die. I don't want to be like my mother."

"Oh, please. Don't use that excuse," Gary countered. "You know she was crazy. You've had everything you need and you haven't had to make any sacrifices. You're a spoiled woman, Kimberly, and I'm extremely disappointed in you. Just because you have that money from your aunt, doesn't mean you can hightail it out of here and shirk your responsibilities."

Kimberly shook her head. "Will you even miss me?" she asked.

"Of course, I'll miss you. What a ridiculous question. You're supposed to be *here* though. You're not supposed to go off and do something bizarre like this cruise. What kind of person even does that? It's like a weird hippy adventure or something."

"I'd get my Master's at the same time."

"Why do you need a Master's? You don't even work."

Kimberly stared at her husband. He was not a bad man. She felt certain that his negative reaction to her news emanated from fear. He would be alone; he would face the social humiliation that his wife had left him; and he would have to cope with their family and household by himself for the first time, ever.

248

"I'm going, Gary. I know it will be hard for you. Things have been hard for me, too. I'm sorry you are unhappy with my plan. I'm not changing it, though."

"There is going to be a huge price for you to pay if you do this," Gary responded.

"Maybe you're right."

Gary stomped out of the room.

"And, maybe you're wrong," she said, exhaling.

Q: Is it important to help younger women achieve their goals?

Probably, thought Kimberly. But she was tired of helping others. She was ready to take a big serving for herself.

PAMELA CARDIN/DODO QUIMBY

With Pamela looking on, Dodo scrolled through the pictures from their trip to Washington, DC."

"These are gorgeous. I'd like to share them with someone I know in New York."

"I'm not sure that's a good idea, Dodo."

"Why not?"

"Bruce."

"Go on."

"Well, he would go ballistic if he saw them."

"Why? Maybe he would be proud of you."

"It's not like that between us."

Dodo tenderly took both of Pamela's hands in hers. "Why don't you tell me once and for all what keeps you from leaving?"

"Are you sure you want to know?"

"Yes, I want to know. I need to know. It's time. You're safe with me."

Pamela searched her face, then said, "There is no love, but it's all I have."

"But, you have me now."

"I do, don't I?" Her eyes welled with tears.

Dodo released her hands and moved them to Pamela's face.

"Let it out, Pea. It's time. I'll take care of you. I'll protect you. We can do this together."

Pamela nodded and smiled through tears. "You're right. You've been so kind. I'm grateful to have you in my life."

"Okay, let's start our new beginning."

HEIDI BELANGER

"You think this supplier is the best one?" Heidi asked Lauren Stahl, her UMass Women's Entrepreneur and Support Group businesswoman match.

"I've only heard good things about them. The ultimate decision is yours, of course."

Heidi fingered the sample tee shirts.

"It's hard to tell the difference between this one and the other one," Heidi said, her eyebrows knit together. She chewed the side of her lip.

"It does take some practice," Lauren advised. "One thing I like to do is check the seams, especially around the collar. I also check the hem at the bottom to make sure it lays flat. And, you've already done one of the most important things which is to wash and dry it several times. That's exactly what your customer will do."

"Okay. That helps. The minimum order is two-hundred-fifty?"

Lauren pointed to the information on the sheet of paper that accompanied the original order. "It says here that the minimum is two-hundred-fifty, but after that you can order upwards in increments of one hundred."

"It seems like so much." Heidi hesitated.

"It's natural to look at things that way when you're just starting, and I understand how nerve-wracking it must feel to make that kind of outlay. However, you have a good product. You know that you have a large buyer for the first two hundred T-shirts, so it's not a bad decision at this price."

Lauren folded the flap of her leather briefcase. It was time for her to leave.

"Lauren, thank you so much for helping me through this process. I know I couldn't have done it without you."

"It's been a pleasure, Heidi, and I'll be with you for the next steps as well. You're doing great! Not everyone takes the leap so quickly."

Heidi laughed. "I guess when I'm ready, I'm ready!"

"I'm impressed."

After Lauren Stahl left, Heidi picked up her phone and entered the number listed on the sheet in front of her.

"Great Gnome Garments," a voice announced. "How may I help you?"

"I'd like to place an order," Heidi responded.

Summoning courage a few days earlier, Heidi had met with the TekNeek human resources manager to present her own family tee shirts as samples. The manager loved what he termed, the "folksy" feel of her stylized concept sketches. Folksy or not, a flabbergasted Heidi exited the appointment with an order for two hundred shirts. Tomorrow, Heidi would meet with Johnson Laser & Print to approve the proof of her design for the TekNeek company picnic order.

That night, she shared a beer with Jim in their kitchen.

"I can't believe this is really happening!" Jim lifted her up in the air and twirled her around the room.

"I know! I'm crazy nervous, though." Heidi looked down at him as he held her.

"If anyone can do this, Hon', it's definitely you. You're just like a little firecracker when you get something in your mind that you want to do."

"Thanks, Jimmy."

"I'm so proud of my girl."

"I'm proud of your girl, too." Heidi beamed.

Q: Have you self-actualized?

Heidi believed that most people would believe she was getting a late start. Was having a loving marriage and family not an accomplishment, too?

DARLY

The black line of the cursor blinked at the end of the sentence where Darly had parked it fifteen minutes ago. She had been busy biting her fingernails, a recently resurrected bad habit. Maybe Professor Grady was right. Perhaps she *had* been swept up by the colorful personalities in her study, and had not adequately followed the guidelines for questioning the five participants. At the onset, her mission was clear: six meetings with interrogative formats designed to elicit rational responses. Unfortunately, this meeting platform had failed from the very beginning. She should have insisted the women give her more concrete answers. As study leader, she had allowed herself to relinquish control and authority to some difficult characters. They were not educated, as she was, in the field of sociology. Only she was the expert in examining the conscious and subconscious ways these women were shaped by cultural and social structures as they moved through life. She was trained to study the connection between broad social forces and personal experiences. She had studied the seminal feminist texts: *The Feminine Mystique* by Betty Friedan, *The Female Eunuch* by Germaine Greer, *Sexual Politics* by Kate Millett, and *The Second Sex* by Simone de Beauvoir. She had scrutinized sociological issues related to the women's movement at the personal level, societal level, and global level. It was her job to examine and assess experiences, collect and organize empirical data, and then develop measurable criteria.

She considered the women in her group to be a good cross section of her target subject, and also representative of an era. Any other researcher who committed to random participants as she had would have been confronted with the same dilemma.

The problem? These real women were confoundedly unquantifiable. None of her training and research could have prepared her for the effect that the Marvelous Mavens had on her.

She recalled Freud's famous question: "What does woman want?" To him, it was rhetorical. Maybe he should have asked a woman and then listened carefully to her answer. She might say that she would like a chance to live her life without hearing the ticking of a biological clock; maybe she would like to decide on a course of action where her family would follow her, instead of her adjusting to them; perhaps she would welcome an opportunity to live in a world where others looked to her for genius, versus duty or beauty; possibly she would appreciate a feeling that she could pursue any solo dream or adventure unaccompanied by another person without fear of potential violence from those around her. These were some of the things a woman could want. But those wants did not consider complicated hormonal realities. Darly knew that Freud could not understand what "woman" wanted because women, by their biological condition, are presented with too many options—none of which are completely fulfilling alone, and all of which cannot be attained separately. With that in mind, she now believed a woman's life transcends what is commonly termed as the human condition. It is the *female* condition. Maybe Dr. Grady, with his PhD and post-doctorate training, paper publications, and peer reviews, was incapable of fathoming what every woman knows. To Darly, the most complex life was that of the female.

She smiled ruefully and shook her head. Where would this perspective lead her? Bitter, docile, depressed, selfish, or selfless? It all depended on which path she chose—or which form of woman she chose to become. She should have known better than to think she would arrive anywhere definitive.

Information gathered at the meetings with the Marvelous Mavens added to her personal confusion. She especially dreaded tomorrow's topic: Self Actualization. How could any of the Mavens respond positively? Every one of them had made major sacrifices that compromised their careers, their families, or themselves. It was hard not to conclude that women shouldered what men would not.

Even her own family was an arena of inequity. After Darly's mother died, her father hired a housekeeper to raise her and her brother Daniel. In his mind, the housekeeper was a surrogate mother to his children. Darly never considered her as such. She could now see that her father was able to compartmentalize his parenting and share it with a hired partner. Could a mother do that? For women, offspring are either in one's heart like the blood that courses through veins—or not.

Darly unabashedly loved her father, but up to this point, she had never considered why he did not step up to a role as primary parent. He was a man, and he had chosen the importance of his own life over his children.

Nothing looked certain to Darly anymore.

From the drawer of her desk, she removed a little black velvet box. Resting it on the palm of her hand, she closed her eyes, straining to conjure the spirit of her mother. After a few minutes, she set the box on the desk and opened it. The lock of Nora's hair lay as it always did, smooth and shining on the black background. In the photo next to it, her mother looked happy. Darly had always assumed her mother had lived the life she wanted; that she had everything figured out, and was heading in exactly the direction she intended. If only she could ask her now.

Her cell phone vibrated with a text. Ian. She scrolled the numerous messages he had left over the last twenty-four hours.

First, *Hey! Why so quiet?*

Then, *Are you ignoring me?*

And, *Darly, really, what's up?*

Finally, *Shane said he saw you on Comm Ave. this afternoon so I know you're okay. Come on. Don't do this.*

They had departed on bad terms. There was no argument, but because she felt Ian did not share her newfound opinions about gender imbalance, a schism had opened between them. His carefree attitude exasperated her. How could he not see the many life choices she would have to make and how serious this was to her?

"Lighten up!" he had said, as if she could weigh all of her options and feel good about selecting any of them, knowing that whatever she chose would shortchange something else in her life.

"I don't like how you seem to think you can just breeze through life and do whatever you want," she had responded.

"Well," he had thrown back, "that's because I can. Why are you so pissy? You can do whatever you want to do, too."

She shook her head at that. "You really don't get it, do you? A woman lives in a totally different universe than a man. She always gets the raw deal."

Ian had run out of patience.

"I don't like what's happening to you, Darly. You really are looking at life in a depressing way. It's all what you make of it."

"That's easy for you to say. You have a penis."

With that, she turned and walked away.

Q: How did the Women's Liberation Movement position you for self-actualization?

Darly was quite certain it had only made it worse.

THE SIXTH DINNER

The Mavens' enthusiasm for gathering together had influenced their arrival time at Vivere. When Darly opened the door and entered the room, they were already in full swing, laughing and sipping wine.

"Hey, Darly!" Heidi raised her glass and called out when she saw her in their midst.

"Hello, lassie!" Sherall acknowledged her as well.

Kimberly, Pamela, and Dodo nodded and smiled to her, not breaking their conversational thread.

Darly's own smile was wan, but it wasn't clear if anyone noticed. She had always been the serious one in the room. She took a seat and slid a tablet out of her bag.

In a few minutes, the others sat down. The food arrived soon afterward.

"How's it going, Darly?" Dodo finally asked.

"Pretty good, thanks."

"How many more meetings do we have?" Kimberly asked.

"This is the last one with a subject. We'll have one more to wrap-up the group at the end of the summer," Darly answered.

"I'm sad about it ending," Heidi said, looking around

the table.

"Me, too," said Pamela.

"Ditto," Dodo added.

"I'm going to miss you guys," Sherall said.

Kimberly was tearing up. "Well, as if you can't tell, I'm definitely going to miss this group."

Darly was all business. "You can still stay in touch." She glanced at her tablet. "Let's get started. Does anyone remember the quote printed at the top of the paper I handed out last time?"

Kimberly held it in her hand. "It's by Abraham Maslow. Do you want me to read it?"

"Please," Darly answered.

"Self-actualization is the intrinsic growth of what is already in the organism, or more accurately, of what the organism is."

"So, can anyone relate to that?" Darly asked.

"I think it just means that you should try to be who you really are," said Heidi.

"And, be your most authentic version of yourself," Dodo added.

Sherall said, "It sounds easy, doesn't it?"

"I may not be remembering this correctly," Kimberly began, "but I think it has something to do with a general way of feeling instead of a constant drive. It's a state of being. Your highest level."

Everyone turned to face her. They had never considered her to be at all intellectual.

"Way to go, Kimberly!" Sherall cheered.

Kimberly laughed. "Well, I did study it a long time ago in school."

Darly brought them back to the topic. "You're all correct. It's not easy to attain though. It's difficult to reach until the basic needs of life such as safety, shelter, hunger, love, etcetera, are managed. Some people search for it the wrong way, too."

Pamela spoke up. "I heard that is the reason some people have a mid-life crisis. They're comfortable in every way until they realize they haven't done what they wanted to do. They have not been true to themselves."

The women in the group nodded.

"How do you feel when it comes to that, Pea?" Dodo asked.

Pamela smiled at her, indulgently. "I think I'm just starting to work on it. I guess it's a long process, but it feels good to take the first step."

"That's great, Pamela," Heidi said. "What kind of changes are you making?"

Pamela looked at the women around the table and said, "Well, at age 58, I'm going to become a model!"

"Really?" Darly asked, incredulous. "That is fantastic. I thought models had to be even younger than me." She shrugged her shoulders. "I'm just ignorant, I guess."

"I'm as surprised as you. Dodo took some pictures of me a while ago and sent them to a friend of hers in New York. Apparently, he knew somebody at Baisers, the French lipstick company, and they want to use me in their ads now. It's amazing."

"Congratulations, Pamela!" everyone shouted.

"Here are some of her test shots," Dodo said, holding two pictures up on her phone for everyone to see.

"Beautiful."

"Gorgeous!"

"I'd buy lipstick from you any day," Sherall said.

Next, Heidi stood and put her bag on the table.

"I have something to announce, too."

She pulled out two tee shirts, one purple and one yellow. TekNeek was printed on them in bold letters.

"Sweet tee shirts, Heidi!" Sherall said.

"I designed them."

"Whoa, good for you!" Dodo said.

"And, they're part of an order that I got from a company because—" An enormous smile spread over Heidi's face. "I started my own business!"

Everyone clapped and cheered.

"Wow," Darly said. "There is so much great news tonight. Heidi, tell us how this came about. Were you planning it for a long time?"

"No, not really. I just connected with a support group at UMass and they assigned me to a mentor. That woman was so encouraging. I realized I didn't have to wait another minute to try out my idea. Everything just fell into place. I'm pretty happy about it."

The tee shirts made their way around the table until they returned to Heidi. She put them into her bag and sat back down.

Kimberly stood next. "I guess if we're all sharing new things, I have something to say, too."

The other women looked up at her.

"I signed up for a year long trip on a cruise ship that goes around the world and while I'm on it, I'm going to get my Masters in International Relations!" She was out of breath at the end of her sentence.

"Oh, my god!" Sherall said. She fumbled under the table for the buzzer to call the waiter.

"That is unbelievable, Kimberly!" Dodo shouted.

Heidi leaned over and hugged Kimberly. Pamela and Darly walked over to her chair to hug her as well.

Marco the waiter entered the room. "What would you like, ladies?" he asked.

Darly looked over in surprise.

"Bring us two bottles of champagne, please," Sherall said. "We are celebrating *self-actualization*!"

"Right away, ma'am!"

Marco turned and ran down the stairs.

The women were all standing now, giving each other hugs, pats on the back, and high fives. Sherall and Dodo had formed a chorus line and the others were on their way to join in. Darly's head was spinning. Where was this meeting going?

Marco returned with the champagne and poured it into six old fashioned coupe-style glasses. The women raised them while Sherall offered a toast.

"To the most Marvelous Mavens and the well-deserved success of those who had it coming."

"Cheers!"

"Bravo!"

"Cheers!"

"To the Marvelous Mavens!"

Darly took a tiny sip of her champagne. She was so very happy for these women, even though she understood them less than ever.

SHERALL SAVARD/KIMBERLY DOLAN

Sherall touched Kimberly's elbow as they walked down the restaurant stairs and back onto Boylston Street. "Do you have a minute to talk?"

"Of course," Kimberly answered.

After the others went on their way, Sherall shared the news she had heard about Gary Dolan's sexting.

"Oh my god," Kimberly responded, stunned by the revelation.

"I wanted to check with you first. The next step is typically a restraining order. She doesn't really want to do that though. She just wants him to stop."

"I can talk to him about it. I'm pretty sure that will do the trick. I'm so embarrassed."

Sherall summoned up the kindness she felt for the other Maven. "Kimberly, this is not your fault. It's not a reflection on you."

"Thank you, Sherall. I would hate to have this get out and affect our children."

"That's what I was thinking, too."

"Especially with me leaving for my trip."

Both women considered the future.

Finally, Sherall asked, "Do you think you'll stay with him?"

"I don't know. This is the first time I've thought of more than a temporary separation. I didn't know he could do something like this."

"Lots of men act out at this point in life. Actually, lots of men act out, period." Sherall rolled her eyes. She quickly added, "Would you please let me know how it goes and if there is anything I can do to help?"

"Yes. I will." Kimberly wiped away a tear. "Sherall, you've been so kind to tell me this privately. You're a good friend. Thank you." She reached out to hug the other woman.

RESULTS

It was unusual for Bruce to arrive home early on a Friday. He looked forward to seeing Pamela's reaction when he handed her the box of long stem roses and chilled bottle of her favorite champagne. He was in a TGIF kind of mood. He pulled his car next to hers and artfully arranged his offerings before he walked through the door.

"Pamela!" he called out from the hallway. No answer. He made his way through the kitchen, ignoring the note propped on the table.

"Pamela!" he called again, louder.

At the liquor cabinet, he poured himself a scotch and took one long sip.

He was famished. Dinner should have been in some stage of preparation. He checked both the refrigerator and the stove. Exasperated, he called Alonzo's Pizza and ordered a calzone, then walked over to the couch to watch TV until the food arrived.

When he recalled the note on the table, he went to it and tore off the envelope edge to pull out the handwritten page.

Dear Bruce,

I'll get right to the point.

I'm leaving you and I will not see you again until we meet in court.

I'm tired of the way you treat me. I deserve more and I want a better life. You almost had me convinced that my fate was to stay with you forever. I was a good wife to you. I can honestly say, for a while at least, that I truly loved you. I have no love for you now, but I am not unloved.

My lawyer will contact Phil so they can work out all of the details.

Good bye.

Pamela

Bruce threw down the note, then picked up his phone to access his online banking. He transferred money from account to account, hiding his assets to the best of his ability. His bankers and other agents would hear from him in the morning.

The doorbell rang. Bruce pocketed his phone and swung open the door.

"Good evening, Mr. Cardin. It's $9.97, please," the personable young delivery man said.

Without a word, Bruce handed him a ten dollar bill, grabbed the box, then slammed the door shut.

The man shook his head in disgust as he walked across the expansive lawn to his dilapidated car.

SHERALL SAVARD

"I think you're right," Scott said to Sherall. "I don't know why we waited so long to do this."

"Maybe we thought if we ignored it, it would somehow turn into a marriage." Sherall sighed.

"Is there someone else for you?" he asked, adjusting the waist tie of his scrubs.

"You first."

"Candace Moore."

"Your personal assistant? I see. Actually, I didn't see,

but okay."

"You?"

"Nobody special up until now," she replied.

"So, there is someone now?"

"Maybe. Yes, I think so."

"We can't forget the kids," he said.

"We always have," she answered.

"We've been shitty parents."

"Both of us, unfortunately."

"They're not doing too poorly, though."

"Let's keep our old nanny Carole Mitchell on a retainer, just to be on the safe side."

"Good idea. They always liked her."

"What else?"

"The house," he said.

"We can make it a trust for the kids. They need somewhere to call home."

"Maybe Candy and I can move in for now, unless you want to stay."

"No. I'll probably get something smaller."

"Fine."

"Okay. I guess the lawyers will do the rest."

"They'll be chomping at the bit," he chuckled.

"Fifty-fifty acceptable to you?" Sherall asked.

"I won't argue with that."

"You're staying here tonight, then?"

"No, I guess I'll head over to Candy's and give her the news."

"All right. Have a good night."

"You, too."

Scott picked up his briefcase and walked out the back

door.

Heidi and Jim were finishing a special dinner in the dining room, relaxing and discussing their day. Justin burst through the kitchen doorway.

"Mom! Dad!"

Their son appeared in the room, his face flushed, his hair disheveled. Jim rose from his chair. Heidi put her hand to her chest.

"Oh my god, Justin! What's the matter?" Heidi cried out.

"It's somebody else's!" he yelled.

"What?" Jim asked.

"The baby. It's somebody else's!" he repeated.

Heidi and Jim exchanged glances, wondering how they should react to this news. It was as they suspected.

Jim spoke first. "Justin, slow down. Have a seat. Start from the beginning."

Justin grabbed a beer from the kitchen refrigerator, then reappeared in front of his parents.

"Sit," his father commanded.

Justin flipped open the can, then sat roughly onto the chair.

"What's happening, Jus'?" Heidi asked.

"I started to hear some things I didn't like, so I told her she would need to get a paternity test after it was born like you said."

"And?"

"It's not mine."

"Who is the father?" Heidi asked.

"The hell if I know," Justin answered.

"Easy in front of your mom, young man," Jim said.

"Sorry." He looked over at Heidi, then continued. "The guy in the cubicle next to me at work said he saw her at a club a few months ago, dancing with some jerk who he knows. He recognized her from the picture I had on my desk. He never talks to me but overheard me telling someone about the baby when I was on the phone. I want him to be, like, my best friend now. I so owe that dude my life." He took a long swig from his beer can. "She's way further along. The dates just don't match up with me. She had to tell me the truth."

"Justin," Heidi said, "you've had a very close call. I hope you never forget this. Are things over between you now?"

"Fuck, yes!"

"Justin!" Jim reminded him.

"Sorry, Mom."

Heidi smiled, forgiving her son.

"Are you... a little disappointed?" she asked him.

For a long moment, he looked into the sympathetic eyes of his mother, then leaned toward her and buried his head onto her chest, strangling a sob.

KIMBERLY DOLAN

"Sign here and here," the mail carrier ordered, then handed Kimberly the envelopes.

She carried them into the kitchen and laid them on the counter. One at a time, she slid the letter opener under each seam. The first contained her new passport, and the other five envelopes contained information about visas which had been newly registered on the passport. She examined each carefully. The visas were not in English and had various stamps and signatures to indicate authenticity.

Kimberly carried the documents into the office and took out the Study at Sea itinerary and brochure. She picked from the list some of the countries she would visit—Morocco, China, Fiji, Panama—then pushed everything else off the blotter and lined the visa documents up in a row. One by one, she looked at each of them and imagined a future that included tasting the food and seeing the sights of that particular country. She had read many stories and seen many movies about adventure travel, but now she would be the one living the fantasy.

Earlier that week, Kimberly called the kids and told all of them about her trip. Matt and Kurt showed little reaction. Brittney opined that her mother was too old and that she should instead be the one to take the trip. Connor thought it was a weird idea. Meghan complained that no one would be home to do tasks for her when she was in college. Kimberly told them all that they would be fine without her and that their dad would take care of everything. He would have to.

DODO QUIMBY/PAMELA CARDIN

Dodo carefully turned the camera over onto the protective pad she had positioned on the counter.

"Here is where you replace the batteries." She looked over at her daughter, Georgie, to make sure she was still interested.

Examining the little compartment, Georgie furrowed her brow and moved closer to inspect the area. "But, what kind of batteries does it take? They're not the usual size, right?"

"Good call," Dodo praised. "These are special lithium batteries. Never risk having a dead camera on a shoot. Always have extras."

Pamela walked out of the bathroom with a towel wrapped around her head, then went straight to the coffee pot to pour herself a cup. "Are you ladies interested in mushroom and cheese omelets, and some blueberry muffins?" she asked.

"Seriously?" Georgie responded. "I love omelets!"

"Okay, then a special order breakfast is on its way to your stomach in about 30 minutes."

Dodo smiled as Pamela set to work in the kitchen. Georgie's weekend visit had been a great success. Although Pamela worried that her presence would be a distraction, Georgie thought that her mother's lover exponentially increased Dodo's cool threshold.

"Wait until I tell my friends that my mother lives with the Baisers model," Georgie had said.

DARLY

On Saturday night, Darly joined her friends Sari, Gracie, and Rachel where they had been waiting for her outside The Scorpion Club. Her eyes were lined. Her hair was tousled and set with spray. She had even shaved her legs. All four of them were ready to party.

"This is so awesome, Darly! You never come out with us anymore," Rachel said, her drop earrings swaying with each word.

"I know. I feel like letting go tonight." Darly responded.

"Yowzah. Sounds dangerous, coming from you," said Sari. She unbuttoned the top of her already low cut dress, then adjusted her cleavage as she examined her own reflection in the nightclub window.

"Come on you guys. I'm not that bad." Darly shifted uncomfortably from one high heel to the other.

"Is Ian busy tonight?" Gracie asked.

"I wouldn't know."

"What's up with that?" asked Rachel.

"It's probably over. I just want to have some fun and not worry about it tonight. Okay?"

"Good mindset, Darly," Rachel scrunched her hair back from her face. "You'll have tons of guys here to make you forget him."

Sari and Rachel entered the building. Gracie grabbed Darly's arm and pulled her through the doors of the Scorpion Club.

Inside, the music pulsed with infectious rhythm.

"Woo hoo!" Sari yelled, "Party!"

It only took a few minutes for the attractive quartet to be approached by several men interested in buying drinks for them. After downing two pear martinis, Darly felt herself get into the spirit of the night.

"What's *your* name?" a tall man sporting a soul patch beard yelled close to her ear.

"Serena," Darly lied, yelling over the music.

"Sexy Serena," he yelled back. "You're looking fine."

"Thank you," Darly mouthed.

"Let's dance." He pulled Darly onto the floor.

A throbbing mob engulfed them, moving like one to the heavy downbeat. When each song neared its end, the DJ cued the next, so there was never a lull in the music or the dancing.

"What's your name?" Darly yelled into her partner's ear.

"Dino. Like the dinosaur," he answered, pulling her hard to him.

Darly was drunk. She would normally have found her present situation dancing with Dino comical, but pear martinis made her feel, not think. She let Dino hold her close and grind against her. He was much taller than her, even with her stacked heels, and the arms she held onto were rock hard with muscle.

Sari and Rachel spotted Darly and danced their way over to her. Rachel raised her arms over her head and worked her hips in time to the deafening music. Dino smiled at the sight, inspired to become more creative with his own moves with Darly. The courtship of dance and drink was irresistible.

"Come with me, Serena," Dino said to Darly after a few more songs. He pulled her through the crowd. "We're going upstairs."

"I have to go to the bathroom first," Darly slurred, gesturing toward the ladies room door.

"Make it fast. I need you bad."

Darly pushed open the door, then entered an empty stall. Her head spun slightly. She felt euphoric, laughing out loud as she almost lost her balance flushing the toilet with her foot.

Gracie was standing in front of a sink, waiting for her

turn to relieve herself.

"Darly!" she squealed, as she saw her friend emerge from the stall.

"Gracie!" Darly laughed back.

The women fell into a hug.

"Who's that hunka-hunka you found?" Gracie asked.

"He's my di-no-saur!" Darly giggled.

Darly stumbled out of the restroom. Dino looked her over, smirking and nodding his head with satisfaction at the sight of her. "You're my queen tonight," he said, then entered the code to the elevator that would take them to the private upstairs lounge.

The door opened to a different scene. Lit by red bulbs, the room was full of tables, couches and curtained alcoves. The music pulsed just as loud as downstairs. Dino nodded to a waitress who then rushed over to them.

"What are you drinking, babe?" he yelled to Darly.

"Can't you tell?" she flirted. "Pear martinis!"

"And give me a Vodka Red Bull," he ordered the waitress. "We'll be in number three."

Reaching his arm around Darly's waist, Dino led her to a far alcove with an opened curtain. He pulled the table away from the leather couch so she could sit. Darly more aptly fell onto it. He sat down next to her and stroked her hair and ran his big hand up and down the back of her neck.

The waitress arrived with their drinks. When Dino gave her two twenties, the waitress flashed him the okay sign with her hand. As she left, she pulled the velvet curtain closed.

Darly picked up her martini and took a gulp, oblivious

to having spilled much of it onto her lap on its way to her mouth. Dino took a swig of his drink, then put his arm around her again. He kissed her as a test, and when she responded with enthusiasm, he pulled back from her and leaned over to take off her shoes and bring her legs up to his lap. He kissed her toes and rubbed her feet with his warm hands. After a while, he rubbed her smooth calves up and down a few times until he reached her thighs. Darly protested only a little. Dino was practiced at his craft. He returned his attention to the back of her neck and kissed it up and down and all around the border of her dress, then moved to her chest. Darly threw her head back and breathed hard.

Dino laid her back onto the couch. She felt him pull off her underpants and push up her dress. For some reason, she didn't care. Pure sensation seemed to be all that mattered. He unzipped his pants and pulled them halfway down. Darly lifted her head to watch him put on a condom until she couldn't hold her head up any longer.

She embraced the sensation of being consumed. It was the pounding she enjoyed most. The raw male energy and violence of the act. No thought; only sensation.

When Dino was done, he sat up next to her.

She closed her legs and lay on her side. "So nice," she slurred.

He patted the naked skin of her rump, pulled up his pants, and without a word, walked out of the curtained booth.

Darly sat up slowly. She adjusted her dress back over her legs. There was a little bit of martini left in her glass, so she swallowed it. She wondered if Dino was coming back. More than dizzy, she wasn't sure she could walk unassisted. After a few minutes, she crashed back onto the couch.

Bright lights woke her. The music had stopped. Searching on the floor, she gathered her underpants and shoes. She forced herself to get up.

Someone briskly whisked the curtain aside.

"We're closing. You have to get out of here," the waiter said. He continued onto the next booth where he wiped the table down with his wet rag.

Darly stood up and shuffled her bare feet over the sticky floor, then pushed the elevator button. It arrived on the first floor where Gracie sat slumped in a chair. When she saw her friend, Gracie jumped up.

"I was so worried about you! It's only VIP access. The waitress told me you were still up there." Gracie rushed over and pulled Darly's arm over her shoulder. "I have a ride waiting for us. Let's go home."

For the next few weeks, Darly dragged herself out of bed every morning. She didn't feel much like doing anything. In preparation for the fall semester, she'd had to vacate her temporary on-campus office. Her apartment was now cluttered with paperwork and books.

She wrote an entry on her computer journal:

I'm in such a funk and I really am so pissy to be around. Maybe I should see a therapist. No, what good would that do? There's nothing wrong with me. There is something wrong with society.

Why did that have to happen at the Scorpion Club? Totally primal. The minute I sat up in that booth, I regretted it. That's the dark side of sex.

But I enjoyed it. God, I loved it. I loved the delicious sensation of knowing I was desired, the flirty negotiation, the quiver of submission, and then the ultimate violation of my body by a man. Except it never feels like a violation. But, it is.

It's completely inequitable. A man takes what he wants and deposits his seed. A woman takes whatever he can give, then pays the rest of her life with a pregnancy. It's a wicked dichotomy but it has to work somehow or our species will collapse.

Women bear the brunt of it all. We're told it's a gift to conceive life and bear children. Do men ever wish they could? Doubt it. How convenient to have that job done by someone else. They don't envy us.

Only women in the civilized world have any choice about sex. Even here, the whole thing is staked on politics. Without birth control, laws, and the benevolence of men, we'd live like animals. Lower forms of human beings. We'd be physical property at the disposal of men. It's only their good will that gives us freedom. What if they change the laws?

But I'll always be a woman. I love so much of it. I love the feeling of a breeze sweeping over my smooth skin. I love practicing yoga with strength and beauty. I love moving my body gracefully like no man ever could.

Why isn't it enough? Why do I struggle with the female reality?

We're stuck forever in these bodies. MAN or WOMAN. I don't want to be a man, but I'm not sure I want to be a woman, either. I'm not queer, I'm not bi, I'm not trans.

How does this femaleness fit in?

These thoughts consumed Darly for days. Everything she saw, she saw in terms of its unfairness toward women. She devoted hours researching goddess worship, and Amazonian and matriarchal societies. Her quest was insatiable. It had become her obsession. She needed answers.

SHERALL SAVARD

Sunlight streamed through the magnificent bay window at the home of Brooks Wilder's late mother. On the long Chesterfield couch, Sherall lay on her stomach, propped up on her elbows. She could see Brooks through the other room at the kitchen counter, pouring seltzer into two glasses. He was scheduled to leave Boston the next week.

"Why not join me in Florida?" he said carrying the drinks toward her. "I have an extra room. You can come and go as you'd like. It would be grand to have your company."

"You wouldn't feel like I was in the way?" she asked.

"Yes, you'd be in the way. I would love that every time I turned around, I'd see your face."

Sherall smiled. Here was a man who gave her autonomy and asked nothing of her, but at the same time, made it clear that he wanted her close and cared about her. It was a yin and yang that offered energy but not the same separateness that caused her marriage to unravel. This mutual respect and attraction was born of two independent beings who not only enjoyed their personal completion, but also the other's past, present, and anticipated future.

Sherall had a chance to start fresh and recreate the person she hoped she truly was inside. A new man, a life away from anyone who knew her, freedom to explore another field of interest, a home in an exciting city—just what she needed. All she had to do was grant herself permission.

"All right. I'll come with you," she said, smiling more sweetly and sincerely than she remembered smiling for many, many years.

Brooks touched her cheek. "We will be happy, Sherall. You can count on me and I can count on you."

Sherall nodded. "Looks like I've met my match."

"And, I, mine."

DISCUSSION

THE FINAL DINNER

Darly sat alone in the dining room at Vivere. Long rays of early evening sun illuminated the walls. The waiter opened the door, but hesitated at the threshold.

"Is it okay if I set up for your group?"

"Yeah, sure. Go ahead, Marco," Darly answered.

She had been working at a breakneck pace over the past weeks to produce the final draft of her study— reviewing written and recorded voice notes she had compiled late at night after their meetings. She often lay awake in bed, tossing and turning, mulling over what the women had said during their hours together.

It had frightened her.

At first, they seemed manageable and even frivolous in their comments. She acknowledged how wrong she had been to feel superior to them. When they first met, late in the spring, Darly was certain of her path in life and confident about how she would achieve her goals. No longer. Her vision was now murky. The Marvelous Mavens had shattered her optimism.

The waiter finished setting the table and arranging the flower centerpiece. He put wine bottles on the sideboard and took out six glasses, inspected each against the light, then positioned them next to the wine.

"Is there anything I can get for you, Ms. Lane?" he asked.

"No, thanks. This is our last night. You've done a great job, Marco. I really appreciate it."

He smiled and nodded, then left the room.

After a few minutes, the door opened again and Kimberly arrived.

"Hi, Darly. You're here early."

"I decided I needed some more time to organize before everyone showed up," Darly responded.

"Can I do anything to help?"

"Yes, please. Would you mind pushing those chairs away from the wall? I'm going to project the screen onto it when I give my presentation."

"Sure thing." Kimberly was happy to help this young woman whom she admired.

Darly sighed and rose from her place where she sat by the window. She picked up her bag and set it onto a chair. She took out her tablet, the stack of papers, some folders, and a portable projector, arranging it all neatly on the floor.

Kimberly had grown uncomfortable with Darly's silence.

"Is everything okay, Darly?" she asked.

"What? Oh, yeah. I'm just tired from finishing up the final work on the study. Sorry to be so quiet."

"No need to apologize," Kimberly said as she adjusted the last chair. "You go ahead and do whatever you need to do to get ready. I always have a book in my bag to read, so I'll sit down and take it out until the others get here."

"Thanks."

Darly sorted the stack of paper into five piles. It had been almost impossible to wrangle what the Mavens had shared over the long summer into a cohesive analysis that addressed the approved thesis premise. She'd done it though. She had debated with Professor Grady as to whether or not she should hand out the study results at this meeting, hoping instead to mail them using the small amount of money remaining in the budget. Grady was adamant that she do no such thing, insisting she confront the women with her findings. Her adviser additionally required her to share their audio responses with him later. Grady reminded her that he would use this information to accurately assess her capabilities as a researcher. This would be the first time Darly did not want to record one of the Maven's meetings.

At last, the others arrived. Heidi carried a large bag. The women stopped at the sideboard to pour wine and greet each other like the sisters they felt they had become.

"Darly," Sherall asked, "how about if I pour you a glass? It's our last meeting." She winked at the others.

"Yeah, Darly," Dodo said.

"No, thanks. I've got a lot to cover tonight. I need to be lucid."

Darly had never shared a glass of wine with the Mavens. It was her way of maintaining the level of professionalism and distance she considered important.

Sherall shrugged at Dodo. The conversation among the other women resumed its natural flow.

Darly walked to the table and took her seat, signaling that the meeting should begin. As soon as the others were seated, Darly spoke. "Welcome everyone. As you know, this is our last meeting together."

"Boo," Sherall said.

"I second that," Heidi added.

Darly blew some lint off the top of her tablet, brushing

its surface with the side of her hand. "You're free to continue to meet."

"Our meetings are the only reason I don't want to leave the area," Kimberly said.

"Kimberly," said Dodo, "we're going to make sure nothing stops you from going on that Study at Sea trip."

"We'll find a way to video chat a meeting with you," Sherall said.

Kimberly smiled. "That sounds cool. I have no idea what you're talking about, though."

The other women laughed, affectionately smiling at this woman who had already grown so much.

Pamela said, "After you return from your trip, you'll be the one who knows more than any of us. It's going to be an incredible adventure."

"I doubt I could know more than any of you, but I'm going to do everything I can to make you proud of me."

"There you go, Kimberly," Sherall encouraged.

Marco arrived, carrying the heavy tray laden with their dinner. He transferred the contents to family style platters, then set them onto the table. "Anything else?" he asked.

"We're good. Thank you!" Heidi said.

After the meal was consumed and the empty plates and platters had been moved to the sideboard, Darly cleared her throat. "I have the results of the study for you but before I hand it out, I want to make a visual presentation of my findings. Also, today I'm required by my adviser to record your reaction to my presentation. He's going to use it as a tool to assess me."

"I'm getting shivers of excitement!" Pamela said.

Kimberly added, "We all know whatever Darly is a part of will be important."

"I, for one, have really enjoyed being her guinea pig," Sherall laughed.

Darly walked over to the large windows and closed the curtains. She stood with the tiny remote in her hand, hesitating.

"Go ahead, Darly," Dodo encouraged.

"I'll do my best to give you the parameters and then you can ask questions at the end."

She turned on the tiny projector. An image of her desktop screen now covered the wall—a colorful and stylized rendition of the Chinese yin-yang symbol. Darly clicked to the first frame of her presentation and read aloud the information everyone could see.

SOCIAL SCIENCE RESEARCH STUDY *on randomly selected target population*

Goal: To examine a population of women whose adult development occurred during the Second Wave Women's Liberation Movement, and to determine the impact, if any, of the Second Wave Women's Liberation Movement on study participants.

Primary Objective: Assessing (anecdotal and observational) the emotional and developmental growth of the subjects relative to the Women's Liberation Movement.

Secondary Objective: Comparing broad social beliefs about the era to specific circumstances in selected study participants.

Exclusion: Men. All women excepting the group who spent developmental years (12- 25) in the USA between

1965-1980.

Withdrawal: 0% withdrawal (All participants completed study)

After reading the page, Darly tapped the remote control in her hand to reveal page two.

HYPOTHESIS: *The Second Wave Women's Liberation Movement (First wave: abolition/suffrage) created an unprecedented opportunity for young women to find success in the workforce and on the athletic field. Women of this generation were able to embrace this opportunity and move forward with careers and accomplishments unavailable to preceding generations. Many women took advantage of these opportunities and it changed every aspect of their lives.*

After Darly finished reading the page titled *HYPOTHESIS*, the room was quiet.

Sherall was first to speak. "Darly?"

"Yes?"

"This hypothesis is what you had *originally* thought you'd find after questioning us, right?"

"Yes, that's correct."

"Just checking," Sherall said, then settled back into her chair.

Dodo and Sherall exchanged glances as Darly displayed the next page.

It was a flow diagram.

Study Schedule
Assemble Participants
Meet and Greet
Introductory Meeting
First Meeting: Ambition

Second Meeting: Family
Third Meeting: Love and Sexuality
Fourth Meeting: Another Chance
Fifth Meeting: Friendship
Sixth Meeting: Self-Actualization
Seventh Meeting: Debriefing

"It looks so official," Heidi said. "I thought we were just having fun!"

Everyone laughed except Darly. She waited for the room to quiet down again.

"Okay, let's get into my results." Darly revealed the next page, then read each line out loud to the group.

AMBITION

•*Only 2 of 5 subjects set career goals*
•*Only 2 of 5 subjects reached career goals*
•*Of those who set and reached career goals, men helped with initial steps*
•*Of those who set and reached goals, 100% were non-traditional areas of work*
•*0% are employed in STEM fields (Science, Technology, Engineering, Math)*
•*3 of 5 attended and graduated from college*
•*Only 1 of 5 obtained advanced degree*

Conclusion: Despite opportunities for achievement, affirmative action, and equal employment laws, only 40% of study participants met expectations.

She glanced back at the group sitting in the dark. Heidi's head hung and she looked at the table. Dodo's arms were crossed over her chest. Kimberly adjusted the scarf around her neck. Pamela carefully folded her hands on the table. Sherall shook her head at Darly.

"I'm sorry," Darly said to the women. "This is what I uncovered. I'm supposed to report facts."

She advanced to the next pages where the details were extensive and similarly formatted.

FAMILY

•Of those working in non-traditional employment, 100% experienced conflict between career and family

•75% of those with children experienced troubled relationships with children

•100% of those with children experienced difficulties with their spouses related to childcare

•2 of 5 reported abortion procedures. 1 of 5 reported multiple abortions

Conclusion: Conception, contraception, raising children, finding and maintaining childcare, sharing family duties, were all sources of friction and disappointment for 100% of participants, with and without children.

The room was silent. Pamela reached into her purse to look for a tissue.

Darly moved onto the next page.

LOVE and SEXUALITY

•100% report some sexual dissatisfaction or disappointment with their partner

•1 of 5 actively pursue variety in sexual relations

Conclusion: Participants generally do not report high satisfaction with sexuality. Traditional roles are typically followed and pleasures are conventional.

Sherall spoke up again. "I feel like a 1 in 5 freak—a flamboyant percentage. Where are you going with this Darly?"

DEBRIFING DARLY

"This is the way the flow chart works when I'm reporting findings and contrasting them with expected outcomes. It's protocol," she answered.

Darly clicked to the next frame.

ANOTHER CHANCE

•*100% of participants had regrets about almost every aspect of life*

•*1 of 4 with children regret having them*

•*1 of 1 without children regret not having them*

•*2 of 5 regret lack of education*

•*3 of 5 regret job choices*

•*4 of 5 regret not being more adventurous*

Conclusion: Family, marital, and employment obligations, as well as fear or lack of imagination, caused all participants to regret major decisions made in their lives.

Bathed in cold blue light from the projector, the faces of the Marvelous Mavens appeared exaggerated. Noses, chins, and wrinkles looked grotesque.

"Hold on, Darly," Dodo spoke up.

"Yes?"

"You make it sound so pathetic."

"I've been careful to remain impartial and not impose my opinion. These results are just a reflection of the information I gathered during our sessions." Darly's tone was distant. She was being recorded.

She advanced to the next slide.

FRIENDSHIP

•*100% of participants regretted not having more female friends*

•*Deterrents to friendships include: spouses, family,*

and employment

•Majority of participants were unwilling to change lifestyle to accommodate new friendships

Conclusion: One of the hallmarks of the Women's Liberation Movement was solidarity between women. The study participants have not indicated that they have women who support them in striving and reaching goals.

Heidi and Kimberly looked at each other, perplexed by what Darly had read.

"Okay, here's the assessment of the final group meeting," Darly announced.

SELF ACTUALIZATION

•3 of 5 participants deferred self-actualization until their 50s

•When taken, steps were on a large scale

•2 of 5 participants report contentment with status quo

Conclusion: Although commendable, the latent effort to reach self-actualization, after one half century of life, indicates a pattern of stagnation. Participants were unable to harness the energy around them at the launch of the Women's Liberation Movement.

The final frame spread across the wall.

RESULTS:

The Second Wave Women's Liberation Movement offered an unprecedented opportunity for a generation of females. Some took advantage of it, and some did not. Participants in this study represent a typical cross section of women affected by this movement. Some had the strength and ambition (like their male counterparts), to seize opportunity and make the most of it. Others, nearly 80% of participants in this survey, did not.

DISCUSSION:

We can speculate why the movement affected some and not others in a way that would cause them to abandon traditional paths and reach for a new way of living and looking at the world. Only they know for sure what held them back.

Or, were they held back? Perhaps the choices they made were the choices all women must make despite a movement that purports to liberate them. Questions of marriage and child rearing are still unresolved. For example, women continue to face the choice of whether or not to change their names upon marriage. It can be a matter of convenience, but one must ask why only women must adapt and change to serve the greater good of the family. Regarding children, although fathers often act as caregivers, the evidence about who responds most authentically to children's emotional needs merits further study. Additionally, research points to the difficulty many women experience when forced to detach from their offspring and effectively delegate the chore of child rearing to others.

In summarizing the results of this study, the researcher found minimal impact of the Women's Liberation Movement to a random cross section of participants. It is unfortunate that the same issues facing women in the 1960s still vex women in the second millennium.

What do women want? It is a difficult question and we may be no closer to answering it than when Freud first asked. A woman struggles because she has too many options and each option has a considerable price to pay. If she doesn't pay it to society in the form of scorn and criticism, she pays it in her heart with guilt and pain.

Darlene Lane

Doctoral Student

Department of Sociology

Boston University Graduate School of Arts and Sciences

Darly left the projector light on while she walked over to open the heavy drapes. Outside, the darkening sky was streaked with spectacular shades of purple, red, and pink. She returned to her seat and turned off the projector. The room was dim.

Kimberly, Dodo, Pamela, Sherall and Heidi stared at her, as if for the first time.

Sherall got up and turned on the lights, then walked over to the sideboard. She picked up an empty glass, filled it to the brim with wine, then set it on the table in front of Darly.

"You're going to need this."

Sherall then reached across and switched off the audio recorder. Darly looked up at her, startled.

"Take a sip," said Dodo.

Darly obeyed.

"Is this what you really think of us, Darly?" Heidi asked.

"What do you mean?" she answered.

The five women at the table stared back at her in silence.

"I had to follow the study protocol. My new adviser is a stickler for the details that must be included."

"Forget him for now, Darly. What do *you* think?" Sherall asked.

"I'm not sure where you're coming from," she responded.

"Darly, you made us sound like our lives were not worth living," Kimberly said.

"I—" Darly started.

"We are so much more than what you recorded," Pamela added.

The muffled steady hum from the restaurant below provided the only noise.

"Take another sip," Sherall said. "We have time. Right, ladies?"

"Right."

"Sure do."

"No rush at all."

"No problem."

"I have a key and can lock up the room, no matter how late we stay," said Heidi.

Darly took another sip of her wine. Her hand was shaking.

"Let it out, Darly," Dodo said.

"It's not my fault," she started.

Five sets of eyes stared back at her, dubious.

"He's such a prick," Darly finally blurted out.

"Go on," said Sherall.

"Well, most men are, aren't they?" Darly continued. She took another sip of wine from her glass.

The Marvelous Mavens exchanged glances.

"I mean, no matter what you do, they think you are either trying to order them around, or one-up them, or seduce them, or do something that they think is like witchcraft—just to get what you actually deserve." She took another sip of wine.

"Keep going," Heidi encouraged. "We're listening."

"Well, my adviser—the new one, not the adviser I started with at the beginning of the study—he's the same age as most of you, and he's a real asshole. He totally does not get it. He thinks if a woman stays home to raise a family, she has failed and has betrayed the movement. He doesn't even believe in the movement anyway." She exhaled forcefully, then took another sip of wine.

"That is disturbing," Pamela said.

"There's more," Darly continued. "Do you want to hear it?"

The women nodded.

"Well, my first adviser was Ian Brown, and I thought he was sensitive to what you all are about, but then he said some derogatory things about you and I just couldn't take it, so we broke up and we haven't spoken for weeks."

"You broke up?" Kimberly asked.

Darly nodded.

"Because of us?" Sherall asked.

"Yeah. Technically, Ian wasn't my adviser because he wasn't going to be assessing me. He was just filling in until Grady got back from Nantucket." Darly finished the Cabernet in her glass.

Sherall reached over and filled Darly's glass, then pressed the buzzer under the table to summon the waiter. Dodo got up and dimmed the lights.

"So, then what?" Heidi encouraged Darly to continue.

"Well, Ian was upset because he thought I was mad at him. I was, but it was such a bummer because that particular night when we had the first disagreement, he had a limo pick me up and there were flowers on the steps and he was making dinner for us and everything. It seemed so sweet. But I just can't be with him knowing how he really feels about women." Darly stopped to catch her breath.

"How do you think he feels about women?" Pamela asked.

"Well, he thinks older women are boring. How can he ever think that? And then, he thinks you are all kind of crazy. He even gave you nicknames."

"Really?" Heidi asked.

"Yeah. It was so disrespectful," Darly answered.

"What were they?" Kimberly asked.

"I don't remember." Darly took a giant gulp of wine.

"Sure you do," Dodo said.

"You won't like it," said Darly.

"Tell us anyway. We're big girls."

"Okay," Darly continued. "Sherall, you were Attention Addict."

"Sounds accurate," Sherall responded.

"Dodo, you were Aging Free Bird."

Dodo smiled. "Can't argue with that."

"How about me?" Heidi asked.

"Tired Cheerleader."

"Ouch. I'm not going to lie. I don't like that," Heidi said.

"I'm sorry," said Darly.

"Me?" Pamela asked.

"Sad Beauty."

Pamela shrugged.

"I'm last. What did he call me?" Kimberly asked.

"Guilty Perfectionist."

"Probably true," Kimberly said, looking around at the group.

Just then, the waiter entered the room.

"Two more bottles of wine, please," Sherall said. "Leave them outside the door."

Marco nodded and quickly left.

"Darly, this Ian guy actually sounds pretty damned smart for never having met us," Sherall said.

"He really is smart. And, handsome. And kind." She took another sip of wine.

"So, it was just the comments that got to you?" Pamela asked.

"No. I've been really thinking a lot. Probably too much. All about the women's movement and how it was supposed to make things so different."

"But, it did!" Heidi said, throwing her hands up.

"Only for some women. It didn't do anything for others. Like some of you." Darly looked apologetically at Kimberly, Pamela, and Heidi.

"Is that what you really think?" Pamela asked.

Darly dropped her head into her hands.

"I don't know what I think anymore. That's the problem."

"Maybe you could tell us a little bit about what you came up with after thinking through things," Dodo said, looking at the other women with raised eyebrows while

Darly still held her head in her hands.

"Like what do you think *should* be different?" Sherall encouraged, as she walked to the door to fetch the wine waiting on the other side. She returned to the table, carrying the two bottles.

Darly lifted her head, then let it fall backward in emotional exhaustion. "Ugh. It's just everything. No matter which way I look, there are problems! You've all had problems and some of you still struggle with them. If you get married, you don't like your husband. If you don't get married, you're lonely. If you have children, you have trouble with them and it makes your job suck and your husband gets to be a drag and even cheats on you. If you don't have children, then you always wish you did and you become unbearably sad."

She stopped and looked over at Pamela.

"I'm sorry, Pamela," Darly offered.

"Darly, I'm fine. Don't worry about me."

"It's just not fair," Darly continued. "I remember my dad always seemed to be nice but maybe he was just a regular man with my mom, too. I don't know."

"Why don't you ask her?" Heidi encouraged. "She would probably love to help you find some answers. Mothers are great that way."

"She died when I was six."

The women emitted a collective gasp.

"Oh, Darly! I'm so sorry to hear that," Heidi said first.

One by one, they stood in line to give Darly a hug. She accepted each one.

"It's no excuse," continued Darly, grabbing the tissue Pamela offered. "I just wish I could believe that every turn was not going to be one with huge negative consequences. I don't feel like ever getting married or having children now, even though I know doing that will probably make me *more* miserable in the long run."

With so many sympathetic eyes focused on her, Darly lost her composure. Months of mounting stress suddenly released. She started sobbing.

The mavens gently pulled her chair away from the table and sat in a circle on the floor, surrounding her. Through her tears, Darly saw a loving face everywhere she turned. A face with wrinkles. A face with mascara caught in creases under tired looking eyes. A face framed by unruly gray hair. A face on top of a sagging neck ringed like a tree. A face marked by a lifetime of pain.

"I'm so sorry!" She said through her sobbing. "I didn't want to hurt you but my professor tried to convince me that your lives were a mess. His life is the one that's a mess. And, my life, too!" she wailed.

The Marvelous Mavens, well versed in the merits of therapeutic tears, let Darly shed hers. After several minutes, the youngest woman in the room collected herself as best she could, despite a lingering shudder.

All five Mavens placed their hands on her.

Sherall spoke first. "Darly, you must trust us."

"I do," she nodded, dabbing her eyes with a fresh tissue, perpetually replenished by Pamela.

"Then, you know that we will not steer you wrong," Dodo continued.

Again, Darly nodded.

"We really do know what is best for you," added Kimberly.

"It's hard not to, when we've all been through it before," Heidi said.

"We care so much about you, Darly," Pamela said. "You're like a daughter to us."

At this, Darly gasped for air and reached out to Pamela. They hugged and the others looked on with approval.

"Okay, let's get down to business here," Sherall started. "Our Darly is in serious need of direction."

"What do you mean?" Darly asked.

"You need *debriefing*. For starters, you have it all backwards," Dodo said.

"Yeah," Heidi seconded.

Darly looked at the concerned faces around her.

"First things first," Kimberly said, tossing to Pamela.

"Women run the world," Pamela smiled.

Darly looked doubtful.

"It's true, Ms. Darlene Lane," Dodo laughed.

"But," Darly said, "It doesn't seem that way."

Heidi put her hand on Darly's forearm. "You're right. It's not true everywhere you look, but overall, it's undeniable."

Darly said, "I don't get it. Women seem oppressed all over the world; even here."

"That's because they choose to be, Darly," said Sherall.

Dodo asked her, "Do you really think that if all women all over the world joined together in conversation and solidarity, either consciously or unconsciously, there would be any stopping them?"

"Honestly," Darly answered, "I don't think anyone could stop all of the women in the world."

"But why do you think that?" Kimberly asked.

"I guess, it's because we have this way of communicating that men can never understand. We have this way of reaching out and connecting on some level that men don't even know is possible. It's like a different vibration or a different dimension that we live in."

The Mavens, seated around her on the floor, nodded encouragingly.

"So, Darly," Kimberly asked, "What are men for?"

"I think maybe they're just here for us to love. Maybe even pity. They will never know what we know, will they?"

The Mavens shook their heads.

Darly continued. "They'll never know what it feels like to bleed every month with the opportunity to conceive. They'll never know what it's like to carry a child and give birth. They'll never know what it's like to have a body equipped to outlive the other sex." She leaned back in her chair. "I'm right, aren't I?" A smile spread across Darly's swollen face.

Street noises outside the window had diminished. The hour had grown late but the Mavens continued debriefing Darly.

She was worried about the success of her study. She knew that her advisor would never approve its submission to The American Sociological Review. Presenting to the International Conference on Education, Sociology and Social Sciences in Vienna was no longer an option either.

Darly knew there was one more possibility. She would not need Simon Grady's permission to submit her findings to the SOCIUS journal. She could then revise the study to reflect the fullness of her findings. She would show the complexity of these women and their life choices. They represented a significant era that was not easily quantified. How could a woman's life be otherwise? The Mavens encouraged her to proceed and said they would be available to answer any additional questions she might encounter.

Darly had another problem.

"I still have to figure out how to deal with Simon Grady."

"Your advisor?" Sherall asked.

"Yes. I have to work with him for the next few years. He holds all the power."

While the other women asked more questions and offered advice, Heidi had been busy consulting her phone.

"I knew that name sounded familiar," Heidi interrupted.

"Really?" Darly hoped to learn more.

"Yup. He went out with my second cousin's mother when they were young. When he found out she was pregnant, he left. She and her family were glad to be rid of him. They used to call him Sigh-Moan because he was always complaining. We use that term whenever anyone is too whiny—don't be such a Sigh-Moan."

"What happened to the baby?" Darly asked.

"She had a miscarriage. It was a close call. Nobody wanted another Sigh-Moan." Heidi answered.

Darly smiled. "That makes me a little less intimidated by him. I'm going to think of that when I meet with him next."

Pamela said, "Darly, what will you do about Ian? He sounded pretty nice."

Darly's face contorted. "I'm not sure he would want to see me again. I was pretty mean to him."

"What did you say?" asked Sherall.

"I told him he could never understand because he had a penis," Darly answered.

The women smiled.

"That's pretty silly in the pantheon of comments," Dodo said.

Darly looked hopeful. "Do you think so?"

Heidi added, "If you really love him, why not just apologize? A good man is hard to find."

The other Mavens nodded.

"What do I have to lose?" Darly asked.

"Exactly," said Kimberly.

DARLY

Only the dishwasher was still working at Vivere when Darly and the Mavens left the restaurant. Once on the Boylston Street sidewalk, the women all went their separate ways. As Darly headed toward the T stop, she heard a horn honk. Her roommate Gracie waved to her from the car window.

"Hey," Gracie said.

"Hi. What are you doing here?" Darly asked.

"I was really worried about you after you left this afternoon. I've been worried for a while."

"Gracie, thank you. You're the best."

"Hop in. It's late."

Even in the dark car, Gracie could see that Darly's eyes were swollen from crying.

"There is another reason why I came to pick you up. I

was curious about the Marvelous Mavens and wanted to see them for myself."

"You did?"

"Yes." Gracie took a deep breath and gripped the steering wheel tighter. "They seem to be ruining your life. You've changed. You always seem bummed out now. You don't look so good. You broke up with Ian. I was hoping you would talk me about it if we had some time alone." She glanced over at Darly. "I miss my old girlfriend."

During the ride back to Allston, Darly told Gracie everything about the evening. They continued their conversation back at the apartment late into the night.

"Oh my god. Those women are awesome," Gracie said. "I knew exactly which one was which when I saw them come out of Vivere. Tired Cheerleader, Attention Addict, Sad Beauty, Aging Free Bird, and —."

"Guilty Perfectionist." Darly helped.

Gracie nodded. "You are lucky to know them."

"Yes. I didn't realize how lucky I was until tonight."

"Do you think I could write an article about them for DIG Boston?"

"What a great idea! I'll ask the Mavens if they'd mind. Grady has to approve his version of my study first, too. Then you can have at it. That would be awesome."

Darly felt better than she had for months.

REFERENCES

SHERALL

At Logan Airport the next week, Dodo, Pamela, Kimberly, and Heidi stood together watching Sherall and Brooks make their way through security. Once cleared, the couple turned to wave to the four women where they could still see them over the crowd. It was easy to spot the group. They were all wearing hot pink tee shirts with MARVELOUS MAVENS emblazoned across their chests. Heidi had handed them out at the end of their last meeting.

Brooks stretched his arm across Sherall's shoulders as they walked through the busy terminal crowd.

"I'm going to miss them," Sherall said, wiping away a tear.

"So, come back and visit them whenever you feel like it. They're good women, Sherall. And, they're important in your life."

"They really are, aren't they?" she looked over at him.

"They're your friends."

"Yes. They're my friends," she repeated.

DARLY

Darly had no time to waste. She woke early every morning and dove right into writing the new version of her study. The SCOCIUS deadline was only two weeks away. She texted and emailed back and forth with the Mavens. There were more questions and she wanted direct answers. She wanted their opinions, not just their anecdotal remarks. What did they think about the women's movement? Did it matter to them? Did it matter to others? Darly did not feel qualified to answer the questions on their behalf, not because she felt academically lacking, but because she knew she had insufficient life experience to process the information. She wanted direct data without any filter.

She was busy, but late at night, her thoughts turned to Ian. She missed him. She knew she loved him. She hoped it was not too late. She did not know how to reach out for another chance though.

KIMBERLY

A few weeks later, the remaining Mavens prepared for another send-off. They stood together at the Black Falcon Terminal at Boston's Cruise Port.

"Are you sure you can carry all of this, Kimberly?" Dodo asked, setting down the large duffel bag.

"I have no choice!" she laughed. "I'm required to handle everything myself. It's only for the walk up the gangway and into my cabin, anyway. Plus, the weight lifting routine Pamela recommended has made my upper body so much stronger."

Heidi, Pamela, and Dodo stood in the hot sun looking at their friend.

"I can't tell you how proud I am of you, Kimberly," Pamela said.

"Me, too," Heidi added.

Dodo moved to massage Kimberly's shoulders from behind. "Remember, we're all here for you. You can reach out anytime you need. Hopefully, the rendezvous in China will work and the four of us will see you there in two months."

Kimberly turned to address the three women in their hot pink shirts. "You are the best friends anyone could ever hope for."

"Right back at you," Heidi said.

"Please take care of Darly," Kimberly said.

"You know we will," Pamela answered.

"Kimmy! Up here!" a voice called out.

They turned their attention to the second deck where a plump woman leaned against the railing, waving with two arms.

"That's Sandy," Kimberly said, waving back.

Kimberly turned to her friends again.

"I guess this is really good-bye."

"You can do it," Dodo said.

"We believe in you," added Heidi.

They formed a group hug, then hoisted Kimberly's pack onto her back, added a shoulder bag onto one side of her and purse onto the other, then gave her the handle to her wheeled duffel bag. They watched her stagger away under the weight of her belongings—a slender solo woman with an enormous adventure ahead.

After about an hour, the ship sounded its horn and prepared to pull away from the dock.

"There she is," Pamela pointed.

Next to Sandy on the second deck, they saw Kimberly waving to them below, her hot pink shirt a vibrant punctuation amidst the others.

DARLY

Darly had just left the first fall gathering of the SocioLites. The resumption of their meetings in the new semester was something she had looked forward to all summer. She felt like a different woman since they had met last. Older and wiser. Now, after this meeting, she could add *hopeful* to that characterization. There had been an unexpected response from the group when she revealed the way Simon Grady had handled her research. According to the SocioLites, he had violated strict regulations when he attempted to aggressively impose his personal bias on her final presentation. Perhaps he did not believe that Darly would share the information about his behavior with others. But, she did. The SocioLites quickly rallied around her cause and drafted a formal complaint on the spot. Their signatures added significant weight to the plea. More importantly, Darly's situation was not unique. One of the members believed that another complaint had been lodged in the past. This additional action would bar Simon Grady from ever again acting as an academic advisor.

On her way home she enjoyed listening to her favorite bus driver call out the names of stops in his thick Boston accent. Darly absently watched passengers get off and on the bus in the early evening sunset. She knew this route well, but today she saw something new that made her grab her phone to capture a picture. There was Pamela's smiling face looking down on Darly from a massive billboard with the words:

BAISERS
La beauté est éternelle.
Beauty is forever.
Darly returned the smile. Maybe she would start wearing lipstick.

Gracie was waiting for her in the apartment kitchen. The latest copy of DIG Boston was on the counter, opened to the article she had submitted as a freelance writer. Gracie's grin was huge.

"The Marvelous Mavens by Grace Granthorne. They kept it all in there! I thought for sure it would be edited down. They loved it, Darly! And, look—Dodo's photos! It hits the stands Thursday, but digital is out now."

Darly searched for the online comments and read them aloud on her tablet:

"The Mavens have grit.

It's about time someone recognized women like these.

They remind me of my mom and I'm going to ask about her struggles now.

They said women of that generation were a mixed bag. Not!

Finally, honesty about real women's lives.

Maybe women can stop pretending now.

Are you listening, men?"

The two young women smiled at each other. "We'll be up all night reading these!" Gracie squealed.

"I can't wait until the Mavens see this!" Darly said.

"Well, their kids will for sure. Reader demographic is 21-34."

The next morning, Darly made a resolution. She would reach out to Ian that very day. She was just going to call him and ask if they could meet. If he refused, she would know where she stood in his life. That would be her answer. She would find a way to live with it. She would have to.

She placed the call.

"You've reached Ian Brown. I'll call you back. Thanks."

Darly hung up. Her heart was racing. She had not planned to leave a message. How could she be sure he had received it, if she did? If he didn't respond, she would always wonder if he never got her message. She would have to try again in a while. She hoped she would still have the courage.

While deliberating her next step, the phone in her lap rang. *Ian.* She clutched at her chest and answered.

"I saw you called," Ian said.

"I did. Yes. I called. I, um, I wanted to find out. Actually, can you even talk?"

"Yes. I have an appointment at 10 though."

"Ok. I just wanted to know if you would be interested in meeting sometime. Just to talk."

"Talk about what?" he asked.

"Um. Well. I just thought maybe we could see where we are."

"Okay." He paused. "Is today at noon good for you?"

"Oh. Yes. So quick. Okay. Yes. I can do that."

"Meet at the tree on the Charles? Do you remember where that is?"

"Yes. I do. Thanks for being so available."

"No problem, Darly. I'll see you later."

He ended the call.

Did Darly remember where the tree on the Charles was? Where he had first kissed her? Did he really think she did not? Darly's stomach twisted in knots. She could not tell anything about Ian's feelings from the neutral tone of his voice. He *had* called her back though. That was something.

She showered and dressed. It was not easy to select an outfit for a meeting whose outcome could decide the rest of her life. How strange to feel such forward momentum, but at the same time know that she was only part of the equation. Ian could rebuff her and send her on her way. Could she handle that? She was not certain.

She recalled the advice of the Mavens. They suggested she take some time to ponder her relationship with Ian and consider the outcome she desired before contacting him. Desire was a funny word, because, yes, she desired him. But the Mavens had shown her that desire is fleeting. It comes and goes. It can fail and be resurrected, if one is fortunate. Darly had never lost her desire for Ian, though. She wondered how he felt about her. She thought she had pushed the boundaries of his desire with her hairy legs and underarms. She had almost dared him to say it repulsed him. He had not, though. He took that part of her evolution seriously. He told her she was a beautiful female mammal, and said she would be sexy to him whatever form she took. She hadn't seen how wonderful that was of him. It was a small thing, the acceptance of hairiness, but it meant that he valued and honored who she was inside. He wanted her to be assured that he saw her true spirit.

How did she thank him? She hurled unfair accusations toward him. She had made numerous and massive assumptions about his perspective. She had not given him a chance to explain his thoughts. Darly had acted as if only her thoughts were the important ones. She had never asked if he would be open to growing and evolving with her as she went through her changes. No wonder his voice sounded flat. For all he knew, he could be subjecting himself to another tirade by her about injustices for which he held no blame.

He was brave.

Or, maybe he didn't care about her anymore.

Darly was early. She waited on the sidewalk with a view of the tree. It was almost noon. Ian had not yet arrived at the spot. If she had looked to her left, she would have seen him waiting just as she was, focused on the tree.

They both began walking. It took quite a few steps for Darly to notice Ian moving toward the tree. He had not yet looked over at her.

Then, they both arrived.

"Hi," Ian said.

"Hi, Ian." Darly's heart felt like it would break. Ian would not smile. The worst outcome could be ahead.

"Do you want to sit down?" He gestured with his hand.

"Thanks."

They adjusted themselves on the grass. Ian removed his backpack and carefully placed it next to him.

For a minute, they just looked at each other. Darly thought that Ian looked incredibly sad. She braced herself to hear the words she dreaded.

Instead, he unzipped his backpack, pulled out one rose and handed it to her.

"Would you please accept this from me?"

"Ian!" Darly felt tears welling as she took the flower.

Next, Ian took two wrapped subs out of his backpack and said, "Do you think if we did what we used to do again, we could fix what went wrong?"

"Yes, yes, yes!" Darly said. Even with tears streaming down her face, she managed to find Ian's mouth to kiss.

FOOTNOTES

ONE YEAR LATER

A soft breeze carried the spicy scent of the butterfly bush through the air and over the white folding chairs filling up with guests. At the end of each row, clumps of lavender caught up in bows dangled from the sides. As the guests looked forward beyond the lawn, they glimpsed a number of loons settling on the pond. It was the quiet time of day when other Island Pond activities suspended in preparation for evening. The golden sun hung low in the sky and the few clouds on either side glowed light pink and purple.

Heidi removed her apron and flew out of the kitchen, brushing hair from her face. She knew the catering staff would do an excellent job preparing food in her kitchen but she wanted to triple check for this special occasion. Stopping to compose herself once she reached the lawn, she walked down the aisle and took her seat in the first row.

Wearing a yellow Vietnamese ao dai that accentuated her graceful confidence, Kimberly paused to survey the decorative atmosphere she had created earlier that day. With a little help from a professional, she had transformed Heidi's Island Pond yard into a magical setting. Off to the side, a clear tent was suspended over two dozen tables set with sage-colored napkins and vases of blue hydrangea. Everything looked beautiful. She walked down the aisle and slid onto the seat beside Heidi.

At the doorway of the house, Dodo waited, camera

ready. Georgie, acting as a symbiotic assistant to her mother, squatted beside her, one hand on the camera case, another holding a circular reflector.

Pamela stood for a moment at the half-opened door. She wore an off shoulder printed dress with a handkerchief hem. After smiling at Dodo and Georgie, she took a deep breath, walked off the porch, and then down the aisle, taking her place at the seat reserved for her—honorary-mother-of-the-bride.

Next, Sherall emerged, wearing a fitted black tuxedo dress. She winked at Dodo, then made her way over the grass and paused at the last row of chairs where Ian Brown waited to join her.

"All set?" she asked him.

"More than I've ever been in my life," Ian answered.

They walked down the aisle together, then stood and turned to face the guests.

Sherall watched the screen door open. Out of it came a resplendent Darly, dressed in her mother's vintage wedding dress, her beaming father at her side. The white lace of the gown looked ethereal in the dimming light of dusk. She stepped off the porch and floated across the green grass.

Sherall motioned for the guests to stand. All turned to watch Darly and her father make their way down the aisle. In the front row, Kimberly, Heidi, and Pamela held hands.

When Darly reached the front, her father kissed his daughter, then turned around to take his seat.

"Welcome family and friends," Sherall began. "Thank you for joining us to witness this happy occasion. Please be seated."

Sherall looked over at the faces in the crowd. In the third row, Brooks Wilder smiled at her. Next to him were her two children, Lina and Luke, smiling as well. Behind them sat tall and handsome Hien Cao, Kimberly's new lover.

Sherall launched into her role as Justice of the Peace.

"Life can be funny, can't it? Just when you think you have it figured out, you realize you haven't. So, you head in another direction until that proves disastrous as well. You lick your wounds, regroup, and try yet another approach. For a while, you're where you think you should be. Then, boom, another unexpected event threatens to unbalance you. You pick yourself up again, brush yourself off, and try something different."

She smiled at Darly.

"This is the way it goes. This is the way life always goes. It's messy, it's heartbreaking, it's euphoric, and it's sometimes dull. No matter what you choose, there will be surprises."

In the first row, the Mavens nodded their approval.

"Knowing how things will turn out is overrated. Things might not turn out the way you hoped. Or, they might turn out the way you hoped. Does it matter? The certainty of not knowing is the only certainty we have."

Dodo made her way around the periphery of the ceremony, unobtrusively clicking away with her camera.

"There is one thing we know for sure, though." Sherall paused to look over at Kimberly, Heidi, and Pamela, in solidarity. "You have to get in there, and I mean really get in there—in life—to find out."

She refocused on Darly. "That's the only way. I'm right,

aren't I?"

Darly nodded at her, then looked back at the Mavens, and nodded at them as well.

Sherall cleared her throat and addressed the groom.

"Ian, will you have Darly to be your wife? To love her and honor her for the woman she is and the woman she will become?"

"I will," he answered.

"Will you promise to support her in every endeavor she pursues, in her effort to fulfill her potential, in her search for balance between emotions and ambition?"

"I will," he answered.

"Furthermore, do you promise to try to understand and appreciate what sacrifices Darly may make to achieve completeness and realize that these sacrifices represent adjustments that she will make over days, years, and decades?"

"Yes, without any reservation," he said, smiling at Darly.

"Please hold hands," Sherall instructed the couple.

"Darly," she continued, "you must understand that Ian is just one man in a universe of many. He is no more able to read your mind than any other man. You must keep him informed, and you must have faith that his promise today is true, and that he is trying his best to be a good mate. Can you do this?"

Darly looked away from Sherall to Ian.

"I can and I will," she answered.

"But wait, there's more!" Sherall went on.

The guests exchanged quizzical glances.

Dodo handed her camera to Georgie, then joined

Heidi, Kimberly, and Pamela as they walked to stand next to Darly.

"We have a promise to you as well, Darly," Sherall began.

Ian nodded to the surprised Darly, indicating that this was a plan to which he had agreed.

"Please hold out your right hand, Darly," requested Sherall.

Each woman held one of Darly's five fingers.

Sherall read from the paper she kept in her free hand. "We, the Marvelous Mavens, hereby declare our steadfast love, affection, and support for you, Darly. We will do all we can to help you through whatever is ahead, be it the completion of your PhD, research travel, pregnancy, birth and child rearing, and any unexpected steps along the way. We will be your mothers, your confidantes, your friends, and your mavens. We will share our experience with the full understanding that you will make your own mistakes that may even rival the ones we have made. We promise to be with you every step of the way, as long as we all shall live."

One by one, Heidi, Dodo, Kimberly, Pamela, and Sherall, kissed Darly on her check. They passed by Ian to kiss him as well, before resuming their places.

Darly pulled a tissue from her bouquet and dabbed at her eyes. Ian moved close to Darly again.

Sherall smiled at the guests, then returned her attention to the couple.

"By the power vested in me by the State of New Hampshire, I now pronounce you husband and wife. You may kiss your bride, Ian."